SWIFT HAT-TRICK TRILOGY

Blissful Hook

BOOK TWO

HANNAH COWAN

First Edition

Cover Designed by: Booksandmoods @booksnmoods

Edited by: Megan Ryan Hughes

ISBN: 978-1-7777818-3-5

Dedicated to anyone who's ever felt like they don't belong.
Never give up. It will get better. Even when it feels like it never will.

Authors Note

Please be mindful going into this story that there are a few topics that not everyone might be comfortable reading.

This book contains:

Depictions of alcohol and drug abuse, physical and verbal abuse, death of a loved one, and explicit sexual content.

Disclaimer

Blissful Hook can be read as a standalone, but it is highly recommended that you read Lucky Hit and Between Periods beforehand.

Between Periods is what I like to call an official prequel, and covers certain past events that carry a heavy impact in Blissful Hook.

Thank you.

Reading Order

Even though all of my books can be read on their own, they all exist in the same world—regardless of series—so for reader clarity, I have included a recommended reading order to give you the ultimate experience possible.
This is also a timeline accurate list.

Lucky Hit (Oakley and Ava) Swift Hat-Trick trilogy #1

Between Periods (5 POV Novella + Blissful Hook Prequel) Swift Hat-Trick trilogy #1.5

Blissful Hook (Tyler and Gracie) Swift Hat-Trick trilogy #2

Craving the Player (Braden and Sierra) Amateurs in Love series #1

Taming the Player (Braden and Sierra) Amateurs in Love series #2

Vital Blindside (Adam and Scarlett) Swift Hat-Trick trilogy #3

Playlist

Someone to You— BANNERS   ♥ 3:39

Easier — 5 Seconds of Summer   ♥ 2:37

I Like Me Better — Lauv and Ryan Riback   ♥ 3:30

Killing Me Slowly — Bad Wolves   ♥ 3:57

Nobody Compares To You — Gryffin and Katie Pearlman   ♥ 3:51

Sober — Bad Wolves   ♥ 3:15

Somebody — Gareth Emry and Kovic   ♥ 3:30

Affluenza — Theory of a Deadman   ♥ 3:36

Stepdad — Eminem   ♥ 3:33

Nightmare — Halsey   ♥ 3:51

Chasing After You — Ryan Hurd and Marren Morris   ♥ 3:27

You Found Me — The Fray   ♥ 4:01

Prayed For You — Matt Stell   ♥ 3:30

I Don't Dance — Lee Brice   ♥ 3:41

Push My Luck — The Chainsmokers   ♥ 3:01

Demons — Imagine Dragons   ♥ 2:55

Better Man — 5 Seconds of Summer   ♥ 3:09

Pieces (Hushed) — Andrew Belle   ♥ 3:18

Loved By You — Justin Bieber and Burna Boy   ♥ 2:39

PROLOGUE
SIX YEARS AGO

Tyler

"GET YOUR SORRY ASS BACK HERE, TYLER. I'M NOT DONE TALKING to you." The gruff slurs echo around the barren room as I walk away from him.

"You haven't been able to tell me what to do since I was twelve, Allen. Stop trying."

I notice a pair of headlights shining through the cracked living room window and pick up my pace.

"Show me some damn respect, you ungrateful waste of skin," he growls from behind me. "Don't turn your back to me."

The old, torn-up, reclining chair smacks against the wall with a thud as he jumps up. My eyes roll back into my head. I come to a stop just mere inches from the front door and turn around to face the old drunk.

Allen's long, dirty black hair is slicked back, his thin scalp emphasizing the bald spot near the peak of his round head. The baggy sweatshirt that hangs loosely off his torso is a deep red colour, similar to the bloodshot eyes that stare back at me. The stench of whiskey seeps from his breath and arouses a gag from my throat.

"You seem to have forgotten your place here. You are *not* my dad," I spit through clenched teeth, broadening my shoulders in front of my stepfather.

"I think it's you that's forgotten your place here, boy. As long as your momma has me here, under this roof, this is my place." Allen seethes the words, his lips stretched back to expose his decaying yellow teeth.

I almost laugh. "The only reason you're here is because I haven't thrown your scum ass out on the street. If I knew she wouldn't follow after your deadbeat ass, you would be long gone."

The same frightening chuckle I used to hear from behind my bedroom door years ago escapes him, sending vicious shivers up my spine. The menacing smirk that dances on his lips used to be enough to send me running away, locking myself in my room from fear. But things change.

"If you have such a problem with how I run things in my house, then why don't you go find somewhere else to live?"

"If *only*. I'm too busy being the only one paying to keep this house from being seized by the bank to focus on finding somewhere else to live. Not all of us can rely on our drug dealing buddies to pay our bills." I throw the words with a force I wish I had when I was younger. It would have saved me a lot of agony if I hadn't been such a pussy back then.

Furious, he closes the distance between us and shoves a long, shaking finger into my chest. "That smart mouth of yours is going to get you into trouble one day. Mark my words."

"I'll be waiting anxiously for that day to come. Now, if you'll excuse me, Allen, my rides here." I flash him an arrogant grin and take a large step back, watching his hand fall to his side. Anger radiates off of him as I dismiss his threat.

Raising my hand, I give him a small wave before walking through the front door. The sticky heat hits me like a brick to the balls as I move down the sidewalk and to the blacked-out car waiting for me beside a busted light post. Pulling out the pack of cigarettes in the pocket of my jeans, I peel it open and grab one, lighting it and bringing it to my lips.

The car honks impatiently, and I throw up my middle finger in their direction before inhaling deeply. With a sigh, I drop the cigarette and stomp it out with my boot.

I reach over and open the car door, breathing in the strong smell of weed. I shake my head and slide into the passenger seat. I hear the other passengers greet me, only to get a lazy, two-finger wave in return before the car takes off down the black tar road.

Here's to another night I can't wait to forget.

1

PRESENT

Tyler

"Are you sure you want to leave already? We're still booked in for a few more days and your brother has already paid for the room. You don't want to waste his money. This trip couldn't have been cheap."

My mom's scolding is as consistent as ever as I shove the rest of my stuff into my open suitcase. No shit, the trip wasn't cheap. Brother dearest got married in Mykonos. How else was he supposed to flaunt his wealth to everyone he knows?

"I never asked for River to pay for my room. If I remember correctly, I didn't even want him to *book* me one." I scoff. "I told him not to. He's the one that wasted his money."

"Can't you just be happy for a few days?" Her eyes shut slowly and her shoulders drop like the weight of her disappointment is too much to bear. "You've been bringing everybody down since the moment you stepped off of the plane," she replies with a weighty sigh.

It's odd hearing her speak in complete sentences. Usually, she's too high to hold a conversation—babbling to herself as if she's the speaker of the house and itching at the skin on her forearms until they're raw and bloody.

"My bad." I push the top of my suitcase down over the

clothes I just threw inside and zip it up. Gripping the handle in a tight fist, I pull it to my side and stretch my neck when the wheels slam against the expensive-looking tile floor. "I already changed my flight. There's nothing I can do."

Mom closes her eyes and inhales a deep breath through her nose and places a hand on a jutted hip bone. The dramatic action nearly makes me laugh in disbelief: Nora Bateman almost looks like a disappointed mother.

What a goddamn sight to behold. It only took twenty-three years.

"Alright, Tyler. Whatever you want to do. You've never been one to listen."

Yeah, it's almost like I had no one to teach me how. "Alright. I'll talk to you later, then."

"Say goodbye to River before you leave. I'm sure he would appreciate the effort."

"I'm sure he would." I snort louder than I intend to and drag my suitcase behind me on my way to the door. A huff echoes behind me as I pull it open and step into the empty hallway. I don't bother looking back when the door clicks shut behind me.

She can enjoy the rest of her vacation drinking bottle after endless fucking bottle from the limitless bar until she crawls to River's room, begging for the toilet bowl. When he flounders at the task of having to take care of his alcoholic mother for once in his life, maybe, just maybe, she'll realize I'm the one that takes care of her, and that she's been taking me for granted.

I shove my palm against the elevator buttons, wincing as the metal cuts into my skin. The doors open, and I all but throw my suitcase inside, grinding my jaw. I didn't plan on coming to this fucking wedding for a reason. My older brother and I detest each other. I can barely remember a time when I didn't want to knock him on his ass and leave him bleeding on the floor.

When it comes to showing our hatred, though, that's where me and River differ. If I don't like somebody, they know it.

There's no point in playing games. It's a waste of time. But River likes to plan—to scheme.

He didn't want me here; I knew that. This was all a power move for him. To show me how much better he was than me. The success, the wealth, and now the wife. A wife who looked like a prisoner at that altar, staring at my brother with eyes vacant of anything but greed. I knew the wedding meant nothing, that it was probably for some sort of money-making plan they were both in on.

I guess it just shows how little my big brother knows about me. I may not run a fortune five-hundred company or have my name on a tower, but I have enough money to retire now and never run out, and my name is stitched on the backs of thousands of hockey jerseys and sold worldwide.

As far as the wife charade goes, if he was trying to make me jealous, he couldn't have been farther off.

Euphoria: A feeling you get from a good fuck, or from stepping off of an airplane after spending almost an entire day strapped into a seat so tiny only your left ass cheek fits. Then there are the crying kids and the old guys with sweaty armpits that won't stop snoring in your fucking ear. Even the deafening music in my headphones wasn't enough to tune it all out. Maybe if I wasn't already on edge from my trip, it wouldn't have bothered me as much. Nah, who am I kidding? Yes, it would have.

My phone hasn't stopped vibrating since I switched it back on. As message after message flashes across the screen, I watch Mom guilt me for leaving. I scold myself for getting her an international phone plan for the trip. I could have at least avoided this for a few days if I wasn't so damn eager to please her. I know it's not worth it—the hurt, anger, and betrayal. It doesn't matter what I do, she will always choose River.

I'm about to turn my phone back off when a different number pops up on the screen. "Yeah?" I grumble, answering the call. I spot my Uber from the front doors of the airport and drag my suitcase to the car.

"Just wanted to make sure you landed safely. The flight that bad?" Matt jokes, a quiet giggle sounding behind him.

"Well, clearly I'm alive. You can rest easy now." I pull open the back door of the black SUV and crawl into the backseat, dumping my shit down on the seat behind me. "The flight was brutal. I'm dead tired."

I buckle my seatbelt and we start moving. *Almost home.*

"You didn't sleep on the flight? Come on! That's the only way to fly. If I don't sleep, I puke."

The only tolerable way to fly, yeah. But in the rush of packing and hauling ass out of Mykonos, I forgot my insomnia meds on the bathroom counter, so that wasn't happening.

"Overshare, Matt."

He laughs loudly. "Get some sleep, Ty. Text me sometime this week and we can make plans."

I nod my head even though Matt can't see me and close my eyes. "Sounds good. Thanks for checking in."

"Anytime. See ya," he says before hanging up. I shove my phone into my duffle bag before I become dead to the world.

Once I get home, I sleep straight through until the following afternoon. And after reintroducing myself to the living world, I spend the next two weeks on the ice.

I never take breaks from hockey—not unless I have no other choice—so I guess pushing myself to get back into my routine so quickly is my punishment for leaving town. I can't afford to lose focus, I've already made it so far, way further than I could have dreamed. Hockey is all I have. I can't fuck it up. I don't have a backup plan.

So, every morning, I wake up before the sun rises, drink a mixture of raw eggs and protein powder, then spend the rest of the day with blades under my feet and the taste of metal in my mouth.

This morning, I showed up at the arena hours before practice was supposed to start. Usually, the arena is empty, but a deep, thundering voice echoes down the hallway as the Vancouver Warrior's new hopeful star player, and my best friend, rips into whoever was lucky enough to be on the receiving end of that call.

My eyes widen the second I hear him yell his younger sister's name. *Shit.*

"You're way too young to be doing this, Gracie!"

"I'm old enough for you to talk to me like an adult, Oakley!"

I stop dead in my tracks as the familiar female voice screams back at him, probably unknown to the fact that the call is on speakerphone.

"You want me to talk to you like an adult? That's rich considering you still act like you're sixteen! What would Mom think?"

"Don't bring up Mom right now. And stop trying to micromanage me! You're not my dad."

My teeth touch and I wince at the harshly thrown insult. The call is immediately taken off of speaker phone. As the blades of my skates dig into the scratched-up cement floor, I debate whether I should save myself the trouble of dealing with the aftermath of Gracie Hutton's erratic behaviour on the ice with her brother or spend the next hour listening to him rant about their conversation in hopes of lightening him up before practice.

"Fuck me," I huff, and proceed to the dressing room.

The door is open when I get there. Oakley sits hunched over on a wooden bench, fingers tangled in his wet, shaggy hair and breaths coming out in pants. He looks up briefly when he notices my presence. He nods once and lowers his eyes back to the floor between his bent knees.

"Hey," he mutters.

"You good?"

"Family drama. I'm fine."

"Ripping your hair out is something you do regularly then? Shit."

His fingers fall from his hair and into his lap. Leaning his back against the wall, he lets his head fall back against the blue brick. "You know the girl that Grant was bragging about? The one he took on the houseboat for three days back in June?" he asks, now staring at me with his lips peeled back in outrage.

"The one with the elastic back?" I recall, my brows furrowed.

"Jesus Christ, Tyler," he hisses. His shoulders shudder as he gags.

Oh. Rage is a familiar feeling as it taints my mind. I fight to keep my expression blank. "I mean, she was a dancer."

A sharp pain shoots through my shoulder when he hits it with his, a pointed warning written across his tightened features.

"I'm joking."

"You're not funny."

I keep my voice level. "You don't have to worry about Grant, Oakley."

Nobody should worry about that fucking dweeb. Of all the hockey players on the team, Grant Westen wasn't one I expected her to fool around with. He barely even makes it off the bench and has the maturity of a twelve-year-old.

Her standards must have dropped since the group of us: Oakley, Ava, Gracie, Adam and I, got back from Mexico last year. After everything that happened between the two of us on that resort, the thought of Gracie with Grant has my molars grinding to dust.

"You don't get it. You don't have a sister."

"Just a bastard of a brother instead." I collapse on the bench beside him.

"True," Oakley laughs while raising his arms above his head in a stretch. "It's just not a topic I want to be brought up around me. I don't give a shit who any of you sleep with as long as it isn't my damn sister."

Guilt paints my insides. I can't say who Gracie does and doesn't sleep with is a topic I want brought up either. Not when I spent a week last year inside of her, hearing her cry my name and learning the different ways to make her soak her panties.

I swallow. That entire trip was a mistake, which is why I've barely seen Gracie since then. I'm already up to my eyebrows in guilt from the last time. Any more and I'll end up choking on it. Whatever happened between us is done. It was the right decision to cut contact.

"Duly noted," I mutter.

"As much as I want to sign with this team, I'm not going to if it means that I'll have to hear about more of that."

I scoff. "Yeah right. You'll sign with this team no matter what."

His laugh is a sign that I'm right on the money. Oakley would do anything to play in Vancouver again. He wouldn't throw that opportunity away for anything.

"Don't tell that to Seattle. They still think they have a shot in the dark."

"They'll have to go through me and the entire VW team to get to you."

Oakley throws his arm around my shoulder as he nods and murmurs dreamily, "Don't make me blush, Ty."

2

Tyler

I FUCKING LOATHE CABS.

The smell of sweat, the lack of decent suspension that sends you jolting around in your seat, and the annoying drivers that can't take your silence as not wanting to hold a conversation with them. I'm nearly tempted to carry a pair of earplugs with me wherever I go as a precaution.

Normally, I wouldn't have agreed to shove myself into one of the tiny back seats with two other wide-shouldered hockey players, but when Matt wants to party, it leaves no other option. I've tried to fight him on it—and failed—more times than I can remember, which is the only reason why I'm not lying in a tub of ice in an attempt to ease the ache coursing through my entire body right about now.

I was finishing up a brutally physical practice this afternoon when Matt called me, insisting I join him at the club that just opened up downtown. My first thought was fuck no, but it didn't matter. And my teammates, being the boozehounds that they are, interrupted my phone call, and took the invite as their own, joining us without a second thought.

"You couldn't have called us a bigger cab?" I grumble,

ignoring the sharp pain in my side as Matt's elbow thrusts its way into my ribcage.

He waves me off, "We're almost there. Stop being a baby."

"Stop elbowing me then," I growl.

"I'm not trying too!"

One of my teammates, Connor, whips around to face us from the passenger seat, his charcoal eyes narrowed. "Will you two shut up already? You're like a fucking married couple."

"Sorry," we mumble begrudgingly.

"We're pulling up anyway," Connor's partner in crime, Aidan, sighs from his spot on my left.

We all jump out as soon as the driver comes to a stop, and Connor reaches through the unrolled window to hand him a fifty. As the cab drives off, I take in the clusterfuck in front of me with a groan of defeat.

The dark red brick building is lit by neon lights that shine brightly down on the long line of people. Two tall, well-built men stand in front of the double doors and the giant line of people as they shove the impatient—and most likely underage teenagers—down the sidewalk when they try to sneak around them.

The rap music is thumping so loud I can feel it pulsing through my legs as we walk across the concrete and toward the club. I follow Matt as he struts toward the front, completely cutting off the four girls next in line to enter the building. I can hear their frustrated scoffs as they're rudely cut off, and grunt in annoyance.

"Joey, my man! How goes it?" Matt roars, the excited greeting directed at the taller of the two bouncers. My eyebrows raise as I watch the intimidating guy break out in a huge grin and pull Matt in for a bro hug.

"Matty boy. Good to see ya, brother. Thanks for the tickets last week. My boys loved the game. The new Saints goalie is nowhere near as good as you were, but what can you do?"

"Tell me about it," Matt boasts, his ego growing tenfold

before my eyes. "Let me know when you wanna go again and I'll grab 'em for you."

"Thanks. Have a good time tonight," Joey says, pulling the door open for us.

"Always do," Matt teases. He looks back at us with a smug smile, like he knows we're the tiniest bit grateful for what just happened. I shake my head and follow him inside Sinners Paradise.

It takes a few moments for my eyes to adjust to the flashing lights bouncing from the metal bars on the ceiling. The thumping bass rolls through my body like a tidal wave as I fall into step with Matt. Despite it being a brand new club, it's not any different from the many I've been to before.

There are four bars set up throughout the building, each one stocked with liquor and plastic cups that look a lot like glass but don't shatter when you drop them. The bartenders vary between an annoyed female and the typical tool in khaki shorts on the hunt for a break time lay.

An enormous dance floor sits dead smack in the centre of the room, completely covered by half-naked, sweaty bodies, and desperate men attempting to grind up on them. The guy who just walked by us masks the powerful stench of sweat with weed. I wrinkle my nose in distaste. Would it kill these people not to wear their drug habits?

"To the bar!" Matt roars in my ear before he disappears from view.

Exhaling, I make my way to the bar, nearly falling back on my ass when a bloodshot-eyed brunette crashes into me, tripping over her foot. I swallow my annoyance and place my arms on her shoulders to steady her. Aidan and Connor are nowhere to be seen, which isn't that much of a surprise to me. They've probably found a discreet place to hide from anyone who might recognize them.

I find Matt leaning on his forearms against the bar, waving

his hands around like a total fuck. He spins around like a one-legged ballerina and sees me standing behind him.

"Here, fuckhead." He pushes a tall rum and coke against my chest. The liquid sloshes against the lip of the glass and onto my black t-shirt. I bite my tongue and take the glass from him. "Please don't be a pouty baby all night, I beg you. Would it kill you to have fun?" Matt's voice is barely audible over the obnoxious rhythm of the techno music.

"Let me get drunk first. Go find the other two. I'm just going to stay over here for a bit."

Slapping a hand down on his shoulder, I give him a gentle shove. He looks like he wants to argue with me, but knowing it won't get him very far, he nods his head once and hurries off.

I love the guy, I do, but I'm more of the lone wolf type.

I turn back to the bar and down the drink in my hand before shoving through the line and ordering another one—or three. As soon as my fifth drink slides across the countertop and into the palm of my hand, I finally begin to feel a buzz spread through my body.

I jolt in surprise when I feel a light tap on my shoulder. Pushing myself away from the bar, I spin around. My eyes focus on a short, curly-haired brunette standing behind me, her hands folded awkwardly in front of her.

Moving my eyes over her, I raise an eyebrow. "You need something?"

Her glasses slip down her thin, long nose. She quickly unfolds her hands and lets them fall to her sides, casting anxious looks around the crowded bar. I lean back with my elbows against the bar and watch, amused as the girl mouths words to her two friends as they stand to the side, waving their hands in my direction.

"Do you speak?" I tease her, grinning as a flush creeps across her cheeks. She turns her attention back on me, her eyes wide with panic. Her lips twitch slightly, and I know she has something to say. "I don't bite. Not hard anyway." I send her a wink, and a mangled laugh crawls up my throat when she gets flustered again.

When she finally opens her mouth to speak, someone bumps her, sending her stumbling back a few steps. As soon as I see a just as slight, but more confident, golden-haired, spitfire, my breathing falters.

There's no time to accept that Gracie is here, in front of me, for the first time in months, because the brunette squeals, capturing my attention again. She trips over herself and barely catches herself before falling to the floor. Her eyes are narrowed to slits when she looks at Gracie.

Ripping my eyes away from the brunette, I finally focus on the blonde.

"Was it necessary to push her?" I shout.

Gracie ignores me, her eyes never leaving the other girl as they stand in some kind of weird, possessive showdown. I give the brunette a half-smile and blink in surprise when she somehow gains the courage to walk back over to me.

"I'm Savannah," she says, introducing herself with a wide smile. As soon as I open my mouth to respond, Gracie cuts me off.

"Hi Savannah, I'm Gracie." Although her words are slurred, the harsh possessiveness behind them is unmistakable.

"I'm Tyler." I nod and take a step closer to Savannah. "Don't mind Gracie. She just doesn't get along well with other girls."

Gracie scoffs and Savannah blinks a few times, looking silently between us with an overwhelming sense of awkwardness that threatens to swallow me whole.

"You're one to talk about not getting along with people of the same sex," Gracie spits, folding her arms under her chest with a glare.

Raising my brow, I chuckle quietly. "You're still on that? It was one time, and you didn't exactly tell me to stop hitting him."

"I didn't know I had to tell you to stop when he lost consciousness."

He shouldn't have touched her the way he was. Not in front of me. It was too soon after Mexico. Everything was still too fresh, and my possessiveness was at an all-time high. I don't feel an ounce of regret for the punches I threw that day.

"I'm just going to go," Savannah cuts in, shoulders tense as she spins around and all but flies away back to her friends.

Gracie moves to stand beside me as she twists her body toward me. "I thought women weren't your priority right now."

The same excuse I told her the last time we spoke has me shaking my head, desperate to fling her claws from my mind.

I turn my back on her and stare down at the bar. I raise two fingers to signal the bartender over and order another drink.

"You shouldn't turn away in the middle of a conversation." Gracie follows me. She wraps a hand around my forearm, and I look at her with eyes as cold as I can muster up.

"And you shouldn't interrupt conversations." I pull her fingers from my arm.

"You should be thanking me. We wouldn't want you too distracted," she throws back.

"Does your brother know you're here?"

"He's my brother, not my dad. Why would he?"

"This place is crawling with creeps; in case you've been walking around here with your eyes closed."

"I can worry about myself, Ty," she says, but her actions contradict her words as her arm snakes around mine. I choose not to say anything.

"Where are your friends? Don't you have anyone else to annoy?"

She brushes off my insult expertly and knocks back the rest of the red drink I didn't see her order and roughly pulls my arm. I reluctantly move away from the bar and sigh as she drags me toward the crowded dance floor.

The temperature is ten times hotter over here than it was by the bar, and the overpowering need to turn around and run in the opposite direction washes over me. Being the asshole she knows so well, I rip my arm from her grasp and rush off toward the front doors.

My head thrashes around in all directions as I search for an exit. When I finally spot the neon red sign hanging above a pair of double doors, I don't look back.

3

Tyler

I CAN'T COUNT THE NUMBER OF TIMES I HAVE TOLD MYSELF TO GIVE up smoking. It's just one of those things that everyone hates, but so many can't give up. Like me.

I was sixteen when I smoked my first cigarette. My stepdad had been smoking around the house for years before that, but I never paid it too much attention. It was just a dirty habit that stunk up the house. It wasn't until he offered me a puff from his that I smoked for the first time.

Every night after Mom left the house for another exhausting night shift at the sketchy restaurant down the block, Allen would offer me a smoke. I suppose in a fucked-up way, it became our thing. It was the only time there weren't any harsh words or fists being thrown in the house.

I wish I had someone back then to tell me how stupid of a habit it was. Maybe I would have quit. Perhaps I wouldn't have. I guess we'll never know.

The familiar burn of the cigarette tears through my throat as I take another hit from the cigarette. The frigid air outside would sting my skin if it wasn't for the liquor rushing through my system, keeping me warm. I relax my shoulders for the time being, thankful for the puddle of alcohol in my belly that has cleared my mind.

It's nights like these that I can understand why someone would want to say fuck being sober, and just stay drunk. For just a few pained breaths, I can sympathize with my mom.

After a few minutes, I decide to head back inside. I drop the cigarette and use the heel of my shoe to stomp it out. Taking one final deep breath of the cool, fresh air, I go back inside. The music is quieter now, although I'm sure that's just another side effect of all of the booze I've consumed in the past two hours.

As I walk toward the bar, I catch sight of her again. It's nearly impossible not to.

Golden curls flow along her back, bouncing with each step. Leather pants cover her long, toned legs and her tight, black crop top does nothing to hide a . . . is that a belly-button piercing?

My eyes stay locked on her and I watch her dance, confidence dripping off of her like honey from a wooden dipper with every move. I catch sight of a short, skinny guy moving toward her and curl my fingers.

He places himself behind her and rests his grubby hands on the exposed skin above her waist. I'm moving toward them before I can stop myself, tension trickling into my shoulders again. I shove the guy off of her without so much as a response from him. I take his place behind her with an aggravated, almost possessive, grunt and shake my head.

Her skin feels hot under my fingertips, scorching my skin in a way that should have made me release her go and turn back, not tighten my grip on her hips. The satisfaction comes next, a few seconds after her back relaxes against my chest. She's swaying so steadily, so confidently that I start swaying with her, our bodies moulding together into a glob of forbidden energy and undeniable lust.

I'm not new to touching Gracie by any means, but this feels new. This touch is public—unrestricted. And fuck, that makes it even hotter. It's getting more difficult to keep from pressing my dick to her ass as more people keep slamming into me.

It's not long before I'm sucking air between my teeth in a sharp hiss. Any previous attempt to keep her from noticing how hard I am becomes futile when I'm shoved a bit too hard. My cock is now nestled against her lower back. And she surprises me as much as she does herself when she spins around, still tucked in my arms, but further back.

Her lips part as she stares at me with wide, startled eyes that have me wanting to wrap my hands around the neck of the guy who was just touching her.

"Ty?" she asks, gripping my biceps to steady herself.

My hands loosen their grasp and my fingers travel across the skin of her lower back, over her hip bones, until they rest just under her belly button. I toy with the metal resting against her lower belly and groan. Definitely a belly button piercing.

The tremor that runs through her body when I swirl my finger around the piercing wouldn't even be noticeable to almost everybody else, but I catch it.

"Yeah. It's me," I murmur.

I beg myself to back away as she takes a cautious step toward me, closing the distance left between us. She pushes against me, and I tense when she places a palm on my abdomen and creeps upwards.

"We stopped for a reason, Gray." I almost choke on the nickname, my eyes not daring to leave hers, no matter how much I beg them to. When she smiles sweetly—innocently—I know that this won't end well.

"Nobody has to know. It can stay our little secret. Like before."

"It's messy and stupid," I mutter.

"Let's just use each other to scratch an itch. That's all it has to be."

I shake my head, but the only word replaying in my head is *yes*. "No."

"Yes."

The word echoes in my mind, and the danger of our actions washes away with my drunken thoughts. The only thing I can focus on is how fucking good she feels against me again. I move my hand up her side, not stopping until I thread my fingers through her hair. I stare at her mouth in nothing but absolute awe as her tongue peeks through her lips and runs along her bottom lip, wetting it.

"Fuck it."

My lips crash down on hers in a searing kiss as soon as the words fall between us. Her reaction is immediate, and she ravishes me with wet, open-mouthed kisses. She's just as addicted to the taste of me as I am to the strawberry lip gloss that is now smeared across our mouths. The hand that was once on my chest has now snaked its way into my hair while her other one rests possessively in the front pocket of my jeans. When I nip at her bottom lip, she lets out a soft moan, and I force my tongue through her parted lips, wrapping it around hers.

She pulls away, lust swimming in the blue of her eyes. "Uber."

"Uber?" I repeat, bemused. She ignores me and takes her phone out of her purse, staring down at the bright screen.

"My Uber is here. I ordered one earlier," she clarifies.

"You're sure about this?"

She just nods her head in response and reaches down to wrap her hand around mine. I pull my hand away, noticing the rejection flash across her eyes, and lace our fingers together instead.

"Let's go then."

Hands are moving, and clothes are flying the second we get inside my apartment.

My fingers skillfully unzip Gracie's leather pants before I push them down her legs. She attaches her lips to my neck with a wet kiss, and I bite back the grunt of satisfaction rising from my throat. She finally kicks the fucking skin-tight pants across the apartment and I pull back.

"Never wear those again," I growl, lifting her up and pressing her back against the wall with a thud.

My lips meet hers again, pressing against them so roughly I fear they'll bruise. She wraps her legs around my waist and her greedy, frantic, fingers fumble with the button of my jeans. It pops open and she pushes the waistband of my jeans down with her feet, her hands occupied, running roughly through my hair. A deep laugh rips through me when she shoves my pants to my ankles.

My vision blurs as I reach down and rub between her legs, the slick heat making me groan. Her breath hitches when I continue to rub my thumb along the soaked material of her lace panties. Gracie reaches for the waistband of my underwear, and I shove them down my legs, pushing her panties to the side.

"I'm still on the pill," she rasps.

I manage to nod before I dip a finger into her. She drops her head to my shoulder, her mouth open and teeth grazing my skin as I slide in another finger.

"You're soaking already."

Her pussy is so fucking tight, clenching around my fingers with a vice-like grip that makes my cock swell against her stomach. She nods against my neck, the sounds of her satisfaction vibrating against my skin, filling the room.

"Are you sure about this?" I grind out the question and kick myself as soon as the words leave my lips. If she doesn't want this, then I'll look like a complete idiot, letting myself get wrapped up in Gracie's web of attraction for a second time.

She responds to my question by reaching down and wrapping her small hand around my dick. She strokes me twice in an attempt to stop my premature chastising.

Gracie stares down at the pulsing cock in her fist, her eyes wide and dark with desire. I know I should back away, tell her to leave and hit my head against the wall for getting myself into this position again, but I can't stop. Her body is paradise against mine, and the familiarity of it is driving me so far up the wall I have to fight off the urge to check myself for a radioactive spider bite.

Choosing to quit wasting time, I cover her hand with mine and guide it up and down, giving my cock slow strokes. The slick wet head bumps her entrance when I line myself up.

"Please, Tyler. Stop teasing," she begs.

Fuck, I forgot how pretty she looks when she begs.

With a growl in my chest, I bury myself inside of her. *"Jesus Christ."*

At the feeling of her squeezing around me, I bite my lip so hard I taste blood. She cries out in frustration when I carry her in the direction of the couch and drop her on the cushions, pulling out.

"On your knees. Grab the back of the couch," I order and settle behind her when she does as she's asked.

Her ass is red from being pushed into the wall, and I take a cheek in each of my palms, squeezing them together and pulling them apart as the memory of how they looked painted with my cum comes flooding through my mind.

"I think about it too," she whimpers, pushing back into my hands.

I swallow a moan and release her, reaching for my cock instead. She's so wet I slide in without any resistance, sinking balls deep.

"Always so tight for me, Gray," I grunt, adjusting my hips and thrusting hard, hitting her soft spot.

"Right there," she says, breathless, even though I am doing all of the work. Not that I mind. She knows I like being the one in control.

Her head falls to the couch and then she's reaching back,

touching every part of my body that she can reach, scratching and pulling at me, frantic as her orgasm approaches.

I collect her hair in my fists and yank her back toward me. My lips touch her ear as I shove my hips against her ass. "Right there?"

"Yes, yes," Gracie whimpers.

I know I'm going to blow as soon as she clenches around me, squeezing me tight. Her back arches and her inner walls flutter as she shouts my name loud enough that it bangs off the walls. She tries hard to keep herself upright as the energy drains from her, so I wrap my arm around her middle and hold her up as I follow close behind her.

Pushing into her for the final time, I come, filling her up as I groan, "Shit. *Fuck yes.*"

Gracie's watching me when I float back down to earth, her lips parted and eyes calm. She giggles, making me frown.

"That was even better than I remember."

4

Tyler

THE FIRST THING I NOTICE WHEN I WAKE UP IS THE SHEEN OF SWEAT on my skin. I find this weird because I've always been someone who has to keep their bedroom window cracked wide open year-round, no matter how cold it is outside. It's just utterly impossible for me to sleep unless I feel like I've spent the past year living in an icebox, meds or not.

I find it even stranger that I can feel the wind flowing in through my open window, yet I suspect that if I were to get up right now, I would leave a giant Tyler-shaped sweat stain on my sheets.

My eyes shoot open, the sun burning them immediately when a small arm snakes its way across my sticky chest. My eyes water from the burn as I glance down at the mess of blonde curls spread wildly across my pillow. The girl's breath hits my ear with every exhale, her mouth barely an inch from my cheek.

I go rigid when a soft moan escapes her lips and her head moves to cover the roaring lion tattoo enveloping my left pec. She pushes the thin sheet that was once covering her lower body to the side as she kicks her leg.

A fist-sized knot forms in my stomach when I drag my eyes

up her bare legs. I stare at the hem of a t-shirt—*my* t-shirt. My breath catches in my throat. I spot the same cursive writing on her collarbone that Gracie got tattooed three months ago. The carefully written quote only makes the knot in my chest tighten. Guilt and regret make my head throb worse than any hangover can.

I made a promise to myself and an unspoken promise to Oakley that this wouldn't happen again. I broke both. And for what? Now I have to pretend like I didn't just sleep with my best friend's sister. *Again.*

My flight or fight response kicks in as I pass a sweaty palm over my face. I'm going to seem like a dick when she wakes up, but I can't be here when she does. I am not ready to have this conversation again.

I very slowly lift her arm off of my chest before sliding off the bed. I pause for a second, hovering over her, waiting. When she doesn't stir, I grab my jeans off the floor and slip them on. I roll my shoulders to avoid taking another look at Gracie, regardless of how badly I want to.

After shutting the bedroom door softly behind me, I see a pair of leather pants and a black shirt lying on the ground beside the front door. You have got to be fucking kidding; we didn't even make it past the front door.

Moving toward the couch, I find my phone lying beside a red-laced bra and another frustrated groan echoes through the apartment. I grab the phone with a heavy sigh before unlocking it and calling Adam. He's the only guy I can talk to about this.

After four unanswered calls and even more unread texts, I run a hand through my hair and give it a hard yank. Of course, the one time I actually need him to be by his phone, he isn't. I know it isn't his responsibility to be here to deal with what I've done, but I'm desperate to throw my anger toward anything but myself.

Why did I think it was a good idea to get blackout drunk last night? And why—of all women—did I bring Gracie Hutton here?

A shiver rushes through me as the memories of last fall come rushing back, making my throat itch. I need to get the fuck out of here. Giving my head another rough shake, I grab my wallet off the armchair. My ringtone blasts through the living room louder than I would have liked, and I almost drop the damn thing as I frantically answer the call before the noise wakes Sleeping Beauty.

"Finally! About time." I force the whisper into the speaker with so much force I'm surprised I didn't cover my phone in spit. I walk out the door, shutting and locking it quietly behind me.

"Sorry, I was sleeping. You know, the thing most people do at this hour?" he teases.

"Fuck off. I'm on my way over," I grunt.

My beat-up Ford shines in the golden light of the morning sun from a few feet down the sidewalk. The chipped paint around the grill mixed with the two loonie-sized rock chips in the windshield should probably embarrass me, considering it really wouldn't be hard to get it repainted or the windshield replaced. But shit like that doesn't bother me. Besides, the exterior problems are the least of my worries. With the engine steaming whenever I drive it further than fifty kilometres, I might as well just wait until the thing kicks the bucket and buy something else.

"It's six in the morning, Ty."

"It's an emergency." I unlock the doors and hop in, cringing at the creak in the door when it closes.

His voice is a lot more serious when he says, "Got it. See you soon."

I rap my knuckles impatiently on the front door of Adam's bungalow, my heart hammering in my chest.

"It's open!" Adam calls from inside the house, and I turn the doorknob and walk in.

A ball of speckled brown fur is heading in my direction before I even have the chance to kick my sneakers off. Adam's dog, Easton, comes barreling in between my legs, and I crouch down to scratch behind his floppy ears.

"Hey, bud. Sorry, I have no treats this time," I apologize, laughing softly when he simply flops over onto his back in response. I stand up and walk toward the kitchen.

"There better be whiskey in that coffee cup," I huff when I see Adam sitting at his small kitchen table.

He's put together like always. His mousey brown hair is gelled to perfection in a small swoop, even though he has probably just woken up, and his clothes are perfectly smooth—not so much as a wrinkle in the mossy button-up stretched along his shoulders.

"You look like shit," he snorts, his eyes looking me up and down.

"Thanks." I sharpen my glare and take a seat at the table across from him.

"What was so important that you had to drive all the way here?" he asks after taking a long sip of what I presume is coffee.

Groaning, I let my head fall back. I know Adam won't judge me for what happened last night. He's not that kind of guy. But he's also even closer to Oakley than I am. I just know that he's going to be disappointed. And fuck, it sucks when Adam is disappointed in you.

"I messed up again." I raise my head, eyes glued to the wall in front of me.

His eyebrows jump to his hairline. "What did you do already? You just got back from Europe."

"Promise me this stays between us. Nobody can know. Especially not Oakley." I sound frantic.

He swallows before mumbling, "Not again."

I nod ever-so-slightly and look away. "I don't even know how it happened. I just woke up this morning, and she was in my bed."

"Gracie?" he asks slowly.

Silence envelopes the kitchen as we sit across from each other, neither of us speaking. Neither of us knows what to say. My head is quickly thrown back again.

"Gracie," I confirm, keeping my eyes trained on the ceiling above me.

"Fucking hell, Tyler."

"I know. Shit, I know." My hands find my hair and tug.

"What the hell happened? I didn't know that you were into her. Shit, are you?"

"No."

Gracie is just doing to me now, what she did before. She's slipping inside any break in my defences and sinking her claws into my chest with the hope I'll never be able to get rid of her. It nearly worked that last night in Mexico, but I refuse to let it happen again.

The damage left behind the first time I yanked her claws free of me is still there today.

"Then explain what happened, because I'm lost," Adam says, his arms folded.

"I have no fucking clue. We were both drinking, and it just . . . I don't even remember how we got back to my place."

"What happened this morning? You said you woke up with her in your bed," he mumbles.

"I woke up and she was sprawled out beside me wearing nothing but my shirt from last night. I freaked out and got dressed. That's when I called you."

His chuckle surprises me as he leans back against his chair. "You just left her there alone? Douche move."

I'm up before he finishes his sentence, heading for his liquor cabinet. I pull out the closest bottle I can find and take a large swig of the amber liquid. It burns the entire way down my throat before it settles in my empty stomach. I'll be paying for that later.

"Yeah, I know. But it freaked me out. Oakley will gut me if he finds out." I set the bottle on the table and sit back down.

"Not only Oakley. You know Gracie will tell Ava, right?"

"I'm fucked." My head drops, banging on the table.

Adam clicks his tongue. "Maybe you should talk to Gracie. You know that last night probably meant a lot to her. She hasn't been around much lately, and I can only guess that's also your fault."

More guilt washes over me at that statement, and I curse myself again for leaving her this morning. Fuck, she's going to kill me the next time she sees me.

I stare at Adam, feeling hopeless. "I don't know what to do. This is such a fucking mess."

"Well, was last night a mistake? Was it like last time?"

"I don't know." The words fall out of my mouth before I can stop them. I shake my head, angry at myself for even debating the question.

"I think that's where you need to start. For now, since you're here so damn early, I need you to take Easton for a walk while I hit the gym." He stands and stretches his arms above his head.

I follow his lead and return the bottle of scotch to its home in the small liquor cabinet. "Yeah, okay. Thanks for this, by the way."

"Always. I'm happy you feel comfortable enough talking to me about this stuff, even if it has put me in a bit of a shit spot. I've been here for you with this since I stormed into your house the day we got back from vacation."

Adam steps close to me and grabs my shoulder, giving it a quick squeeze before leaving the kitchen. Easton trots in after him, staring up at me with excited eyes and a wagging tail.

"You heard the W-word, didn't you?" I breathe out a laugh and grab his leash from the hook by the door and clip it to his collar.

At least Easton doesn't care about who I sleep with. He's too busy licking his balls and sleeping all damn day.

5

Gracie

I'VE HAD MY FAIR SHARE OF REGRETFUL MORNINGS.

The ones where you crawl out of a stranger's bed with your hair sticking up every which way and your mascara smudged all over your face as you collect your clothes and scurry away as fast as possible. It's in those very awkward, shameful moments that you rethink your entire existence.

You ask yourself questions like: How did I end up here? I didn't let him put it in my butt, right?

You wonder why you didn't just stay at home in bed smothering yourself in fuzzy blankets while inhaling an entire pizza.

Now, even I can admit that not every mind-boggling night out turns out bad. I've had my fair share of good mornings, too. The mornings when you still wake up in a stranger's bed, but instead of running away, you stay in bed next to them, talking for hours until it's time to grab your shit and leave without uttering another word to them.

Unfortunately for me, today I woke up to the former rather than the latter. The morning of regret. Yet somehow, it is even worse this time.

The first thing I notice as the grogginess fades is the faint, familiar smell of Tyler's cologne. I've never been able to pinpoint what exactly it smells like, just that it smells like him. Spiced with a slight splash of something forbidden.

A grin plays on my lips as I wrap a hand around the silky comforter covering my t-shirt-clad body, pulling it up over my face. A squeal rips through the silence before I throw a hand over my mouth, stifling the sound before he can hear me.

Once I calm down, I gradually lower the blanket until it rests just under my chin, and dart my eyes over to the spot beside me. When I see nothing but black sheets, I sit up quickly, a chill sweeping over me.

He better be cooking me breakfast right now.

Huffing, I narrow my eyes and throw the blankets off before touching my bare feet to the carpet. I groan at the ache between my legs and curl over because *shit*, that hurts After a few moments, the pain subsides enough that I can stand again and continue my hunt for the asshole who left the ache.

Light streams in from the cracks in the curtains. How long have I been asleep? Shit, Jess is probably freaking out. Leave it to me to abandon my best friend in a brand-new bar for a guy.

Maybe the fact that the guy was Tyler will lessen the severity of her rage.

"Tyler?" I call out, opening the bedroom door and peeking my head out at the practically bare, cold apartment he calls home. He could definitely use a girl's help to spruce the place up a bit and make it less. . . frat-like.

When I get no response, I push the door open and step out. Not seeing him in the living room or the bathroom, I head to the kitchen. My stomach drops when I realize it's completely empty, with not even a single pancake or drop of coffee waiting for me.

I put my hands on my hips and straighten my back. So this is how it's going to be, eh? Tyler Bateman, you are in for one hell of a rude awakening.

After spending half an hour scouring the entire place for my cell phone, I finally found it squished between two couch cushions. And no, I really don't know how it got there.

Calling Jess was . . . an experience to say the least. At first, she screamed in my ear, nearly shattering my entire eardrum as well as my phone. But after hearing my explanation, she relaxed a bit and agreed to pick me up.

I take full advantage of the fact Tyler isn't here to bitch at me for using his shower and eagerly skip into his bathroom. The tap lets out a sinister screech as I turn the water on and remove his t-shirt, laying it gently on the closed toilet lid.

When I look in the mirror above the sink, I watch my cheeks turn a crab-apple red. The glow you get after having mind-blowing sex is a real thing. I mean, there's no other way to describe the lively gleam in my eyes or the special twinkle in my smile right now. It's a familiar, welcome sight.

My hair, on the other hand, is even worse than I was expecting. It looks like I just spent the past few hours doing the Kylie Jenner lip challenge. Spinning around, I hop into the tiled shower and let my shoulders drop as the hot water pours over my skin. The water pressure massages my scalp as I look for the closest available shampoo.

Of course. A two-in-one—a girl's worst nightmare. Would it kill one freaking guy to want to have silky hair and use a conditioner? Ugh.

I dump the dreadful substance in the palm of my hand and coat my tangled strands of blonde hair in it. After my hair is washed and my body is scrubbed, I get out of the shower and put on a pair of basketball shorts I found in one of Tyler's drawers, and the same shirt from earlier.

I shove last night's clothes into a grocery bag and wait for

Jess outside. Ten minutes later, I'm in the passenger seat of her new car.

"So," Jess drawls, eyes darting between me and the road in front of us. The wind blowing around the beige interior of the car is causing her onyx-coloured hair to bite her round cheeks. I giggle when she attempts to blow it out of her face before giving up and rolling her window up.

"So?" I muse. My arm rests against the window frame, and I stare at the lush green trees that fly past us. It really is beautiful here in the summer. Everything is so green, way greener than in Penticton.

"What are you going to do now?"

We turn down the road leading to our apartment, and with a click of my tongue, I smirk.

"If I told you, I would have to kill you."

She looks at me. "Yeah, maybe I shouldn't know. You can go a bit bat shit."

I shrug. She's not exactly wrong.

We park in the underground parkade connected to our building before getting out of the car and heading for the elevator.

Never in a million years did I expect to be living somewhere as fancy as this place. Growing up with barely enough to survive off of, to suddenly living in a downtown Vancouver apartment complex with an infinity pool and a giant gym is a lot to adjust to. Not that I'm complaining.

When I first talked to my older brother about moving to Vancouver, it didn't shock me in the slightest when he was completely against the idea. Nor did it surprise me when the only way he would agree to it was if he got to pick where I lived in Vancouver.

He's always been far too protective over me, but I could never blame him for that. Not after we lost our dad.

What did surprise me, though, was his offering to pay for the place he chose. But I guess being Mr. Money-Bags now, he has the money to spend. Either that or his girlfriend, Ava, made him pay for it.

When we exit the elevator on our floor, one of the guys that live next door is unlocking his front door. "Hey, Cody."

Startled, he drops his keys and looks at me with wide eyes.

"Oh, hey, Gracie," he mumbles while ducking down to grab his keys and quickly opening his door and stepping inside his apartment.

As soon as he shuts the door shut behind him, Jessica laughs.

"It's hilarious how into you he is. Poor guy doesn't stand a chance."

Giving my head a small shake, I follow her down the hall to our place and once the door is open, step into the bright open space. The summer sun beams through the floor-to-ceiling windows, outlining the entirety of our open-concept apartment. A smile twitches at the corners of my mouth. It's a gorgeous view.

I set my purse down on the entryway table and kick off the tennis shoes that Jess brought me. "He's just friendly, Jess. Give him a break."

"The guy can barely make it through an entire sentence without stuttering when you talk to him, Gray. You're too blind when it comes to anyone but Tyler," Jess informs me. I glare at her as she flops down onto the tray leather couch and flicks on the TV.

"Blind or optimistic?" I ask, joining her on the couch just in time to catch the intro to *How To Get Away With Murder*.

Jessica turns to me and raises a judgmental eyebrow.

"Optimism is for those too scared to go for what they want," she replies dismissively.

My first reaction is to argue with her, but knowing it won't get me very far, I swallow back my defiance and put all my attention on the show in front of me.

6

Tyler

I CAN DO THIS. I'M TYLER GODDAMN BATEMAN. I'VE DEALT WITH worse situations—worse women than Gracie Hutton.

I tell myself the same confident words until they're impossible to ignore. I'm sure I would make the day of the prissy-ass receptionist in Gracie's building, dressed in a white-collared shirt and well-ironed slacks if I spun right around and left.

He's been watching me from the moment I stepped inside the building. Curiosity and maybe even fear dance in his eyes, almost like he's waiting for me to pull a baseball bat out from under my tattered leather jacket and rough up the place. I'm almost tempted to do it just to see how fast he would run out of here with a wet spot in the crotch of those expensive pants.

Every ounce of my self-control is being tested the longer I watch him stare at me like a puzzle he just can't solve. I can't pinpoint the exact reason behind his rigid demeanour, but I would assume he's trying to figure out why I look so familiar.

It's clear I'm not from around here. I'm used to the judgmental looks by now. It's not common to see a millionaire pro-hockey player walk around looking like a kid from the wrong side of the tracks, but I've stopped caring about shit like that a long time ago.

Harsh words are on the tip of my tongue, just aching to be spat at the blonde-haired boy, but I swallow them down. Pulling out my phone, I check the text message that brought me here once again.

> Apartment # 313, floor 10. You're already on the list of people allowed up. Just tell the receptionist your name. Think before you speak this time Tyler, or I'll kick your sorry ass all the way back to Greece.

The firm warning makes me chuckle. Ava always knows what to say to make me pull my head from my ass, even when I've been so adamant about keeping it there. She knows me too well.

I slide my phone back into my pocket when I reach the front desk. I grind my teeth when the sunshine boy's eyes widen, and his Adam's apple bobs with each nervous swallow. My nose scrunches. The smell of his expensive cologne is suffocating, and I have to bite back a cough before I draw even more attention to myself.

"Buzz me through. I'm visiting a friend," I say, eyeing the name tag above his right pec with an amused grin. "Ryan."

He stares blankly back at me, mouth gaping like a damn fish. I debate reaching over and clamping it shut but think better of it.

"If you wouldn't mind getting a move on, I have other things to do today."

"Your name please," he rushes, staring at the computer screen with wide eyes.

"Tyler Bateman." I rest my forearms on the desk and stare as he nods his head, his shaking fingers typing frantically.

A few moments later, he nods once more and buzzes me in.

"Thanks for your time, cupcake." I fake a smile and walk through the now opened glass doors beside the front desk. My smile drops the second I'm out of his view.

I'm a pretty brave guy, and I don't scare easily. Hell, I get paid to beat hockey players into curled up balls of pain for a living. So why does the thought of apologizing to a small, nineteen-year-old girl terrify me?

I like to think it's because said girl happens to be my best friend's sister. But I know that deep, deep down, it's because she's one of the few people who can go head-to-head with me without breaking a sweat.

It's pretty clear to anyone who comes across Gracie Hutton that the woman is a fucking spitfire. I've known it since the second I first saw her. And I know for a fact her confidence and sometimes overbearing personality is was what caused the inevitable breakup with that loser she was dating for way too long after high school. Although, I know she would never admit it.

So, as far as she knows, we all think she left him to "find herself," or whatever lame-ass bullshit she's tried to spin since they broke up.

The ding from the elevator snaps me out of my thoughts, and I take a deep breath before exiting the small space. Triple checking Ava's text, I square my shoulders and march down the hallway. The fluorescent lights burn my eyes, and I stare down at the carpeted floor beneath my feet. The carpet is rich with intricate designs that remind me of something out of a seventies movie.

Gracie's always been a bit over the top, but she wouldn't have picked out this place alone. I'm sure of it. It's way too rich for her blood. Just like it is mine.

After a solid three minutes, I reach apartment 313. A brown doormat sits in front of the door—the words Welcome To The Shit Show etched in the rough brown material. *How fitting.*

I knock on the door and take an anxious step back as I wait for it to open.

I don't have to wait long before a dark-haired beauty pulls open the door. She's turned to the side as she yells something back into the apartment, not sparing a glance at the stranger in her doorway. The short, velvet pyjama shorts she's wearing do little to hide the ass peeking out from underneath them. Her lack of a bra is made well-known when I see two rock-hard nipples saluting me through her thin top.

"Expecting company, Jessica?" I ask, cocking a brow.

"That depends on who you're here for," she flirts, as if her best friend isn't just down the hall. She puts a hand on her hip. "If you want another round, you only have to ask."

I take a confident step toward her, pressing our chests together. Her breathing slows and she looks up at me through hooded eyes.

Bending down, I whisper, "I would rather rip my fingernails off one by one with a rusty pair of pliers than spend another night with you." We're so close I can feel her flinch.

"Who is it, Jess?" Gracie's voice echoes down the hall.

The question makes Jessica jump away from me, nearly tripping over her feet. "It's Tyler!" she calls back, eyes moving to the floor as a look I can only assume is shame passes over her face.

Thumping footsteps crash down the hallway, making me chuckle. Clad in an oversized t-shirt, Gracie comes barreling into view. She has tossed her unruly blonde hair up into a lump on the top of her head. It bobs from side to side with every unbalanced step. It's a pretty comedic sight, but I won't test her patience by laughing at her. Not until she accepts my apology at least.

"I'm going to go to my room. Let me know if you need anything." Jessica mumbles before scurrying away.

"What did you say to her?" Gracie demands in an accusatory tone. With hands on her sides, she walks closer to me. I brush off her irritation with a grin, frustrating her even more.

"You don't wanna know, princess. Trust me." With a roll of my eyes, I walk inside, not waiting for the invitation I know I will never get.

Gracie shakes her head at my reply and waves her hand

toward the living room, sarcasm thick in her words. "Sure, come on in."

"This place is a little extravagant, don't you think?" I ask when she moves around me to close the door.

"Don't bother with the small talk. What are you doing here, Tyler? I thought you wanted nothing to do with me."

My stomach sinks when I notice the pain in her eyes, and I fall back against the couch cushion, letting out a regretful sigh.

"I shouldn't have left you alone."

My eyes dart around the room before landing on the picture of her and Oakley that sits on the fireplace mantle—proud and unforgiving.

"Yeah. You shouldn't have. That was a real douchebag move." She crosses her arms and stares me down with narrowed eyes.

"We shouldn't have gone there again," I say. My eyes search hers for the hope that I already know is there, making me feel even guiltier than I was before. "I still can't give you what you need. When I saw you lying there, I knew you would wake up and see me and think what happened was something more than what it was."

Her eyes squeeze shut as I speak, her jaw set.

"You do not know what I *need*. And you do not get to decide what I'll think without even talking to me. You left me in your bed alone, Tyler, like I was some twenty-dollar fuck you picked up on the corner," she growls, her eyes wide and dark.

"Never say that about yourself again," I growl, taking a step toward her. "You have no idea how wrong you are."

Her words have triggered horrible images—memories—almost as if she had just switched the light switch on in a haunted basement. They run through my head, painting my vision with a thick crimson red.

The bruises covering Mom's legs as she stumbled into the house hours after I was supposed to be tucked away in my bed. The ripped diner uniform that would cover her frail body as she dragged herself up the splintered wooden staircase. The muffled cries that spilled from beneath the closed bathroom door, the shower not loud enough to swallow them.

My head swims as I turn away from Gracie's curious gaze and stare at the floor-to-ceiling windows taking up the far wall.

"Okay. I'm sorry," Gracie says a few moments later, her tone gentle, calm even. She places a cautious hand on my right arm, letting it rest there for a second, testing me. Then, when I don't shrug her off, she comes closer and places her other hand on my left arm, pulling me into her embrace.

Just like that, all thoughts leave my mind. The warm feeling stretching up my spine is foreign. I'm having a hard time figuring out what it is as her fingertips rub over the tough material of my jacket.

"What are you doing?" I murmur, my words barely audible.

"I didn't mean to upset you."

Her words roll over my body before fading into nothing. Slowly, she presses her cheek against my chest. Her steady breaths brush against my shirt, soaking through it and hitting my skin with an open, unspoken promise.

"I know."

7

Tyler

VULNERABILITY ISN'T SOMETHING THAT COMES NATURALLY TO ME. When you're raised the way I was, you learn that feelings aren't something that you should share. Instead, they should be locked away and forgotten in a place where nobody can find them.

Maybe that's why I have always been so withdrawn. If there was nothing for me to feel, then there was nothing to spend my time alone worrying about. I guess in a really messed up way, I'm almost thankful for that. I mean, lord knows my fucked up childhood has left me with enough terrible memories to scare a prisoner on death row. So I choose to shove them in a dark room far back in my mind where I won't dare touch them, lock the door, and let them rot. But as the heat radiating from Gracie's delicate body coats my flesh in a soothing blanket, the lock on that door rattles, terrorizing me worse than what lies behind it.

My arms stay rooted to my sides, much to their displeasure, and I don't miss the soft sigh that hits my t-shirt as Gracie realizes I might not shove her away in a fit of rage.

"Ty?" she breathes and pulls away slightly, just enough to look up at me. The blue in her eyes is more vibrant than usual as she stares curiously into the dark pits of my own. I'm not sure what she's looking for, but I can only assume it is something I don't want her to find.

With a strangled cough, I place my hands on her arms and move her away. "I need to go," I grumble, running a hand through my hair and turning around. Her arm wraps around mine just as a vexed huff rings through the room.

"What happened? Did I freak you out or something? You don't have to go," she babbles, a sudden helplessness drips from her words. Her wide, wounded doe-eyes send a jolt of pain to my chest as soon as I turn my head to look back at her, a mistake that only intensifies my need to get the hell out of here.

I'm moving through the door as her words fall on nothing but the space I left behind. Finally, I escape the shrinking confines of the apartment. My eyes focus on the hallway carpet as I stalk my way to the elevator. The soft smacking sound of her feet against the rug just outside of her door makes my stomach twist. She calls out for me to turn around and talk to her. But there's no good in that plea for either of us.

Everyone has their "thing" that helps them focus. Something that gives them the strength to drag themselves up off of the ground and walk on their own two feet again. Something that sends jolts of happiness through your entire body, lighting you up with the feeling that you crave whenever it's not there. Something that makes all the horrible stuff you've gone through in your life nothing but a slight tingle living in the back of your mind.

That something for me is throwing my fist in someone's face. In a boxing ring, mostly.

"Fuck, man. You're almost as good as me now," Braden praises. He pulls the ropes apart and shoves his six-foot-five, two-hundred-and-fifty-pound body through them before jumping down onto the cracked concrete floor. Following his lead, I untie my gloves and yank them off my sweaty hands. I reach the bags thrown against a lone red wall in a dungeon of black, courtesy of the busted-ass paint job a group of us did a few weeks prior.

Brooks, the owner of this boxing gym, had been on one of his renovation benders and decided that the place needed a bit of sprucing up. Now, most would think the obvious choice would be to clean up the obscene number of smoke butts lying around the back of the gym, or maybe scrub the sweat stains off of the concrete, but nope. Instead, Brooks wanted a red wall.

Yeah, yeah. We all give Brooks a hard time. But he's the closest thing to family most of us around here have. So if the dumb ass wants a red wall, he's getting a red wall.

"Yeah, right," I grumble, not bothering to bug him about the sickening amount of confidence he has in himself before lifting the top of my t-shirt to wipe the beads of sweat sticking to my forehead.

"Come on. You could be if you didn't practically live in that damn rink all year. We miss you around here."

"You see me all of the time." I can sense his sarcastic eye roll even after he turns to grab the water bottle from his duffle.

"Yeah, okay," he snickers.

I give my head a shake. "Got something to say, fuckhead?"

"Not a single word." He shrugs. Braden isn't the first one of the guys to give me a hard time about ditching them. It's not that I am not aware of the fact that I am held up in the arena all the time, but hockey is everything to me. It's a once-in-a-lifetime opportunity. One that gives me the chance to take care of my mom the way she should be taken care of. Not to mention that hockey was the first sport I found I was actually good at. Turns out, I was a natural at shoving guys into end boards and slamming a wooden stick against a small rubber circle—something I guess I can thank Allen for.

The fast-paced, physically exhausting game was an immediate addiction for an anger-fuelled kid desperately trying to keep his emotions at bay. At first, I would stay out late, hunkered down at the neighbourhood basketball court using two busted old milk crates tipped on their sides as a makeshift hockey net. Rocks were the perfect pucks, and I would shoot as many of them as I could with the beat-up hockey stick my mom got me for my ninth birthday.

Eventually, the late-night practices in the back alley two houses down became late-night practices in a freezing hockey rink. I got good. Not exactly Oakley Hutton good, but my skill level was way above the remaining forwards on my team by the time I reached my college years. And by some odd twist of fate, I entered the league undrafted a year after my best friend.

Braden speaks up when he gets no response from me. "We just miss your arrogant ass around here. You're always either at the arena for a game or practice. I'm surprised you haven't set up a tent there so you don't have to bother ever going anywhere else." He's offering me a small smile, and although he didn't mean to guilt me, my stomach twists. I swallow quickly and return a forced smile.

"I'll come around more. I'm sorry."

"Alright." He nods, although I know he doesn't believe me. "Now go shower. You're pretty ripe, dude." He wrinkles his nose to emphasize his point. I cringe at the fact that he is right and squeeze his shoulder before heading toward the locker room.

My mom is sitting outside my apartment building when I pull up. Her head is hung low from where she sits on the concrete stairs leading up to the door. Dark hair blends with the night sky. Her bare hands pull tight at the sides of her unzipped, well-loved jacket as she tries to make do with the broken zipper.

My heart feels heavy as I wonder what happened this time. It must have been bad for her to come to me knowing the mouthful she might end up receiving. Sighing, I count down from ten before I get out of the truck. Then, with my bag thrown over my shoulder, I take quick strides toward her.

"What are you doing out here, Mom? Did you forget your key?" I bend down and wrap a hand around her arm, gently helping her to her feet. She throws a frail arm around me as I lead us to my apartment.

"Oh, your key. Right. I think I lost it. I'm sorry, sweetheart," she murmurs, the pungent stench of vodka rolling off her tongue.

"Don't be sorry. It's getting colder at night now though, so call me next time instead of waiting outside." The last thing I need is to be taking her to the hospital because she's gotten sloshed and wound up with hypothermia.

She nods her head against my shoulder but doesn't offer any verbal acknowledgment. When we reach my door, I quickly slide my key in the lock and usher us inside. I flip on the main light switch and gently guide her straight to my room. Not bothering to turn on any more lights, I lead her to the bed in the dark and sit her down on the edge.

We easily fall into our usual routine. I crouch down, pull off her favourite pair of black heels, and slide her coat over her thin shoulders. Standing up, I turn around and set her shoes down on my dresser and drape her jacket over the side.

"Crawl in, Mom," I whisper, and place a hand on her shoulder, slowly pushing her until she takes the hint. She lies down slowly, stretching out on the lumpy queen bed and adjusting her position until she's comfortably laying her head against the pillow.

"Thank you, sweet boy. You take such good care of me."

Nodding despite the fact I know she can't see me in the darkness of the room, I sigh, relieved that she isn't putting up as much of a fight as the last time and pull the covers over her. I take one last look at her before I go to collect the essentials she will need when she wakes up.

With a new pound in my temples, I place a bowl, two Advil, and a glass of water beside the bed.

It has always bothered me—not knowing or understanding how someone can treat themselves as if their life means nothing to them or anyone else. Thinking about how selfish I think that makes her makes me feel nothing but guilt. I don't know the struggle of addiction—not the way she does.

So that should mean that I shouldn't get to judge. Right? But I do. Because even though she is the parent, I have been the one taking care of her my whole life. And it isn't always as easy as it was tonight.

8

Tyler

"THERE'S MY FAVOURITE KILLJOY!" OAKLEY SHOUTS, JUMPING UP from where he sits beside Ava when I walk inside Adam's front door a week later.

"If it isn't my favourite hockey dud. I was expecting better from you this season, ya know? I might have to tell the team that our new captain is a flop," I tease, a genuine smile on my lips for the first time in a while. One that only this group can bring out.

"Soon to be captain," he corrects me with a wink. "And if you wanna play dirty then I'll have to make sure you don't see a minute of ice time all of next season."

As we shake hands, I look over his shoulder and catch sight of Gracie trying to sneak a glance at her brother and I from behind the kitchen door frame.

"And miss out on reliving our glory days? Yeah, right," I scoff, my attention still fixed on Gracie's wide blue eyes as they meet mine from across the room, making my stomach dip.

When Ava comes barrelling into the room, the curious blonde whips her head back around in a feeble attempt to avoid getting caught gawking at me by her future sister-in-law.

"Well, aren't you a sight for sore eyes?" Ava asks, hand on her hip. "Finally decided to join us, eh?"

Chuckling at her light tease, I shake my head and accept the hug that is quickly offered to me. "Trust me, I would have rather been with you guys," I mumble, quiet enough for only her to hear.

She squeezes my arm in response before pulling away, her eyebrow raised. Her green eyes are clouded with judgment but the last thing I feel is judged. Funny how that works.

"Well, are you going to come say hello to the fat pregnant lady or not?" Morgan quips, her sass level at an all-time high. I still don't know how Matt has handled her this long. God knows I wouldn't be able to. I can barely handle an hour alone with her on a good day.

"Not with that attitude I'm not," I scoff, and walk toward her regardless. My eyes widen as I round the couch and see her protruding bump. "Holy shit."

"I know! I'm fucking huge!" she cries, her eyes swelling with unshed tears.

"Sorry . . ." I trail off, not sure how to pull my foot out of my mouth as I lock my wide eyes with Matt's tired ones. "What is happening?" He shrugs his shoulders in response and places a comforting hand on Morgan's back.

A hand slapping against my ass sends a shock through my system. I quickly spin around and throw daggers at Adam.

He looks back at me with a shit-eating grin. "Hey, buddy. Ready to get this show on the road?"

Excitement rolls through my bones. "Always."

Adam moves to sit down on the couch, and as I turn to follow his lead, I see the only open spot is beside Gracie.

The hurt etched deeply in her features is undeniable as I reluctantly sit down beside her. Our thighs brush together, and the urge for me to lean as far away from her as possible rolls away with the immediate need to let more than just our thighs touch. Thankfully Oakley stands before I can do something I'm sure I'll regret.

"Ava, baby," Oakley murmurs, pulling Ava to the front of the room with him. "You know I love you, right?"

This is the moment every one of us has been waiting for. It's why I helped Adam order a congratulatory cake from the most extra cake shop in Vancouver. Oakley's finally going to do it. It only took him a few years too many. Ava's eyebrows tug inwards as she nods.

"So you know that I would be an even bigger idiot than I already am if I waited any longer to lock you down? To finally give you my last name? Forever?" His tone has changed from nervous to unmistakably confident at the turn of a dime.

As Ava catches on to what's happening, surprise takes over her features. Wide, shiny, emerald-green eyes stare back at Oakley as he slowly gets down on one knee. Gasps break through the room as the other two girls watch the heartwarming sight in front of us and my own proud smile grows.

When a small hand wraps around my much larger one, my breath catches in my throat. I fight to keep my eyes trained in front of me and silently pray that this dangerously stupid move remains unseen.

A soft sniffle breaks my concentrated gaze and my eyes dart to the girl sitting beside me. A sudden pang shoots through my chest, causing my brows to scrunch in confusion. Gracie's bottom lip is caught between her teeth and quivering furiously as she tries to hold back her happy cries from tearing through the room and interrupting her brother's special moment. My eyes focus on the lone tear cascading down her cheek, and my thumb is swiping it away before my brain registers what I'm doing.

The second the pad of my thumb makes contact with her skin, an unnatural heat flares through my body while she seems to freeze in response. My mouth dries up like a wet sponge in the sun and I stare at the small beauty mark on the right side of her mouth.

The sound of clapping and booming voices pull my attention

away from Gracie and toward the happy couple who I'm assuming deserve congratulations.

I'm getting up off the couch to do just that when a sharp pain shoots through my foot. I turn to the side and hiss, "What the fuck was that for?"

Gracie clenches her fists and ignores my irritation as she leans in and whispers the words "follow me" in my ear. She's walking away from me before I get the chance to argue. Closing my eyes and taking a deep breath, I look over at the group one last time and follow her. When I reach the room at the very end of the hallway, Gracie pulls me further into the room and carefully closes the door behind us.

"What the hell was that back there?" she spits, an uncontrolled fire burning brightly in her eyes.

"What are you talking about?" I ask, my eyes locked on the wall behind her and a fake tone of confidence drips from my tongue. The corners of my lips tug up as she lets out a small growl, shooting daggers into my chest. Her fists open and close by her sides, and her cheeks have become a dangerously dark shade of red.

"Don't touch me like that and then act like . . ." Her voice trails off, yet she takes a brave step toward me. I raise an eyebrow and stare at her expectantly. "Like you have no idea what you did! Stop acting like you feel nothing for me when we both know that you do! You're a giant pussy," she finishes, her jaw clenched in anger.

Pulling my lips back, I cross my arms and glare down at her as rage builds deep in my chest. "You need to think carefully about what you're going to say next, princess," I reply, my eyes narrowed into slits. I take a menacing step toward her.

Our bodies are flush, heat radiating off of both of us in waves. My chest is rising and falling at an alarming rate as anger blurs my vision. For a second, I wonder whether I should run through the door behind her.

"And why would I do that? So you can run away again?

Pretend like nothing happened and move on with your life? News flash Tyler, it didn't work last time, and it won't work this time." She pushes back like always.

I can feel my dick straining against the zipper of my jeans as flashbacks of last summer flicker through my mind like a movie reel. The hot Mexico sun beaming down on my back as she lay under me on nothing but a thin beach towel. Her nails ripping into my shoulder blades while mine gripped the soft white sand with every jaw-grinding thrust.

We spent hours on that beach, hiding away from reality until we couldn't anymore. It was fun, even exciting, hiding the late-night meetups from our friends. But it was also selfish. Stupidly selfish. And after we got on that plane and flew home, I promised myself I wouldn't betray them again. But I did the night I took her home from that club and I hate myself for it.

"It was working," I mumble, closing my eyes in a weak attempt to keep myself from staring at the black bra peeking out from her sheer shirt. My feeble attempt is made futile when I grip the thin material between my fingers. "Have you worn this in public before?" I grit through clenched teeth. Jealousy burns in my veins, forcing images into my head that I don't want to see.

Looking down at her shirt, she plays with the hem before looking back up at me again with a widespread smirk. "Oh, this? I usually only wear it when I'm looking to get laid. The guys usually can't keep their eyes off—"

I slam my lips against hers before she can finish the rest of her sentence, knocking her back into the wall as she gasps in shock. She responds to me instantly and runs a hand through my hair, pulling me harder against her. I cup her face tightly in my hands and snake my tongue through her parted lips. Any self-control I had is long gone the second she pushes off my hat and scratches her fingers along my scalp. She then gives a harsh tug to the hair on the back of my neck, and a gravelly groan falls against her mouth.

Letting go of her cheeks, I run my hands down her sides, grabbing tightly on her exposed hip. I pull her toward the bed that is waiting for us a few feet away. When my knees brush up against it, I sit down and pull her onto my lap. As she readjusts her ass on my thighs, she pulls away slightly, beaming at the obvious hard-on nestling between her spread legs. Then, without warning, she tugs at the shirt covering my torso. Taking the hint, I raise my arms and yank the shirt off for her and throw it away carelessly.

"Does this feel familiar, Tyler?" she coos, and my blood runs hot with lust. Her hand inches down my stomach and grabs me through my jeans. My head falls back at the sudden contact, and I fight back the moan that's itching to be set free by tugging my bottom lip between my teeth and gnawing roughly at it.

"Words, Ty," she purrs into my ear, fingers moving up my length until they reach my zipper. "Tell me you remember how good we felt together."

"Yeah." I choke, every inch of my body needing more friction between us. "You know it does."

She tells me she liked my answer by grasping the waistband of my jeans. I raise my hips, allowing her to pull them down enough for the cold air to hit my cock through my boxers. "What about this?" Her hand wraps around me through the last boundary, gently rubbing where I need her touch. Her baby blues stare at me innocently, just begging me to fuck her and give us what we both need. As I open my mouth to speak, a loud knock on the door echoes through the room. I freeze, my eyes on the locked door. Gracie jumps away from me and her body makes a loud crack as she hits the hardwood floor. In any other situation, her clumsiness would have made me laugh.

"*Shit.* Shit, shit, shit. Put your shirt on! That could be my brother!" she whispers. Her expression is frantic as she runs her shaking fingers through her hair. I stand up quickly, jumping as I pull my pants back on. "Fuck, I'm so stupid! It's definitely my brother," she rambles, hands still wrapped in her hair.

I brush her concern off with a light chuckle, "He won't suspect anything."

Another knock on the door sounds and she pushes me back forcefully, eyeing the small spare room. "Where's your shirt? I can't find it!"

My heart drops when I don't see it either.

9

Tyler

"I HAVE TO SEE WHO IT IS," GRACIE SAYS WITH A SHUDDER, AS SHE struggles to make it to the door. She grasps the door handle and barely pulls it open an inch. "Adam! Thank God! Where's my brother?"

I've never been happier to see Adam than I am right now. Relief floods through me and I relax a bit.

"He's too preoccupied with his new fiancé to be paying attention to your little disappearing act," Adam gripes, disappointment radiating from every inch of him. His tone rubs me the wrong way as he rips into Gracie. My feet finally move, and it's only a couple of seconds until I'm right behind her, pulling the door wide open to narrow my eyes at Adam. "Oh, you don't even have a shirt on. Even better. What a fantastic time to get laid." He's scolding me as if I'm a child. "Did you forget your brain in Europe or something? I thought you were smarter than this."

My face flames as my dormant anger makes an ugly return. Tearing my eyes away from him before I blow a gasket, I turn in search of my shirt once again.

"You both need to get your shit together before Oakley finds out about this. We're all fucked if he does, and nobody told him. You know that, right?"

Sitting down on the bed, I watch Gracie drop her head, her shoulders sagging with shame. My hands wind themselves in my now very messy hair, and I can't help but let the guilt devour me whole.

Oakley has been nothing but a great friend to me, even when we both knew I didn't deserve it. Bringing me to family dinners, always calling to check in on me regardless of his crazy schedule, and what do I do in return? Fuck his sister. In a giant fucked up way of saying thank you.

"Oakley won't find out. Not until we tell him," I mutter. I want nothing more than for this conversation to be done with. I need to get out of here and have a smoke.

"What even is this anyway? Is this a fuck-buddy situation, or is this actually something worth him knowing about? Because if I'm about to get dragged into this shit storm, I need to know what I'm going to be dealing with." Adam crosses his arms against his chest, letting out an exasperated sigh.

"Who has a fuck buddy?"

My head snaps up, and my blood runs cold as I stare wide-eyed at the other two. Gracie's mouth falls open, and her hands shake at her sides. Our worst nightmare is about to become an even nastier reality.

Gracie turns to me, motioning toward the walk-in closet beside the bed as Adam tries to cover for us. "Oh, uh, just some buddy of mine."

"Fuck no!" I whisper, shaking my head fervently.

"Please, Tyler," she pleads "He's getting closer. Go!" She grabs my arms and shoves me in the direction of the closet door.

Holding back a growl, I angrily pull open the door and walk inside. Empty clothes hangers stab me in the back as Gracie pushes me even further into the closet, not stopping until I hit the wall. She smiles apologetically before shutting the door, locking me in the dark space.

Laughter carries in through the closet soon after, and for a second, I think we might just get away with this. That is until Oakley's booming voice shakes the room.

"Is that Tyler's shirt?"

"How would I know?" Gracie asks, her voice steady. I envy her.

"That's definitely his shirt. What is it doing here? Where is he?" Oakley demands.

"Man, just take a step back for a min-" Adam tries to reason with him.

I take the nerves in his voice as my cue and walk out of the closet. I throw my hands up in surrender when Oakley spins around to face me. Oakley throws my shirt at Adam the second his eyes narrow in on me. And if looks could kill, I would be ten feet under already.

"You better start talking before I throw my fist clean through your skull," Oakley hisses through clenched teeth. He clenches his fists tight at his sides, and I notice the vein in his forehead throbbing painfully. I would be lying if I said that fighting a guy Oakley's size doesn't scare me.

"Oakley, let's not do this today. Come on." Adam tries once again to reason with Oakley as he takes a cautious step toward him. But, it's a move he quickly learns was a mistake because Oakley turns to him, a face full of rage-driven disappointment.

"You knew about this, didn't you? You're just as much a shitty friend as this fucker." His hand flies in my direction, stopping just a few inches from my chest.

"At least let me explain," I plead as I try to bring his attention back to me and not to Adam. "Adam has nothing to do with this."

"I don't want you to explain anything to me. I want my sister to do the honours." Oakley snaps at me, bringing his narrowed gaze to rest on his guilt-stricken sister.

Gracie snorts. "This isn't any of your business to begin with. I'm not a little girl anymore."

"Are you sure? Because you're sure as hell acting like one." Oakley stiffens. "You're not sixteen anymore. This obsession has to end before you get hurt."

"Obsession? Nice." She shakes her head furiously. "You always know just what to say."

"Don't flip this on me. I've spent years trying to ignore the way you look at him but I'm done. You two would only end badly," Oakley states smugly.

"And that's your decision to make?" she questions.

"It is when I'm the only one with common sense! I know Tyler better than anyone, and any relationship you could have with him wouldn't last outside of the bedroom."

This sibling argument quickly becomes a free-for-all. The insult makes me grind my jaw. I take a warning step in Oakley's direction.

"Let's not pretend like you're some saint," I scoff, finally stepping in between the heated siblings.

"I am compared to you!" Oakley snaps back, cocking his head. "I wouldn't have taken advantage of my best friend's sister, that's for sure."

"You seem so sure that I took advantage of her but you don't even know what happened before you came bounding in here acting like a damn bodyguard with an axe to grind."

"Don't, Ty," Gracie pleads, her posture rigid. It's clear that she doesn't want her brother to know about us, but I can't act like I wouldn't like for it to just be over and done with already.

"Unless you can look me in the eye and tell me you weren't in here trying to sleep with my sister, then I don't want to hear what was happening. I can figure out enough of it on my own."

"What the hell is going on in here?" Ava shrieks, storming into the room, confused. Gracie stares at her intently, her eyes pleading. Ava picks up on the tense energy quickly and looks at Oakley with narrowed eyes. "What did you do?"

"Me? Why don't you ask the little girl silently begging for

your help?" Oakley speaks to Ava but his words are directed at Gracie.

"Somebody better talk."

Nobody speaks. I know I should be the one to say something, anything, to make this better, but my mind is blank. I am too focused on the guilt and hopelessness this entire situation has brought. I should not have slept with Gracie in Mexico and I sure as hell should not have done it again here. Or anywhere. I've gone and fucked this up way worse than I ever thought I could.

"Tyler didn't take advantage of me, Oakley. Quite the opposite actually. And this isn't the first time we've been together like this. This is just the first time you have caught us," Gracie says softly, her cheeks flushed. "And you can be upset if you want, but it doesn't change the fact that we're not going to stop. You don't control my life anymore."

My jaw goes slack. I am surprised that she had the nerve to not only tell the truth about what we have done but to make a bold statement that could end up not being true. A sharp pain radiates through my face as Oakley's fist connects with my jaw. I lose my footing at the sudden force, flying back on my ass as he launches himself at me. I'm pinned to the ground before I can react, the back of my head throbbing from hitting the floor.

Oakley's fist winds back again, but Adam moves to pull him off me before he can hit me again. His weight is lifted from my chest and my lungs fill up like empty balloons.

"You can have him then, Gracie." Oakley turns to me. His lips are twitching but remain in a tight line. "Because I want nothing to do with him anymore."

My gut twists and pulls as Oakley shakes free of Adam and storms out of the room. Gracie kneels down in front of me and I throw an arm over my eyes as she asks where it hurts. I can't find it in me to reply so I just continue to lay here, dead to the world.

The pain shooting through my cheek is nothing compared to how I feel after hurting Oakley and destroying one of the most important friendships that I have ever had.

10

ONE YEAR AGO

Gracie

I SLIP MY ROUNDED SUNGLASSES BACK OVER MY EYES AND LEAN against one of the many colourful lounge chairs spread out along the infinity pool. The sun is hot against my tanning-oil-lathered pale skin, making the frozen drink in my hand more noticeable as it melts into a slushy.

Ava gave me a hard time about using such a hefty amount of tanning oil before I left her room, considering I burn even under a thick layer of SPF, and tanning lotion *probably* isn't the smartest choice to avoid that. But if there's one thing I'm going to get on this trip, it's a freaking tan.

It's just after lunchtime and the resort is packed full of bikini-clad women and shirtless men. A sight I can't say isn't the least bit enjoyable.

Back in Vancouver, the guys are either wearing white tees with rolled sleeves and chinos, or fancy business suits that have short-legged pants to show off their ugly socks covered with pot leaves. I much prefer glistening washboard abs and brightly coloured swim trunks.

The five of us have been in Mexico for just over a day now, leaving me with only five days left to drink as many complimentary alcoholic beverages as possible and kiss as many random half-naked beach bums as it takes to forget about all of my petty problems back home.

It had been way too freaking hard to convince my new boss to let me take this week off, so I think I deserve not to worry about a damn thing for a few days.

When I first started working for Cleo at her small dance studio in downtown Van, I half expected to spend my days standing off to the side as an extra in case she needed someone to cover for her or help the odd kid remember a missed step. I didn't expect her to throw all of the routines for our upcoming recitals onto me.

I'm not new to the world of dance or to creating my own routines. I've been a dancer for all my life for Pete's sake. But until now, I've never had to come up with a complete performance, top to bottom, for someone else; let alone multiple little ones with overly involved parents ready with their pitchforks freshly sharpened in case I embarrassed their children.

I know that I should be looking at the situation in a more positive light considering it will give me experience with something I've never done before. But the stress from the bucket load of new responsibilities is already building up, and with my unwanted anxiety rearing its ugly head whenever possible, it seems like more of a chore than a learning opportunity.

"You couldn't have worn a bathing suit with a bit more fabric?" I hear Oakley ask as he comes up on my left and sits in an empty chair. "What kind of bathing suit is that, anyway?"

Ava follows shortly after, a large sun hat flopping in her eyes and an adorable white one-piece with crisscrossed straps covering her lean body.

"Leave her alone, babe." She swats his arm and flops down on his lap. Oakley wraps an arm around her middle and pulls her closer to his chest. "I think she looks beautiful."

I grin. "And that's why you're my favourite." Wiping the beads of sweat from my forehead, I look at the crowds of people in the pool ask, "What took you guys so long? I'm going to burn if I stay out here for much longer."

"It's better if you don't know," Oakley says smugly, a smirk on his lips no doubt. I don't look to find out for sure.

Ava snorts when I scrunch my face in disgust. "I told you not to put so much oil on. Been there done that, Gray."

She reaches into the large bag she set beside her chair and pulls out a pair of sunglasses and a bottle of sunscreen. She slides her sunglasses on and holds the sunscreen toward Oakley. "Heads up."

As my brother reaches forward to grab the bottle, a stray hand pushes him away and swipes the sunscreen.

"Thanks, Ava. I left mine upstairs," Tyler teases. He joins the group with a beautifully rare and relaxed grin. The same one that never fails to awaken the family of butterflies in my stomach.

Oakley scoffs and shoots his elbow back, hitting Tyler above the band of his swim trunks. A pained groan slips from his lips, and I become way too easily distracted by the hand that's begun rubbing at the two deep lines leading to what hides beneath his trunks.

"Asshole," Tyler mutters and smacks the back of Oakley's head on his way to the empty chair beside mine.

Coincidence? Maybe. *Maybe not.*

I immediately look away and chew on my lip, praying that nobody caught the eggplant emojis in my eyes just now. Oakley would have a hay day with that. I probably wouldn't see another day outside of my hotel room.

The legs of the chair squeak as Tyler sits down. I peek over at him to find him watching me, his head tilted and the ghost of a grin tugging on his lips.

"You know, if I wasn't such a confident guy, your staring would have made me self-conscious."

The teasing whisper has my eyes bulging as I gulp air like a fish out of water.

"I wasn't staring," I argue.

He arches a brow and leans toward me, elbows resting on his knees, his fingers mere inches from my thigh. "No? Because I was."

I twist in my seat and stare at him open-mouthed.

"Pink is your colour," he murmurs. His eyes trail over my skin and goosebumps follow.

"I didn't know I had a colour. I thought I looked good in everything."

My heart thumps against my ribcage the second his eyes meet mine. His eyes hold mine for a few seconds before his gaze falls somewhere else. *Dismissed.*

I empty my lungs and sneak a look at my brother and Ava. They're completely locked in their own world. Neither of them are paying any attention to us.

"Are you searching for another compliment, Gray? Because I'm all out." He turns to face me again, his mouth set in a tight line. He spreads his legs wider, and the urge to get up and stand between them swims to the surface.

"I don't need one." I shrug. "There's already so many written across your face. Now if you'll excuse me, I have to get out of this sun before I combust."

I stand confidently and immediately feel a rush of pride for not letting Tyler get the better of me like I usually do.

Turning my back to him, I reach down and grab my beach bag, smirking when I hear the sharp intake of breath behind me. Sliding my bag to rest on my shoulder, I tighten my ponytail before looking back and raising my brow.

"You know, if I wasn't such a confident girl, your staring would have made me self-conscious."

11

PRESENT

Tyler

"Are you okay? I am so sorry, Ty." Gracie kneels down beside me, running soft hands across my jaw as if she can't believe what just happened. I narrow my eyes, shove her hands away, and push myself into a sitting position. I don't bother looking at the hurt expression that I know she's wearing as my rejection stings her fresh wounds. Instead, I get to my feet. The room spins. Great. Just what I needed. Another fucking concussion.

"Where are you going? You need to go to the doctor!" She's fuming now. She spins around and pins me in place with a glare.

I scoff and dismiss her with a shake of my head, stalking out of the room. Her footsteps echo behind me as I walk down the hallway, her overbearing stubbornness not allowing her to leave me alone. Fuck, the Hutton's are stubborn as hell.

"Screw off, Gracie. I'm not in the mood," I mutter. I walk into the bathroom and slam the door shut behind me, twisting the lock quickly before she has a chance to follow me in.

I inwardly wince as soon as I turn to look in the mirror above the sink. A subtle blue has made its way over my olive skin, almost perfectly outlining a set of knuckles. My lips are swollen too, only I don't think that's from Oakley's beat down. Turning on the tap, I splash my face with cold water, hoping it will cool my raging body temperature. I lean my elbows on the counter and hang my head.

What the fuck am I supposed to do now? My best friend hates me. My other ones are probably right there with him, and I've muddled lines I swore I would keep crystal clear.

"Can we at least finish talking about what happened? I don't want to keep pretending there's nothing between us!" Gracie shouts from the other side of the door.

My fingers tug on my hair as I groan louder than I probably needed to and yank open the door. "There's nothing to talk about. There's nothing between us," I snarl, my nostrils flaring in anger. "You need to move on. I'm done."

My words hit her like a slap. Her jaw drops and tears well in her eyes. The ache in her chest is reflected in the film across her baby-blue eyes before she drops them to the ground. Her fingers curl into fists, and for a second, I wonder if she will do the same thing as her brother and actually toss one at me.

"You know something, Tyler?" she asks, her sad eyes lighting up with a fire so fierce I feel my mouth dry up. I set my jaw, and raise an eyebrow in response. I cross my arms and lean back. "I feel sorry for you."

Heat rushes through my body, forcing its way over my tingling skin and through every inch of muscle as she stands in front of me, wearing a grin so smug I want to suck it right off.

"You what?"

Her smile is enough to convince me that I should push her up against the wall and remind her what happened earlier. Probably not the best idea though.

"Maybe you are just as broken as everyone says."

I take a menacing step toward her, and her eyes widen slightly. "And maybe you're smarter than I give you credit for, princess."

She swallows visibly. She parts her lips the tiniest amount

and continues to gawk at me. Her cheeks flush a deep shade of pink.

"What's wrong? Cat got your tongue?" I blow out, bending down to let the soft words touch her ear. I softly nip her earlobe and a powerful shudder racks through her body. Her head falls on my shoulder. "I am broken. But don't ever feel sorry for me. I don't need your sympathy." I back away from her, letting her head fall into empty space, startling her.

She regains her composure and narrows her gaze. I am walking around her and heading for the front door before she can speak another word.

"You're coming out with me tonight. You've been sulking for like the past week," Braden demands. His stern tone leaves no room for negotiation. "Enough of this bullshit." The jingle of keys is the only sound on the quiet street as he locks the gym's front doors and shoves them back in the pocket of his hoodie. Inhaling the end of the cigarette hanging from my lips, I fall into step beside him down the chipping sidewalk.

"I'll pass," I mumble, trying to fight him anyway. We stop beside his blacked-out Honda and he scoffs. "Funny, I don't remember giving you the option."

I roll my eyes and take a last puff of my cigarette before stomping it out with my shoe, turning to him with a scowl. "I'm going to take a shot in the dark and say it won't be just us. Am I right?" I ask, opening the passenger door once the beep sounds from his remote starter.

The thick smell of body spray clings to the car's small, red-stitched interior, and I nearly cough. Like any playboy with an inability to keep his dick in his pants longer than a few hours, his car reeks of past conquests. It doesn't surprise me. Braden is as douchy as they come with his adoration for beautiful women. His fleeting expression answers my question, and I snort when he pretends that I didn't notice.

"Would that be so bad?" he asks, sticking his key in the ignition and starting the engine. A pained groaning noise echoes through the once quiet neighbourhood.

"Oakley won't come."

"Yeah, he will. Ava will make him," he chuckles, stealing a look at me before looking back at the road.

The first drop of rain that hits the windshield makes us both groan. One thing this city does not need is more rain. Despite having to spend most of the year driving in the frequent downpours, drivers here seem to lose all sense of direction the second they hit a wet road. They either start going fifteen kilometres under the speed limit or fifteen over it. There's rarely an in-between.

"You really think he isn't going to smack my head against a brick wall the second he sees me?" I challenge. I don't miss the fleeting scowl that appears on his lips just before it disappears. "It's only been a few days."

"Not if he wants Ava to let him come home anytime soon. He has a home game in two days, so unless he wants to spend his night in a hotel room instead of at home with his girl, then he needs to talk to you. Not slam your head against a wall."

I close my eyes and lean back against the headrest. "Does he know I'll be there?"

"I already told him," the sneaky fucker says, bursting with pride.

"You're a pretty brave guy, just assuming I would come."

"That's the sweetest thing you've ever said to me." He sniffles and lifts his thumb to wipe an imaginary tear from his cheek. He turns to look at me with a dramatic pout.

"Fuck off." I shake my head and let the quiet music from the radio wash over us as we sit in silence for the rest of the drive.

The effects of the whiskey Braden made me gulp down before we left hit me as we pull up outside the small bar. This bar used to be the place to be during hockey season in college—back when the team was at the top of the social circle, I guess.

"Everyone else is inside already." Braden opens his door and rolls up the sleeves of his plain black shirt to show off the detailed sleeves of black tattoos on his forearms as usual. We step out into the warm rain. Thankfully my nerves have been calmed by the excessive booze my liver is trying to filter through, and I follow after him.

"Always gotta be fashionably late eh, buddy?" I tease as we walk up to the entrance. I pull open the door and walk inside. It's nearly empty here. The only people present are the bartender and the massive huddle of hockey players with their plus ones. They take up the back of the restaurant, taking up all of the brown booths.

"About time!" Matt slurs as he stumbles in our direction, skimming the bartender's shoulder as he does so.

"Careful," Braden laughs and places a hand on his shoulder to steady him as we make our way over to the group. My eyes land on Oakley. He stands with his back to us, a full drink in his hand and the typical Seattle cap resting backward on his shaggy hair, his back straight. His shoulders are squared as he nods his head to whatever Adam is spewing in his ear. It isn't until Braden shouts some inaudible greeting at the group that he turns around and sees me for the first time since throwing a fist into my face.

We both freeze, our feet glued to the floor as we glower at each other. The air grows thick with tension as the rest of the group catches sight of our stare-off. Adam is the first one to speak up with an over-exaggerated shout.

"It's about to be one hell of a night, boys!"

12

Gracie

"I SWEAR TO GOD, OAKLEY. THIS IS SO NOT FUNNY ANYMORE. IF YOU don't call me back like *right now,* I promise I will drive home and tell mom all about your anger issues. Don't test me," I hiss into my phone as I leave what seems like my hundredth voicemail this week.

I know for a fact that he's been listening to them. There's no other way he can possibly have more space in his voicemail. I thought after he had left his own voicemail the day after our . . . unfortunate night that this would be done with. But I guess not.

I throw my phone on my bed with a groan. I toss myself down beside it, and my body sinks deep into the mattress. I swing my fist down on my pillow in anger. I can't believe Oakley is ignoring me just to prove a point. If I didn't know any better, I would think *I* am the older sibling.

"Still nothing, eh?"

A shrug is the only response I can offer Jessica as she moves to the bed and flops down beside me.

"Clearly," I mumble into my duvet, hot breath fanning my face. A hand rubs across my back, making slow circles on my tense muscles. Turning my head to the side, I raise my eyebrows at her. Her hair is done flawlessly and the fancy braided bun resting on the top of her head looks extremely out of place in my messy bedroom.

"Are you going somewhere?" I ask, gesturing at her over-lined, dark-stained lips.

"Yes. We both are. We are going to the Brew tonight."

I flip over and stare at the bumps on the ceiling, laughing. "The puck bunny bar? Are you serious?" The last time I stepped foot in that place, I had to watch Tyler swap spit with some busty blonde supermodel all night. I ended up getting sloshed and puked all over her. It was by far one of my finest moments.

"I never joke about a fun time, Gray," she scoffs and pushes off the bed. She stares at me with her hands on her hips, shifting her weight between her two feet.

"Wanna tell me why we're going to that abandoned shack tonight?"

I watch her roll her eyes before walking into my closet. She comes out seconds later with a handful of hangers in her hand and drops them beside me. I stare as she picks through them, eyeing every piece carefully.

"This is definitely the one." She launches the dress at me. The gold sequins covering the dress were the reason why I had bought it a few weeks ago, and the off-the-shoulder sleeves flatter my body type quite well. I cock my head. "Don't change the subject, Jess,"

She sighs. "I heard it's going to be the hot spot for hockey players tonight."

A smirk spreads on my lips as she finishes her sentence. Hockey players, hey? This night just got interesting.

"Which ones?"

"Uh oh. I know that smirk." The shake of her head answers my question. There are only a few that would have invited her. "You have a plan, don't you?"

"Of course I do. I always do."

As soon as we step into the humid bar, I can feel the beads of sweat form on every inch of my exposed skin. I always wondered how it got so hot in these places. I mean, there's barely even anyone in here. I'm pretty sure it's to get people to buy drinks in hopes of cooling down. Kinda lowlife-ish, honestly.

Jess and I link arms as we make our way through the bar. As we turn the corner, my eyes fall on Oakley's broad back. He's standing in between Matt and Adam, one hand resting on Adam's shoulder while the other leans against the bar top.

Their laughter is contagious, and I have to suppress my own as I feel it swelling in my chest. We walk up confidently and grab the attention of a few of the players as we pass. No surprise there. The sudden lack of attention the rest of the guys receive from our new admirers draws their eyes to us as they turn around.

"Little H!" Adam roars when he sees me, his eyes glazed already as he holds his arms open for me.

"Hey, Adam," I giggle and move into his warm embrace.

"I'm also here. In case you boys forgot," Jessica nags, her hand resting cheekily on her hip. A twinge of annoyance settles between my shoulders but I shake it off.

"Oh, we didn't forget!" A guy shouts from beside Matt, shooting her a flirty wink. I don't remember his name, but I know Jess will be more than happy to tell me tomorrow morning.

Adam and I pull apart. I turn to face Oakley, my eyes filled with hope. "Hi, Lee," I murmur. I hate fighting with him. He's my best friend.

Oakley brushes me off like a fly buzzing in his face. His attention doesn't even fall on me for a brief second as he moves toward the bartender and orders himself another drink.

His rejection sends a piercing pain throughout my chest. My heart pounds against my rib cage. I can feel numerous sets of eyes fall on me as I stand in place, my eyes dropping to my feet in an attempt to push back the oncoming tears that are just aching to be shed.

"Follow him," Adam says, his voice dropping low so only I can hear him as he gently rubs my arm. Looking over at him, I force a fake smile on my lips. I take his advice and follow my brother.

I find him leaning against the bar with a long neck in his hands. His baseball cap is pulled low over his eyes as he hangs his head. Tension ripples off him in thick, painfully angry waves. I join him nervously. "You here for a specific reason, Gracie?" The tone of his voice is sharp and commanding.

"So he *does* speak!" I grin and sit down on the empty barstool beside him. The slightest tug on the corner of his lips brings the slightest glimmer of hope back.

"I assume from the lack of angry calls from Mom that you didn't tell her anything." He looks surprised, but he shouldn't be. I would never snitch on him. Not *really*.

"So, you did get my messages," I point out before flagging down the bartender and ordering a beer. When one is quickly slid in front of me, we both lift our bottles, gulping. Awkward silence covers us like the most miserable, scratchy blanket.

Our relationship has never been awkward. Yes, we have had our fair share of fights—mainly due to his overprotective nature, but things have never been this bad. I'm still not even sure how we got here, to this standstill.

"Look. I'm sorry, okay? I'm sorry you found out the way you did, and I'm sorry you disapprove of it." I sigh and down the rest of my bottle. He stays silent, his eyes focused on the mystery drink splattered across the bar-top.

Taking a much-needed deep breath, I collect my footing and shove the empty bottle toward the bartender and step down from the stool. If he wants to play it like this, then we will. I'm not getting down on my knees to beg him for his forgiveness. This is my life.

As I readjust my purse on my shoulder and whip around, more than ready to get the hell out of this situation, he calls out my name. "Sit. Please," Oakley begs, lifting his head for the first time and bringing his eyes up to meet mine. The hurt in his eyes is enough for me to set aside my own feelings and repair what I broke between us. I nod and sit back down. I place a hand over his where it rests on the dingy countertop.

"Talk to me, Lee. Let's figure this out."

He pulls his hat off with his free hand and rakes his fingers through his hair. He shakes his head once and slips the hat back on before smoothing out his overgrown beard.

"I'm sorry for the things I said to you. I was an awful brother and you didn't deserve any of that."

"Damn right, I didn't deserve it," I tease and lightly bump my shoulder against his. A small dimple appears on his right cheek as a smile starts to take over his features, lighting up his face. "Next time though, it won't be me you'll be dealing with. It will be Mom," I threaten.

His smile drops and is replaced with a shaky grimace as his eyes bulge. Grinning wide at his newfound distress, I give myself a mental pat on the back. "You're evil, Gray," he says with a click of his tongue. Our laughter brings a warmth to my chest that I've been missing this entire week.

"Can you promise me something, though?" I ask when our laughter dies down. The dreaded question now hangs in the air, darkening the mood slightly.

"Anything," he promises without hesitation.

"Fix things with Tyler. For me, for Ava, and for you. We both know you need to go home," I say gently, my hand squeezing his tightly. He sighs deeply, staring at me with regretful eyes as my words sink into him.

"I will." He swallows with a tight grimace. "This has been by far one of the hardest weeks of my life. This isn't what I wanted."

"It isn't what any of us wanted. Which is all the more reason to fix this."

"I promise I will fix this. Okay? Just trust me," he says, his signature confidence instantly convinces me that he's serious as it finally makes its glorious return. Everyone knows that a confident Hutton is a force to be reckoned with.

"I love you, big brother," I murmur into his shoulder, soaking up this moment for as long as I can.

"I love you too, little sister," he replies, placing a kiss on the top of my head and resting his cheek where his lips were just seconds ago.

Maybe I was too easy on him, and perhaps I forgave him too quickly after all of the things he said to me. But the only thing I'm sure about right now is that no matter how much we go through together, it will always be us against the world.

13

Tyler

Adam's unnecessary shout of welcome garners far too much attention. Everyone at the booth turns around to face us. I can see the slight tensing of Oakley's jaw from here and I straighten my back in response.

Braden slaps a hand on my shoulder and pushes me forward as he starts walking toward the group, smiling like the damn Cheshire Cat. Choking down my grumble, I shove my hands in the pockets of my jeans and try my best not to look like I'm being led to the guillotine.

"As fashionably late as ever, big man," Adam slurs, his statement clearly aimed at the brute beside me. Adam's arm is slung loosely over Braden's shoulder.

"Isn't that Gracie?" Braden asks nobody in particular, staring off to the side.

My throat tightens as I follow his line of sight.

She's standing tall with her hands placed firmly on her hips, barking harsh words at the girl standing in front of her, replicating her stance. It takes me a few seconds before I realize that the girl in front of her—wide, square-framed glasses and all—is none other than Beth Winston, stalker-extraordinaire.

Beth always creeped me the fuck out with how she was

always watching Adam with big, beady eyes back when they were in Uni, and the hatred she felt toward Ava was like something straight out of a horror movie. She didn't even know Ava any more than you could know a random person in a coffee shop that accidentally spilled steaming hot coffee all over you. We all knew that she was only after Ava because she was closer to Adam than she was. The entire feud between them was just confusing and weird. But it's been three years since then. So why the hell is Beth acting like a deranged ex shoving around a girl who has never so much as looked in her direction before?

I'm as surprised to see her as much as the next guy, but as I watch her take another step toward Gracie with a spine-chilling sneer, I know that I won't be able to sit back and watch whatever's going to happen next.

Gracie's head smacks against the brick wall behind her and she lets out a gasp of pain, falling back against the wall. Adam rushes past me before the growl rising through me has a chance to escape. I stare at him. His cheeks are flushed in anger, eyes cold and hard, jaw set. I haven't seen him this angry in a long time.

"Keep your hands off me!" Gracie shouts, the urgency behind her words cuts straight through me and urges my feet to start moving toward her. In my rush to get to Gracie, I push past a guy I have never met before, I catch a glimpse of the two girls before I am shoved out of the way by a couple of gawking asshats. I growl when one of their elbows digs into my ribcage, sending a jolt of pain through my side. My fists clench at my sides. I turn my attention to the two frat-boy-looking douchebags.

Walk away. Walk away. Walk away. This is not the time to start a bar brawl.

My gaze is torn away from the two guys when someone shoves past me, pushing me out of the way. I whirl around and see Oakley forcing his way through the crowd. An outraged cry rings throughout the bar and I'm focused only on getting to

Gracie. I follow after Oakley as we both head toward the same girl.

"What is your deal, you psycho?" Gracie's eyes are wide, bewildered, and her lips are slightly parted. Beth stares at her in anguish. Her hands are twitching at her sides, and her foot taps the floor to an off-tempo beat. She looks manic.

"Where's Adam?" Beth spits. My eyes move slowly over Gracie, tuning out the catfight as I look for any piece of her out of place or, even worse, *hurt*. Even the thought of it makes my chest throb.

My teeth grind together as soon I see the red patch of hair at the back of her head, and a stream of blood cascading down her cheek. Locking my steely gaze on Beth, I start toward them only to have my arm squeezed in a tight grip. The hand yanks on my bicep, sending me faltering back as I look down at the familiar, tattooed forearm.

"Let go over me, Oakley. I won't ask again," I hiss.

He ignores my comment with a shake of his head, but lets go of my arm.

"She can take her. Trust me."

"She's hurt."

"I know. If Beth wasn't a girl, you know I would be out there beating the life out of the sorry fucker. But Gracie won't want us to interfere. Not with this one."

Pride ripples through me as I watch Gracie pull her shoulders back and huff, clearly exhausted from this entire thing. She takes a menacing step toward Beth. Beth tilts her head, taunting Gracie.

Gracie's lips move slowly as she takes another brave step toward her opponent, face set in stone. Then, she finally snaps. Her arm shoots out. Gracie's clenched hand flies toward Beth, hitting her smack on the bridge of her nose.

Beth reels back, and her eyes go wide. An animalistic scream rips through the air. My jaw goes slack. That's my fucking girl.

"Don't ever touch me again," Gracie spits.

Beth's top lip curls and her right hand forms a fist. Gracie takes a step back and starts to lift her hands to protect her face when she sees Beth pull her arm back. "I always thought you were just a pretty face. Guess I was wrong—"

"Beth. You need to leave."

Gracie whips her head around, searching for the person who decided to insert themselves into the stand-off. Confusion mixed with a wave of fierce anger is clear on her face. When her eyes find Adam, she relents and drops her hands.

Adam takes a cautious step toward a very clearly unstable Beth. She is staring at him lovingly from where she stands in front of Gracie. He raises his arms slightly as if he is trying not to scare a wild animal when he moves closer to her. He doesn't pay attention to the buzzing group of onlookers surrounding us. He focuses all of his attention on her.

"You don't need to make this any more of a scene, okay? Let's go outside," he pleads, in a gentle tone. Beth nods her head in agreement, smiling broadly at him. Adam visibly relaxes.

Relief floods through my body, and I let out a breath I didn't know I was holding. Adam leads Beth away from Gracie and through the crowd.

Gracie stays where she is, her feet planted firmly on the floor, eyes wide. She raises a hand to the back of her head and winces.

Her eyes meet mine through the dispersing crowd, the lack of drama doing little to entertain their drunken minds. A brave group of stragglers stand off to the far side, watching her, almost as if they can't believe the small, innocent-looking girl in front of them could have possibly stood up to a complete maniac.

I tear my eyes away from hers and glance around me, searching for her scary big brother to no avail. Oakley is nowhere to be seen. It's almost a relief. The space around me is empty now as I dart my eyes around the bar, the tightness in my chest from being squished shoulder to shoulder with complete strangers fading into nothing.

"You okay?" Gracie's voice runs down my spine, sending

chills down to the bone. My eyes lock on the thin, red cut above her eyebrow and the several scratches on her arms as soon as I turn back around. I'm shocked that I resist the sudden, almost overbearing need to run my calloused finger around her wound in hopes of taking the pain away. Her hair is knotted and her cheeks are flushed. I almost chastise her for asking if *I'm* okay after what just happened to her, but I don't want to upset her.

I swallow harshly and nod. "We need to clean those cuts and make sure you didn't crack your damn skull."

Her lips part slightly, a hiss slipping between them when she reaches up and touches the back of her head, flinching back at the sting. "Okay."

"Were you . . . you know? Watching that back there?" she asks after a few beats of awkward silence as we walk side by side toward the dingy bathroom.

"Only the last part," I lie. I keep my eyes trained in front of me, swerving us between stumbling idiots as I try to force this uneasy feeling deep, deep down and leave me the hell alone.

The stupid stick man rests above the men's washroom. I don't hesitate to push the creaky door open and place my hand on her lower back, leading her inside.

"Stay here," I order and leave her beside the door before she can argue with me. I move toward the closed stalls, kicking open the closed doors one at a time, which luckily for us all happen to be empty. I turn to the door and twist the lock.

"Can I move now?" she asks, sarcasm dripping off her tongue as I watch her fold her arms across her chest. My eyes flash down to the prominent cleavage showing as she unknowingly pushes her tits up with her arms, but I manage to pull them back to the dried cut.

I turn on the creaky faucet and grab a wad of paper towels from the holder as I wait for the water to heat up. She leans back against the countertop when I turn back around, bright eyes glued on me, greedily watching me gather everything I need to clean her up.

"Get up on the counter," I tell her, wetting a piece of paper towel in the now-warm water. Looking back, I watch as she raises an eyebrow at my somewhat forceful command and cocks her head to the side.

"What's the magic word?"

Setting the wet towel down beside the sink, I turn to her, taking slow—almost predatory steps until we're close enough that I can watch the desperate swallow she takes. Her eyes trail up my torso until they rest hungrily on mine.

"Now."

Her surprised yelp makes me smirk again as I place my hands on her waist and lift her effortlessly onto the cold counter. I reach over and wrap the wet towel in my hands, moving between her legs.

"Wasn't that so much easier?" she teases.

"Sit still. I don't want to hurt you," I mumble as I raise my hand and gently pat the dried crimson with the rough paper towel.

"You don't have to do this, you know. I am a big girl."

Ignoring her comment, I spin her to the side before parting a section of blood-soaked hair, finding nothing more than a small cut. I sigh in relief and carefully wipe away the blood. "How did this happen anyway?"

She scoffs and rolls her eyes dramatically. "I saw Beth when I finished talking to my brother. Apparently, she lost Oakley and wanted someone to take her to Adam. I said no."

I toss the last paper towel into the trash and back up to examine how iffy of a job I did and I nod my head in approval. That is as good as it was going to get. I move to take a step back but her fingers wrap around my wrist to pull me back in place.

"Thank you," she whispers, tangled in each other's gaze as we stay surrounded by the silence given to us by the private bathroom.

The feeling of her fingers rubbing across the top of my hand consumes me as fast as the heat behind her eyes has. I want nothing more than to sit here and feel her delicate touch on my imperfect skin all night long.

"Let me in," she murmurs quietly, inching closer to me. The seconds flick away slowly around us.

"You wouldn't like what you would see."

The air surrounding us is thick, heavy with tension, almost like the world is begging me to open up and let her see the deepest, darkest parts of myself that have been expertly hidden from everyone, including myself. She has no idea what she's asking of me. Of herself even. She doesn't deserve any more heartbreak in her life.

She's too pure.

14

Tyler

THEY SAY THAT TO LET GO OF YOUR PAST AND MOVE FORWARD, YOU need to start by accepting whatever it is that you're holding onto so tightly. Only then can you allow yourself to finally be set free of those haunting restraints. Personally, I think it's a giant load of shit.

There's a reason why we distance ourselves from the memories that haunt us. We do it to protect ourselves—to help keep the façade of happiness intact. Why the fuck would we willingly want to revisit the demons living in the deep dark closets in the back of our minds? The ones that we purposefully locked away?

I know I sure as hell don't want to. Nor do I ever plan on it.

Maybe that makes me a cynical bastard. I mean, it isn't that far of a stretch for those that know anything about me. Not even the closest people to me know what hides behind the smirk that's expected to reside on my seemingly always chapped lips. It's just easier that way.

Nobody expects anything from you when they know there isn't anything for you to give. Or at least that's what I have worked so hard trying to prove to everyone around me. Unfortunately, though, I wasn't expecting a sparky blonde to throw me for an absolute loop.

Of course, I should have expected that a certain Hutton would give me a run for my money. She's always been obnoxiously confident in ways that I have never been able to fully comprehend in my broken mind. It used to be easy to brush off her obvious shows of affection with a throaty chuckle and a roll of my eyes back when she was just a kid. The sixteen-year-old teen with curly blonde hair and wide, innocent, blue eyes didn't warp my thoughts into unthinkable static or send shivers down my spine like the grown, confident spitfire that she so proudly is now.

Mexico was the first time I ever acted on the new attraction I felt toward her. We were both looking for an escape on that trip. She needed a break from her overbearing job and boy problems, and I needed to hide from the family drama and pain that haunted my dreams every night. We both agreed that whatever happened in Mexico stayed in Mexico. But it got more complicated than that the further into the trip we got. And now, having her so close to me, looking at me the way she *always* does, while she sits on this bathroom counter just inches away from my chest, sends endless unholy thoughts through every single inch of my heating body.

She wants me to let her in. To spew my deepest thoughts to her like word vomit. To tell her that somehow, someway, I feel something for her. A confession that deep down, we both know will only bring her disappointment.

Gracie Hutton deserves everything that I could never give her. She always has and she always will. Gracie deserves the fairy tale love story with the wrap-around porch, white picket fence, and the Dalmatian named Spot. She needs someone who will get married in an old barn with her, surrounded by family and friends as everyone drinks champagne and boasts about their happiest childhood memories.

Unfortunately, I don't have family or happy memories worth sharing with anyone. Especially not her. She doesn't deserve the drama that I carry around with me like a suitcase of unfortunate events. The evil step-father, the junkie mom who, regardless of being offered help from her youngest son, relies on other junkies and a shitty job at a worn-out diner for money. Then let's not forget about the older brother who ran away when he hit the cash motherlode, abandoning his underage brother and helpless mother in the hands of a manipulative son of a bitch as he did so.

I suppose I could always take the risk and share my burden with her. Maybe she'll be strong enough to handle it—to take some of the weight from my shoulders and set it on her own. But if that were to happen, how long would it be before it got too much for her? Before the weight of all of my issues crushes her?

That's what worries me.

Soft fingertips brush against my cheek, the feather-like touch urging my eyes to flutter shut as warm breath hits my lips. The music thumps faintly through the empty bathroom, just loud enough to remind us that we are not totally alone.

"I think I will surprise you," Gracie whispers, her fruity breath hitting my nose in a soft puff. My head shakes before my cheek is engulfed in her now open palm, my eyes still pressed shut, not wanting to open and be blown back to the harsh reality waiting for us outside this room. In this bubble, right now, everything is okay.

"When Jacob broke up with me, I was relieved."

I know right away that this is her attempt at trying to show me how to open up. My eyes open slowly, and I watch her pull her bottom lip between her teeth nervously, something I have noticed she seems to do quite often.

"I know that probably makes me an awful person, considering I dragged him along with me when I knew I should have just let him go," Gracie adds, her voice wavering slightly.

"You're nowhere close to being an awful person," I laugh with a shake of my head. My eyes swim in hers as I try to search for the pain I can hear in her voice. She gives her head a quick shake and drops her hand from my cheek, leaning her forehead against mine instead.

"I was with someone else when the only person I've ever really wanted was you."

Her hand latches onto mine as soon as I start reeling back, keeping me in front of her. My frantic breaths meet her steady ones as she runs her hands up my back before using them to hold my cheeks.

"I've waited this long, Ty. I can wait until you're ready to admit to yourself that I'm not going to run from you. You can trust me. I won't hurt you," Gracie says softly. Her words snap me back to a time I try to forget.

"You can trust me, Son. I won't hurt you," Allen slurs as he crouches down in front of me, cigarette smoke blowing across my face and painfully down my throat as I inhale. I look around his shoulder, staring up at my mom with an unfamiliar urgency.

"Mom?" I murmur, my attention still locked on my new stepfather and resting on her. The diner uniform is clean tonight, with not a single stain tarnishing the white material. It must be new.

"Look at me when I'm talking to you," Allen hisses, placing a firm hand on my shoulder. He shakes me until I'm forced to turn my focus on him again.

"Sorry, Allen," I apologize quickly, not wanting to upset my mom. She found me and River a dad. I should be respectful.

"Ty? Tyler? Are you okay?" Gracie's frantic voice cuts through the room, successfully and thankfully, snapping me out of my reverie.

"Sorry. I'm fine," I cough. Taking a step back from her, I create some much-needed distance between the two of us. Her face drops at the slight rejection, and her hands fall from my cheeks, resting at her sides.

"We should get back before your brother comes looking for us." I walk over to the door without daring to steal another look at her. I can hear the change in her breathing from where I stand.

I would be lying if I said every inch of me isn't fighting off the need to walk back to her and slam my mouth against hers.

Fuck I need a smoke.

"Right. My brother." She sighs over the sound of water rushing from the tap. I look back despite my better judgment to see her staring down at her hands as they rest limply in the harsh flow of water.

I'm doing the right thing. I know I am.

"Those are going to kill you one day."

"No shit," I say and take another drag pointedly. What did I do to deserve this? Tonight of all nights? Oakley scoffs, putting his hands in his pockets and standing awkwardly off to the side.

"If you're here to punch me again, at least wait until I'm done," I mumble before taking another deep inhale. The thump of sneakers against the cement sounds behind me, and my shoulders tense. I prepare myself for the inevitable pain coming my way.

"I am not going to punch you."

I throw the cigarette on the sidewalk, stomp on it and look over at Oakley. The crisp night air chills me straight to the bone. Or maybe that's just fear. I'm not sure. I really don't want to be punched again. My eyebrows shoot up as I silently question him.

"Then why are you here? I highly doubt you came out here to smoke a dart with me."

Wouldn't that be a scene to remember? Goody two-shoes Oakley Hutton smoking.

He clenches his jaw tightly and shoved his hands in his pockets.

"I'm assuming she's okay? After earlier?" The suspicion is

obvious in his tone as he tries to see if I'll tell him the truth about where I have been.

"She will survive. It was just a small cut."

He chuckles at my answer and rolls his eyes. "You know that's not what I meant, smartass."

"And you know that's all you're going to get from me, hotshot," I retort before a genuine laugh pushes through my slightly parted lips.

"Look, Tyler. If you want to date my sister, all I ask is that you don't hurt her. Or lie to me again." He sighs and leans against the tree standing to the side of us. "That wasn't cool, man."

"You have nothing to worry about. There is no Gracie and I. Okay?" I huff slightly at the curious expression on his features as he watches me thoughtfully, judging every slight movement I make. I don't blame him for not believing me; even I don't believe it right now.

"But you'll tell me if there is, right? You're both my family. And I know my sister better than to think she's going to roll over." He laughs genuinely and holds his hand out in front of him, taking a step forward.

"Scouts honour." I wink and grasp his hand in mine, giving it a firm shake. "You're my family too."

"I'm not going to apologize for punching you, by the way."

"I wouldn't expect anything else."

I really wouldn't.

15

Gracie

BEING RAISED IN A HOUSEHOLD WITHOUT A FATHER WAS PROBABLY the hardest thing I have ever had to go through. Unlike my brother, I was too young to have spent a lot of time with our dad. My most potent memories of him come from family movie nights and the old fairytale storybook he used to read to me every night before he tucked me into bed. Everything else about him I had to learn from someone else.

Sad, right?

My shy, awkward, seven-year-old self couldn't quite comprehend why two cops were on our front steps in the middle of the night or what they had said that made my mom fall to her knees as she broke right in front of us.

The weeks after finding out that our dad would never come home again were spent planning a funeral and sitting back, watching as Oakley tended to our mother the way she used to tend to us.

No kid should have to grow up as fast as Oakley did. One day he was a happy-go-lucky thirteen-year-old boy, then the next, he was a serious, grown-ass man taking care of his family. It was unfair, really. Thankfully, we made it through it—through everything. Because of him. I helped him as much as I could, and together, we managed to take care of Mom and each other as well, as families should.

The tragedies that we went through also helped bring me closer to Mom. She's now not only my best friend but my inspiration too. She showed me what a strong-minded woman can really do and what she can overcome when she puts her mind to it.

I always found my own pride in knowing that I was making her proud by being the most powerful form of myself. But now . . . now I'm not so sure I even remember what being a strong woman feels like. I have let myself slip into an inescapable hole of desperation— a hole filled with nothing but an obsession for the only person who's ever made me feel pure bliss and agonizing heartbreak at the same time.

I know love isn't easy, but is it supposed to be this hard?

Leave it to me to fall for the guy who doesn't want to be loved. I'm quickly running out of ways to convince him that I'm not going to run for the hills the minute he shares one tiny part of himself with me. We have already seen each other naked multiple times. I don't think it gets more intimate than that.

"Hey, girly. Your not-so-secret-admirer is asking for you at the door," Jessica says teasingly, sticking her head through my partially open door. I jump up off the bed as my heart starts picking up—shamefully, might I add. I skip toward her. Maybe what I said to him at the bar has finally sunk in. It only took three freaking days.

I hear the faint voices of the *One Direction* boys flowing from the living room, meaning Jess was more than likely finally cleaning up the mess her friends made from the night before. On days like yesterday and today, I have to remind myself that she is my best friend and that I would do anything for her. If I didn't force myself to remember that simple fact, I'd have her ass kicked out on the street corner for acting like a complete idiot.

My embarrassingly wide grin falters when I see our neighbour standing timidly in the entryway, his chocolate-brown eyes curiously scanning the apartment.

"Cody, hey." I greet him, my words coming out duller than I had hoped. He jumps when he hears my voice. He recovers quickly and straightens up, standing rigidly in front of me.

"Hi, Gracie. I-I hope this isn't too abrupt of a visit."

I shove my hands in the pockets of my frayed shorts and offer him a much brighter smile this time. "Course not. What's up?"

It's not like he *meant* to get my hopes up. I shouldn't punish him for my own problems. Plus, it's kind of adorable how nervous he is—the complete opposite of Tyler.

Dammit, Gracie. Knock it off. I wish I could hit myself in the face without looking like an idiot.

Cody's cheeks flush instantly, the deep red overpowering his pale complexion. I hold back a giggle when his eyes dart off to somewhere across the room as I rest on my back foot and watch him.

"You okay? Want some water or something?" I offer, my eyes twinkling with mischief.

"Would you wanna go get some ice cream with me?" He blurts the question, and my eyebrows shoot to the ceiling.

"Now?" I ask, mouth gaping open in surprise.

"Is it a bad time?" He stares down at his sneaker-clad feet. "We can go another time if that works."

Is now a bad time? It's not like I had much planned for my day other than sitting in bed and eating shitty food.

"Now works. Just let me grab my bag," I say finally.

A wide grin spreads across his lips, and I let a giggle escape when I notice the adorable dimples on both of his cheeks.

I rush out of the living space and quickly down the hall until I make it to my room. After grabbing my purse from the back of my desk chair, I run a few frantic hands through my wavy blonde hair and take a deep breath. I can do this. It's just two neighbours going to get some ice cream. I love ice cream. It's not a big deal.

"I hope you aren't a frozen yogurt kinda guy," I joke as I make my way back into the living room. His attention is pulled away from the vast floor-to-ceiling windows before landing on me again. He shakes his head as I make my way over to him.

I offer him one final look of encouragement while I slip my shoes on. Oakley always teased me about how small they are growing up. I'm sure they haven't grown since I was a tween.

"I'm going out!" I shout to Jess before leaving the apartment with Cody.

The awkward silence threatens to choke me to death once we reach the elevator. The stuffy heat of the elevator almost pushes me over the edge as eerie music fills my ears. My eyes flicker over to Cody, desperately trying to search for something I can use to break the thick silence. The ironed khakis and matching polo shirt do little to spark my imagination, and his short, perfectly gelled blonde hair is certainly not helping either.

"So, how long have you lived here?" Is all I can manage to ask, my enthusiasm clearly lacking. I stare helplessly at the floor numbers as they light up, one by one, the closer we get to being out of this damn elevator.

"In this building or Vancouver?" he asks. The overwhelming urge to roll my eyes at his response takes over, and I give in.

"Both?" Thankfully, the long-awaited bell dings and the metal doors are pulled apart soon after, setting us free.

"I've lived in Vancouver my whole life, but I've only been living in this building for a year. You?"

The snob behind the desk sends us off with a half-hearted wave as we step out of the open doors. The fresh air welcomes me with open arms. "Both for only a few months."

"Where are you from then, if you don't mind me asking?" We fall in step with each other down the sidewalk.

"Penticton."

"Ah, a country girl. I never would have guessed." he teases, clearly missing the unimpressed expression on my features. *Country girl?* Maybe it was better when he was too afraid to speak to me.

"Not exactly. It's not that small," I say with a laugh so I don't say something that would most likely hurt his feelings.

"Compared to Vancouver it is," he states matter-of-factly, turning to raise an eyebrow at me.

"Every city here is small compared to Vancouver," I shoot back before letting out a thankful sigh when we reach the small ice cream shop.

"After you." He smiles widely, holding the heavy glass door open for me. I breathe in the sweet smell happily as we move to the cashier, the different flavours displayed in the open coolers make my mouth water. Oddly enough, we are the only ones here.

The young girl standing behind the counter forces a smile—obviously not wanting to be here—before asking for our orders.

"I'll get two scoops o—" I begin.

"Two vanilla cones please," Cody says pointedly, cutting me off, ordering not only for himself but for me as well.

Oh, I don't think so.

"Just one vanilla cone, *actually*. I'll have two scoops of bubblegum." I smile at the girl, ignoring Cody and stand off to the side. Mister Pushy can pick up the bill.

I fold my arms over my chest as I watch him pull out his wallet and hand the employee a twenty-dollar bill. He makes his way over to me sheepishly. "I'm sorry. I don't know why I did that," he says apologetically

The doorbell rings, signalling another customer. When no one walks past us, I turn around only to see that we're still the only people here. Sighing, I drop my arms and turn back around, nodding my head.

"It's okay."

"I just wanted to get to know you finally, and I've already

screwed it up," he grumbles, his jaw clenched. He is clearly frustrated with himself.

"You didn't screw it up. It's okay, really." I insist, wearing a small smile. The quiet lyrics of whatever song is playing through the speakers help ease the tension as he simply nods his head in response. I try to hide my annoyance for the remainder of the date. I can't help but wonder if staying in bed would have been a better decision after all.

16

ONE YEAR AGO

Tyler

I SLAM BACK ANOTHER DRINK AND SCOLD MYSELF FOR BEING reckless enough to flirt with Gracie not even ten feet from her brother—*my best friend.*

The sun has set now, and the pool deck is otherwise empty except for the odd cleaning person walking around or myself, calf-deep in the chlorinated water.

A bottle of tequila sits in my closed palm, providing me with a sense of burning comfort every time I tilt it back and swallow. I know there are other ways to deal with my feelings, but none are as easy as letting the thoughts get completely washed away by a wave of clear liquid.

When I saw Gracie sitting by the pool with Oakley and Ava earlier, I was tempted to pick her up and carry her back to my room. That tiny triangle bikini top that barely covered the tits that seemed to have grown overnight, and the matching bottoms that tied on the side—so easy to undo—made my cock stiffer than a fucking wooden board. I nearly put a towel over my crotch.

I don't know what caused the sudden urge, but I wanted to slip one of my t-shirts over her toned stomach and carry her away to my room more than I wanted air to breathe.

She isn't the nervous word-vomiting teenage girl she used to be back when I would come over for Anne's famous lasagna or to practice shooting with Oakley in his backyard.

No.

Time had changed more than just her brother and me. It had changed her too. In all the right places.

I know she's struggling with work and Anne's recent health struggles. I know that her dipshit of an ex-boyfriend dumped her on a limb and that she pretends not to be hurt by it.

There isn't a day that Oakley doesn't talk about his sister. He misses her—living in a different country and all—and doesn't miss a chance to gush about how proud of her he is or how badly he wishes he could have been there to shove that dweebs face into a brick wall.

Right now, I hate that I'm treated like a part of their family. I hate that at this very moment, my dick is on high alert, tenting the crotch of my basketball shorts just thinking about Gracie Hutton.

I gulp down another swig of tequila and scrunch my face as it tears down my throat, leaving it raw. Grunting, I let my neck go limp and close my eye, kicking my feet in the water.

"The pool closed an hour ago."

"Fuck," I mutter under my breath and set the bottle down off to the side a little firmer than necessary. "Then what are you doing here?" I ask, louder than before.

I force my eyes to open and lift my head so I can stare at the last person I need to see tonight.

Gracie wears light blue jean shorts with a rip in the front pocket and a yellow tank top as she stands a few feet away with her arms crossed. She lifts a curious brow but smiles slightly, almost knowingly. The idea that she knows more about me than I want her to pisses me off.

"Same as you. I needed to think."

She sits down on the edge of the pool beside me but doesn't

relax her tense shoulders until after a few beats when I still haven't told her to get lost.

"You don't know me."

"Don't I?"

I ponder her question as if I care about the answer.

"Go sit by yourself if you need to think. This spot is taken," I grumble, too tired to put up a real fight. I'm not going to admit it, especially not to her, but her company isn't all bad.

"Here's good," she chimes, smiling a megawatt smile that nearly knocks me into the pool.

She used to have braces; I've seen the old pictures of her in middle school that hang on the staircase at her mother's house. They paid off; big time. Her teeth are perfectly straight and so white that she could be in a White-strips commercial. I drop my blurred gaze to my knees, itching for a smoke.

"Your loss. I'm not exactly the best company," I grunt.

"Who said that? Whoever did was a tool. I think you're pretty great company." She sounds so sure, so sincere that it makes my stomach churn.

I squint my eyes at her before I can stop myself. Gracie giggles in response, moving her feet in slow circles in the water. Her hands are spread out behind her, and she leans back on them, tilting her head back and letting her hair swing along her back.

"I mean, you're not *always* the best company." She laughs again, meeting my stare. The twinkle of the string lights hung above us reflects in her blue eyes. "You can be a real asshole."

It's my turn to laugh. "Yeah, I can."

She doesn't reply this time, just looks away and gnaws on her bottom lip. Something is bothering her, but I'm too stubborn to ask what it is. So instead, I guess and mumble, "Jason was never going to be able to keep up with you, Gray. He was a fucking loser."

Her lip slips from between her teeth. "His name is Jacob."

"Jason, Jacob." I roll my eyes. "Either way. He was mediocre, amateur at best. We both know you need someone better. Someone who isn't going to tell all his friends how good you are in bed and all the things you can do with your tongue. A real man would want to keep that shit to himself, to fantasize about when you're not together and he thinks about you in bed with his hand around his cock."

Her eyes widen in surprise before she gulps a few times as though she's struggling to breathe. Fuck, I wasn't supposed to know that, was I? Great, now Oakley's going to punch me for spewing out secrets.

"Is that what I need? A real man?" she asks slowly, almost in a whisper. Her eyes bore into mine, gripping onto them with claws out.

I force myself to look away. "It's what you deserve."

And that man's not me.

It's about time we both remembered that.

17

PRESENT

Tyler

"Oakley's finally gone, eh?" Braden huffs, bent over and gripping his knees while he tries to catch his breath.

I ran him to the ground in the gym today. It's a rare occurrence for Braden to work out anywhere other than his dad's boxing gym, but he's a sucker for the equipment at the private gym that my teammates use on our days off. The treadmills happen to actually be from *this* century.

"Yeah, he couldn't get on the plane fast enough this morning."

"You think he's getting laid tonight?" He wears a shit-eating grin, his lack of filter makes my nose wrinkle in disgust. The thought of what Ava and Oakley do when they're alone time is not something I often find myself thinking about.

"You're fucked," I shoot at him.

"Not as fucked as you, apparently. Tell me, why wasn't I filled in on your newfound love fest with baby Hutton?"

I clench my jaw and glare at him, stiffening my back to try and stand taller than him, but I fail. He's got a solid three inches on me.

"I hit a soft spot, did I?" he taunts.

"I'll be the one hitting if you don't shut up," I snap before relaxing my shoulders and trying to steady my racing heartbeat.

I brush off his watchful eyes and start walking to the locker room. Bringing my right hand up, I push open the heavy door and leave him laughing proudly to himself.

Braden joins me in the locker room a few seconds later. "I don't blame you for finally caving. Gracie's a fucking dime."

The mirrors on the wall shake dangerously beside us as I slam him up against the wall, my arm pushing up under his jaw to hold him in place. "Don't talk about her like that," I growl, keeping a dangerous amount of pressure on his throat.

"Aye, aye, captain," he gasps, wearing a grin despite the fact that I am cutting off his airway. He eyes my arm tucked under his chin. With a huff, I step back. He lurches forward, catching his breath.

"You good now?" Braden gasps, colour coming back to his face.

"I will be once I get the hell away from you." I open my locker, and a pile of dirty clothes falls onto the ground.

"Shit, dude. I think it's time to do some laundry." His fake gag causes my eyes to roll as I bend down and hastily grab the clothes, shoving them in my open bag. Deciding to save myself from the unwanted company, I shrug on my jacket and slam the locker door shut.

"See you tomorrow." I slap his shoulder a little harder than necessary as I walk past him. I don't wait for a response and leave him standing there alone, a smirk on his face no doubt.

There's not a single cloud in the night sky tonight, only millions upon millions of shiny dots laughing down at me. My driver's side door creaks when I pull it open, and I remind myself yet again to oil the damn thing. I'll add that to the endless list of things I need to do. The engine comes to life with a low rumble, blowing a large cloud of black smoke into the night. I roll down the window before pulling out into the empty street.

I'm pleasantly surprised to see the absence of my mother when I pull up outside my building. She's been here every day this week like clockwork, always sitting in the cold, forgetting all about the key that rests in her jacket pocket. I have come to the realization that Allen must have been gone again, most likely knocked out in an abandoned alleyway high out of his mind. She's always here more when he's gone.

I throw my bag over my shoulder and head inside, not wanting to stay out in the street longer than I have to. The neighbourhood's not great, but I would rather live here than in some fancy building that I don't feel comfortable in.

I know my friends don't understand why I continue to live in a neighbourhood filled with police sirens and potholes the size of Texas that the city can't be bothered enough to fix. It's where I feel the most at home. But I guess I can see where they're coming from. I make enough to live anywhere I want. But I can't seem to make the move, so I just don't.

Every last breath of air leaves my lungs when I slide my key into my apartment door to find it already unlocked.

"Fuck."

I shove the key back in my pocket, carefully place my hand on the knob, and turn, pushing the door open inch by inch. The lamp beside my couch is pouring a dull, yellow light throughout the small living room, illuminating it just enough for me to catch sight of my mom passed out on the couch.

I let out a sigh before moving entirely into the apartment, shutting and locking the door behind me. Turning back, I almost let an exhausted laugh slip past my lips.

"When are you going to get it, Mom?" I whisper, shaking my head. I guess I should be thankful for her finally remembering her key and that she has also managed to make herself a makeshift bed on my couch.

Taking careful steps, not wanting the creaky floorboards to jolt her from her sleep, I tuck the blanket in beside her and place a kiss on the top of her head. As I flick off the lamp, I start to wonder if this will always be my life.

A continuous pounding on my door tears me from my third hour of sleep.

After spending the entire night stuck in deep thought, I finally managed to drift off at around four in the morning. Not like it did much good, though. The knocking stops as soon as I throw my legs over the side of the bed and stand on wobbly knees. I run a hand over my face, rubbing the sleep out of my eyes before I throw open my bedroom door.

"You have the silkiest-looking hair!" I hear Mom exclaim from the kitchen. Narrowing my brows in confusion, I look to the front door and see a pair of pink polka-dotted Vans lying beside my boots.

Fuck no.

I head to the kitchen, my strides larger than usual as fear digs its jagged claws into my skin. A giggle rings throughout the room, sending very familiar tingles up my spine.

"Thanks! It's all in the conditioner."

I round the corner and catch sight of her. Her hip is pressed against the counter as she shows off her perfectly straight, milky white teeth to my mom with a widespread grin.

"I wasn't expecting guests." My gravelly tone carries through the room, surprising the two women in my kitchen as they turn to face me.

"Don't be so rude, Tyler," Mom scolds. "And put some clothes on."

A chill breeze rushes over me as I look down at my bare chest, an involuntary shudder shaking through me. As I look up again, my eyes are pulled to the stiff guest in my kitchen. She's openly staring at my exposed torso without a care in the world, her mouth hanging slightly open and her pink tongue resting slightly behind her bottom teeth.

Close your mouth unless you want me to fill it, Gracie.

"I'll be back," I mutter, ripping my gaze away and moving to my room before I have to explain why I'm sporting a boner in front of my mother.

After finding an old hockey shirt in my drawer, I toss it over my head and head back out to what I am pretty sure is going to be a complete fucking disaster. The smell of freshly brewed coffee greets me as I brush past the beige armchair that separates my living room and kitchen. If it wasn't for Adam, I'm pretty sure I wouldn't have a damn thing in this place. But of course, he insisted we go furniture shopping the day after I moved in. He's more of a girl than any girl I know some days.

"How's your brother doing? Is he still playing hockey? Tyler doesn't tell me anything these days."

My back tenses at her jab. I brush off Gracie's questioning stare as I head to the cupboard that holds my coffee cups.

"He does." Gracie tries to hide her confusion as to how the woman in front of her doesn't know that her brother is the biggest name in hockey right now. "He just got engaged, actually."

I jolt at my mom's sudden squeal, a groan slipping past my lips when the coffee sloshes onto the granite, missing the round lip of the mug.

"That's so exciting! Congratulate him for me, would you?"

"Why would she do that? You don't even know him," I snap, clutching my cup in a tight fist and whipping around. She feigns ignorance from her seat at the table, mouth gaping open in shock as a subtle "oh" falls in the silence.

"Tyler," Gracie mutters, rising from her seat. Her wide eyes watch me cautiously as if she is trying to understand my behaviour.

I ignore Gracie and raise an eyebrow at my mother. "I don't have time for this. I'm assuming you have things to do today?"

Gracie snaps this time. *"Tyler!"*

I turn my attention to her now, my eyes narrowed into sharp slits as I wait for another scolding. If she had any idea how my mother really is, outside of this facade she likes to paint, I wouldn't be the bad guy right now.

"It's okay, sweetie." Mom smiles slightly and stands, placing a gentle hand on Gracie's shoulder. "He's not much of a morning person. Actually, that reminds me." She turns to me again. "River called while you were sleeping. He is going to be in town this weekend."

My stomach drops. A dull pain starts to make its way through my skull. Gracie doesn't need to hear about my ever-so-perfect big brother.

"Tell brother dearest, I said to get fucked," I snap. Walking to the sink, I pour my full mug down the drain. Placing my hands on the edge of the steel basin, my grip tightens until my knuckles turn a ghastly shade of white.

"You can tell him yourself when you join us for dinner Saturday night."

A sarcastic laugh rips through me as I let go of the sink and turn around. "It will be at one of his fancy restaurants, right?"

I lock eyes with Gracie in an unspoken apology. She gives me a comforting smile. I can feel some of the overwhelming tension seeping from my body at the soothing action, my appreciation for her growing tenfold.

"As a matter of fact, yes, it is. I would love it if you brought Gracie along."

"I don't think s-"

"I would love to, Mrs. Bateman," Gracie cuts me off and moves beside me to place a hand on my arm. Her eyes dare me to argue.

"Perfect!" Mom beams, her gaze fixed on the not-so-subtle show of affection Gracie decided was the best way to get me to shut me up.

"Walk me out, would you Tyler?" she asks happily, almost as if she has no clue as to how I am really feeling, which she probably doesn't.

"I don't mind walking you out! I need Tyler showered and ready to go as soon as possible," Gracie says, giving my arm a quick squeeze. She winks at me and ushers my mom to the front door. I sigh heavily once they are out of my line of sight and lean back against the counter, my body feeling weighed down. Listening for the click of the front door, I close my eyes and run a hand across my prickly beard.

"She's gone."

I nod my head in response, my eyelids not daring to open even an inch.

"I didn't know you had a brother."

I peel my eyelids open with a sigh. "Clearly, that was on purpose."

Watching as her shoulders rise and fall, a sudden feeling of guilt washes over me. I give my head a shake and walk toward her. I come to a stop when there are only a few inches of space between us.

"Thank you," I mumble, my eyes locked on hers before I pull her into my chest. Her body tenses from the odd action, but she relaxes quickly and wraps her arms around my waist. Our chests move perfectly in sync as we breathe in time. All thoughts of my brother are tossed from my mind as quickly as the breaths from my lungs. I move my focus to the soothing motion of her hand, rubbing slow, wide circles on my lower back until I feel my eyelids start drooping.

"Are you planning on staying?" I mumble into the top of her

head. I know that I shouldn't ask her to stay—it's not fair. But I don't care. Not right now.

She pulls away slightly, just enough to be able to look up at me. "Is that okay?"

"Yeah," I breathe, too exhausted to question myself.

"Then I'm staying," she murmurs, pressing her cheek against my chest.

I hum a response as I let my eyes close once again and move us back until I feel the edge of the counter against my lower back.

She's the first to pull back what feels like hours later. "Are you going to pass out on me, Ty?"

I grin sleepily before simply taking her hand in mine. I lead her out of the kitchen toward my bedroom.

"You're not planning on getting lucky, are you? Cause I am so not ready for that right now," she says, all in a rush. Her cheeks flush a bright pink as she stares down at her feet.

I chuckle and shake my head, squeezing her hand. "I just want to sleep." She raises a suspicious brow. "Scouts honour." I wink, opening my door and leading her into the dark room before slipping my shirt over my head. After I adjust the covers I had so hastily discarded earlier, I hear her suck in a sharp breath of air. Turning around, I look at her, confused by her sudden change in mood.

The light, teasing energy has quickly morphed into a tense, hard-to-breathe one I learn very quickly I don't like. Gracie's eyes are dull as she stares vacantly at the half-made bed, her bottom lip jutted out slightly before it's pulled rapidly between her teeth.

I scratch my neck awkwardly as I stare at the sad girl, my heart pulling painfully.

"Uh, Gracie?" I clear my throat with a cough. "You okay?" My question seems to snap her out of the trance. She shakes her head once and looks at me with a forced smile.

"It's just been a while since I've been in this room. I'm sorry."

Right. Since the time I completely abandoned you after a night of seemingly mind-blowing sex in my own fucking bed. Yeah, I know.

"You have already apologized. Please don't do it again. It was embarrassing enough the first time," she rambles as she strides over to the bed. Gracie slips under the covers, facing away from me as she pulls my duvet over her small body.

Swallowing down my apology, I nod to myself and crawl in after her. The heavy duvet wraps around me as I lay frigidly beside her, deciding to keep a smart amount of distance between us, not wanting to upset her even more. "You don't deserve to be left alone in anyone's bed. Especially not mine."

The room remains silent, our breathing the only sound in the space, taunting me almost, reminding me that I hurt her again. Maybe I *should* apologize? We both know she deserves it. But she deserves a lot more than some ridiculous apology after I treated her like a used puck bunny.

The air from my lungs evaporates when she turns toward me, her perfectly sculpted features illuminated from the faded hallway light. Her veil of blonde hair sprawls out on the pillowcase. She stares at me, the familiar gleam in her round eyes sparking a fire deep in my chest.

"I forgive you," she whispers and inches closer to place a cautious, gentle kiss on my lips.

My mind is a jumbled mess of guarded, unwanted thoughts as she pulls away, not giving me time to respond. She rests her head on my chest and lets out a deep sigh.

Fuck. What are you doing to me, Gracie Hutton?

18

Tyler

"THIS IS FUCKING RIDICULOUS," I GRUMBLE, AND YANK ANGRILY ON the tie hanging loosely around my neck. The tight, navy-blue material stretches awkwardly around my arms, pinching me with every slight movement I make. I know that I should be used to wearing suits by now, but I don't think I ever will be.

My brother doesn't deserve me going to this dinner tonight, let alone dressed up in a suit that cost more than I care to admit. It usually hangs in my closet, serving as a constant reminder never to go suit shopping with Oakley Hutton. The guy has a nasty habit of forgetting I'm not anywhere near as successful as him while piling dress shirt after dress shirt over his arm and waving around a black card.

I untwist the cap of my hair gel and dip two fingers in the thick, teal, goo. As I run it through the tips of my hair, there is a gentle knock on my door, followed by the sound of it opening and closing.

"You really shouldn't leave your door unlocked, Ty!"

"Like that would have stopped you from finding a way in any way," I scoff, keeping my eyes on my reflection in the vanity mirror.

The clacking of Gracie's shoes reverberates through the apartment, reminding me that she is, in fact, meeting my brother tonight. There wasn't much I could do to convince her not to come after she had all but promised my mom she would be there, so I've just kept my mouth shut and left it alone. I don't want to stir the pot even though it will probably overflow tonight anyway.

"Aren't you going to tell me how amazing I look? I got this dress especially for you," she teases, her voice much closer now. She sends my imagination into overdrive with such a simple phrase.

I pull my fingers out of my now slicked-back hair and open the door. My mouth goes dry the second I see her leaning against the doorframe, a sly smirk on her nude lips. The first thing I see is skin—exposed, smooth, pale, skin that shines in the low glow of the bathroom light. The gold dress fits her figure like a damn second skin. Her collarbones jut through the thin straps on her shoulders, pulling my attention to the two perky tits staring at me, taunting me as they ache for my touch.

"Fuck," I moan, and stare into her sparkling, ocean-blue eyes.

Her gentle laugh is music to my ears as she pushes a curl behind her ear. "I don't think so. You owe me dinner first."

A cough crawls up my throat quickly, her silhouette blurring as my eyes water from the burn. "Do you know how to tie a tie?" I ask hopefully, swiftly changing the subject.

"Who do you think tied Oakley's?" She scoffs, moving toward me. "I think the better question is how don't you? Don't you wear one to your games? Now stand still."

Her warm breath fans my face as she grabs the tie between her fingertips. Her small face is taut with concentration. I look down at her in complete awe. I know I should tell her that she looks gorgeous tonight, but I let the words die on my tongue when her touch lands on the ridges of my jaw.

"No." I shiver slightly when she locks eyes with me. The grey hue in them is more prominent tonight. "I don't wear one."

"You really need to shave," she murmurs ever so gently.

Nodding slowly, I lean my forehead against hers. I hear her sharp intake of breath as she watches me carefully, not wanting to spook me. Then, cautiously, she stands on her toes and presses her lips softly against mine. Her hands stay on my jaw as her thumb rubs gently across my stubble.

My eyes close in response to her feathery touch. The moment we are in rests heavily on our shoulders. Until my phone rings, that is, bringing us back to reality.

"Shit," I mutter under my breath and take a much-needed step back to grab my phone off the counter. I could punch myself in the groin right about now. I can't keep letting myself get into these positions with her.

"Hello?" I clear my throat, my gaze on Gracie as I wait for the person on the other side of the call to speak. She watches me silently, begging me to drop the phone into the toilet and carry her off to my bedroom with nothing more than her heavy swallowing and lidded eyes.

"I hope you are on your way by now. We're waiting for you," Mom scolds, and I hear River shout something in the background.

"Yeah. We're almost there," I lie, my lips twitching, aching to be lifted in a smug smile. "See you soon." I shove the phone into my pocket and move toward Gracie, throwing an arm out in front of me theatrically. "After you, Gray."

She giggles and wraps her arm around mine as we walk through the doorway.

"I'm sure you're worrying over nothing. It'll be fine, Ty."

We pull into the parking lot of River's restaurant, and I'm immediately overwhelmed by the sudden need to vomit. The extravagant building annoys me as soon as we hop out of the truck. With the unnecessarily large windows and giant pillars, you would think that you are heading into something a lot more impressive than the overpriced, unoriginal corporate restaurant that you really are.

I grab her wrist, halting our movements when we reach the automatic doors. "You don't know my brother. Just be careful, okay? Promise me." She tilts her head as she stares down at her wrist before lifting her clouded gaze to mine. "Promise me."

She nods her head instantly at my words. "I promise."

Breathing out a sigh of relief, I place a firm hand on her lower back and lead us inside.

"Bateman," I mutter when we reach the tall, giraffe-like hostess, cutting her off before she has a chance to spew the same old bullshit I have heard a million times.

"Oh. Right this way, Sir." She forces a smile while she leads us through the packed restaurant.

I roll my eyes at the oversized crystal chandeliers hanging above the tables, knowing full well they look fucking tacky to every single person in this place. Yet, none of these overdressed businessmen would ever dare admit to that. What would be the point?

It's bright in here, making it way too easy for every set of eyes to gawk openly at the two of us as we pass by them on the way to the back of the restaurant.

My body tenses the closer we get to our table. The unknown reason behind this dinner worries me. Our family doesn't *do* dinners. We don't do much of anything, actually, besides throw low-blow insults and call each other nasty names like children who have just learned swear words. We're as far from a real family as they come, and I know for a fact that I wasn't brought to one of my brother's fancy restaurants so we could all hash out whatever has been bothering us. No. He wouldn't risk losing whatever fake persona he's shown his employees just to have it out with me. He would have just come to my apartment to do that.

"Relax," Gracie whispers.

"I'm trying," I mumble, squeezing her lower back.

The hostess comes to a stop in front of us and I look up. I spot my mother first. Her chair is pushed up close to the man sitting beside her. The sight of the two of them sitting so close together is enough to make me want to turn and run. Mom looks so cozy beside him, as if he actually treats her well. As if he isn't the reason she's so damn broken inside.

Allen couldn't even bother to dress up tonight. I would have laughed at the stained Metallica t-shirt he's wearing if it wasn't for the anger thumping in my chest. They look as out of place as I feel right now.

"We're going home," I spit, seeing red. My arm wraps all the way around Gracie's waist as I pull her flush to my side and spin us around. She lets out a sound of surprise but lets me get us a step away without arguing or pressing me for answers.

"Brother! Where are you going?" His voice makes me tremble. Gracie halts her steps and squeezes my hand, pulling my attention back to her.

"What happened? What's wrong?" she asks, her eyes searching mine for answers I can't give her.

"I didn't think he was coming," I stammer as fear sinks its uninvited claws into my skin.

"Who? Your brother? Of course, he would be here," she says in utter bemusement. I can't blame her for her confusion. I shake my head and squeeze my eyes shut.

"Talk to me." She squeezes my hands tighter.

"My stepdad. He's sitting beside my mom." The words burn my throat and they stumble off my tongue.

I open my eyes to watch her, scouring the seats behind us for the man who loves to refer to himself as my father. She nods when she sees him and turns her head back to me looking at me with obvious concern.

"It'll be okay. I'm a big girl," she says lightly in an attempt to calm me and places a hand on my cheek. I lean into her touch, trying desperately to wash away the feeling that is now swallowing me whole. She doesn't know why I am shamefully terrified of the scrawny man waiting for us at the table, and I hope it stays that way. River knowing about Gracie was bad enough without adding Allen into the mix. He doesn't need anything else to use against me, and that's exactly what he will do with her. "If it gets bad, we'll leave. Okay? Just give me a sign, and we'll blow this popsicle stand."

She's watching me with a determined glint in her eyes. One I have come to know very well—well enough to know that it would be stupid of me to think I could make her leave now anyway.

"Okay." I nod.

"Okay." She smiles up at me, grabs my hand, and leads me back toward the table.

I set my jaw as the three of them turn their attention to us.

River watches us with a smug smile on his face. He sits back against the silk chair that sits at the head of the table, hands clasped in front of him.

"About time. Did you need a pep talk before you could come talk to me, Tyler?" He smirks, baiting me into starting a fight with him already.

Gracie grins as she sticks a pin in his pettiness. "I'm Gracie. It's so lovely to meet you, River." I sit down across from Allen and keep my eyes focused anywhere but on him.

"What a beautiful name. It's so nice to meet you. Mom has told me all about how wonderful you are." River winks at her and flashes her a cocky grin as she sits down in the remaining chair next to me.

"I wish I could say the same, but I didn't even know you existed until a week ago," she replies politely—casually even— an easy smile resting on her lips. She grasps my hand in hers.

River's eyes narrow as he stares at her, head tilting slightly. "Is that so? He has always been so scared of me stealing his toys," he sneers, his top lip curled.

My teeth grind together as my anger starts to grow. "How's your wife? Where is she tonight? The whore house?" I cock my brow and watch as his confidence falters.

"Don't you fucking—" he starts, his voice tight with unsuppressed rage.

"That's enough, you two. We are here to have dinner together as a family, not to bicker like children," Mom snaps from across the table.

I look forward, my eyes zoning in on the hand that is wrapped so tightly around hers. "Do I not get a proper introduction, Tyler?" Allen speaks up, his gravelly voice rubbing roughly against my eardrums the way it always has. "I thought I taught you better manners than that."

"Allen, this is Gracie. But you already knew that," I add quietly. I look at him for the first time in months. His gaze is already fixed on mine. The unforgiving dark shadows still hang prominently underneath his sunken eyes, and his top lip is curled, revealing the same yellow still staining his rotting teeth.

"It's nice to meet you," Gracie says with a forced smile. I feel her inch closer to my side.

"Do me a favour and keep my son under control tonight, would you, doll?"

19

Gracie

I squeeze Tyler's thigh tightly at Allen's demeaning words as a familiar fire comes to life deep in my chest. "I see you've mistaken my kindness for stupidity," I laugh softly and take a sip from the glass of water in front of me to clear my throat.

Allen's brows raise as he eyes me, his distaste for the entire conversation written clearly on his less-than-appealing features. I can't say that I'm surprised. He doesn't seem like the type of guy to hide his emotions very well.

"And how did I do that?" he scoffs. The glasses and cutlery rattle when he slams his hands down on the white-clothed table.

This guy is barking up the wrong tree. I don't know who the hell he thinks he is—talking to me as though I am nothing but a random girl his stepson snuck into his house after his bedtime—but I do know that I sure as hell won't put up with it.

"I may not know a damn thing about you, Allen. But it isn't hard to see that you radiate toxic masculinity. Not to mention that your lack of respect for not only your son but also the girl he brought with him tonight is extremely offensive." My face flushes when I finish, embarrassed by the various sets of eyes gawking curiously at our table, marvelling at the lack of manners I have shown. I guess I should just let them stare. The only eyes I care about right now are the deep brown ones currently burning holes into the side of my head.

"One last thing," I continue. "If anyone is going to be doing you a favour tonight, it will be Tyler by keeping me under control before I end up saying something I really shouldn't."

I barely manage to finish speaking before my breath catches in my throat.

A large hand wraps around mine, sending familiar tingles up my arm, letting me know that it's Tyler's. I peek over at him, a smile tugging at the corners of my mouth when he starts rubbing his thumb along my palm.

He looks at me fiercely, a deep feeling lighting up his eyes but as he turns back to his step-dad, the light fades.

"You really know how to pick them, don't you, boy?" Allen fumes at Tyler.

"So does Mom," Tyler spits.

My stomach forms a knot as I feel the air tighten around us. It's almost suffocating.

Allen smashes his fist against the table. The dishes clatter once more. Red wine spills from the rim of our glasses and soaks into the expensive silk tablecloth.

"Tyler, come on. Not here. Don't embarrass me," River warns, his voice low and threatening. He rolls his eyes and snaps his fingers at a nearby waitress.

Nora sits still in her seat, dead silent. She picks at the skin around her fingernails, not paying any attention to the scene in front of her. My frustration only grows when I see how Tyler is staring at her, silently begging her for help.

The waitress pales as she rushes over to the table. River waves his hand aggressively and snaps orders at her. "So, Gracie," he says with a sigh as the stained tablecloth is being replaced with a clean one. "What is a gorgeous, strong-worded woman like yourself doing here with my little brother of all people?"

"I just really didn't want to spend a night away from him, if

I'm honest." The words flow far too easily from my lips. The truth behind them is embarrassingly clear to the entire table, Tyler included.

"How much did he pay you to say that?" River chuckles. His arrogance makes my skin crawl. "With that new hockey contract he just signed, I'm sure no number was too high for looking good with you by his side tonight."

"Keep your mouth shut," Tyler snaps. He shakes his head incredulously. He pushes his chair back and stands up, pulling me out of my seat as he does so. River mutters something under his breath that I don't care enough to listen to. I take a step toward Tyler and give his hand a squeeze. "I don't even know why I came here. It's always the same shit," he spits before turning to look at me, his expression softening slightly. "Let's go."

I nod my head in agreement and narrow my eyes at the people who dare to call themselves his family. We spin around and start walking side by side through the restaurant. Neither one of us turns back.

His body tenses beside me as the hushed whispers meet our ears, a quick, bitter reminder that we're not yet alone. He lets out a low growl beside me and flips the bird to an overly curious daddy's boy muttering about us a few tables away.

"I need a smoke."

He really does need to kick that habit. Although I don't think my commentary would really help the situation right now.

"We're almost outside," I say gently. The automatic doors slide open a few seconds later. The cold breeze blows over my bare skin as shudders rack furiously through my body.

"Stop," He comes to an abrupt halt beside me. I look over and grin as he shrugs his shoulders out of his suit jacket. He avoids my eyes as he takes a step behind me, holding the jacket out as an invitation to slip my arms through the sleeves. Heat rushes to my cheeks, and the fading light of the sun hides my flush as I slide my arms into his jacket. It's warm and smells like him—like whiskey and the same spiced cologne he has worn since we first met. The familiarity washes over me, and my heart rate speeds up to an abnormal rate. He lets out an awkward cough and darts his eyes around the parking lot.

"Thank you." I smile up at him and slide my hand in his once again, the long sleeves of his jacket bunching at my wrist.

We reach his truck quickly, and he slowly drops my hand and places his own atop the cold body of the truck. I stand silently beside him as he lets out a deep breath and leans on his hands. My brain selfishly decides that now is the perfect time to check him out as my eyes rake over the muscles cording through the thin material of his white dress shirt as his grip tightens on the hood. The veins in his hands pop out as he clenches them, his teeth grinding together. I stay rooted to the spot and play with the cuffs of his jacket.

As much as I want to ask him how he's doing, I know he won't talk unless he wants to. This was no doubt embarrassing for him—to have his family behave like such assholes in front of everyone in that damn restaurant. I wasn't expecting tonight to go well by any means, considering how against going he was in the first place. But I definitely wasn't expecting it to go *that* badly.

River is a pompous ass, and although his mom didn't seem bad when I first met her, I can honestly say that I can't stand the woman now. And then there's Allen. Everything about that man screamed skeevy. From his greasy hair to his yellow teeth, there wasn't a single nice thing about him. The snide remarks, the menacing looks, and the intimidating aura were enough to send shivers through my entire body—and not the good kind. My heart aches for Tyler, knowing he had to grow up in that kind of family—in that house. It isn't fair. He deserves so much better than this. Than what he had.

He pushes himself off the truck and slams the hood. I don't have time to prepare myself before his hand grabs my hip and pulls me to him, leaving a small step between us. He finally meets my eyes again and inhales deeply through his nose.

"I'm sorry you were there for that. I should have never brought you," he murmurs, the brown of his eyes deep, melted chocolate as they twinkle under the parking lot lights. I place my hand on his chest and slowly drag it upward until his strong jaw rests in the palm of my hand. The warm skin stings my cold fingers as they rub over a long scar hiding in the overgrown stubble.

Questions pop up in my brain, demanding to be asked and answered as I stare at him, hoping he'll tell me what I want to know. His lips part and Adam's apple bobs. For a moment I think that he's about to tell me everything, but he shakes his head and says, "Let's get in the truck."

My heart drops to my feet when he brushes me off and moves toward his door without sparing me a second look.

I was so freaking close.

After a silent half-hour truck ride, Tyler pulls up in front of my towering apartment building. The quiet, droning rap song plays from the speakers but provides no sense of comfort. We both sit awkwardly in our seats, neither of us wanting to make the first move. I peer out the window and watch the groups of people walking down the sidewalk, most of them carrying expensive purses or wearing designer suits. A wave of nausea rolls over me and I grip my knee. Since when did I become a girl that lives in a penthouse, pretending I'm not a broke dance teacher using my brother's money to stay afloat?

"You okay?" Tyler asks quietly, turning to face me.

I nod my head and pull my hand away from my knee before brushing an invisible hair away from my face. "Are you?"

"They didn't used to be like that," he sighs, gripping the steering wheel. "My mom and River, I mean."

I raise my brow and turn my body toward him with my hands in my lap. "I didn't think they did," I whisper.

He squeezes his eyes shut and pushes out a harsh breath. "He ruined us. Allen is the reason we all struggle with addiction. He forced that on us. We didn't choose it. "

I stare at him, head tilted and confusion running rampant in my mind. Addictions? With Allen, it's clear to see, but everyone else? Not so much.

He must sense my confusion because he quickly blurts out an explanation. "River can't go a day without a bag of white dust in his suit pocket, and my mom can't sleep at night without draining an entire bottle of Vodka."

My lips part and my jaw drops slightly, his words taking me by surprise.

"Looks can be deceiving, I know," he chuckles darkly. His gaze is fixed on the trees lining the painted road in front of us.

"Where does that leave you then? What's your so-called addiction?" I ask curiously. My skin flares when he turns and locks his eyes with mine.

"You, Gray. I think I'm addicted to you."

20

Gracie

It seems my mood is shared with the entire city as rain continues streaming outside my bedroom window. The unrelenting raindrops pelt against the thick glass, creating a depressing visual of how I feel inside.

Tiny balls of sweat stick to my skin, yet I can't bring myself to push off the thick duvet that covers me. I lay in a tight ball instead, and continue to drown in my puddle of regret. The faint smell of Tyler's cologne still lingers on my clothes from last night, making me feel guiltier as the seconds tick on.

His face keeps flashing through my mind, terrorizing me whenever I think sleep might be possible. The rejection that had washed over his features when I didn't respond to his words grips my stomach in its fist, yanking me around as the image continues to burn itself deeper into my memory.

You, Gray. I think I'm addicted to you.

His words took me by surprise. It was like someone flipped off the lights in my head. Those eight words might not have been an obvious declaration of love, but I know better than anyone that to Tyler, they may as well have. That was his attempt at letting me see the big heart that he keeps stored safely away from this world. But I was too caught up in my own feelings to think about his.

I just stared back at him—for how long I'm not even sure—just opening and closing my mouth like a damn fish. I tried racking my brain for some sort of perfect response. But I took a few seconds too long. He took my silence as a sign of rejection, and in good old Tyler fashion, closed up immediately, not letting me get another word in before he was hiding that part of him from me again. He all but pushed me out of his truck with a clenched jaw and a wave of his hand. The black smoke was the only remainder of him as I stood on the curb, watching him speed away through blurry eyes. Little did he know he was taking a fragment of me with him.

It's safe to say that I haven't moved from my bed since then, not even for the McDonalds Jess tried to bribe me with this morning. I've been staring at the flat screen hanging on the wall across the room for so long my eyes burn. But I don't dare turn it off now. My brother is skating across T.V as his team wins with another unsurprising blowout score. With him being so far away, it's almost soothing to be able to see him play, even if it is just through a small screen. Days like today, though, I wish he was just a drive away. I know he's out doing what he loves, but I miss him and his horrible advice a lot more than I would ever admit to him.

Sometimes I need my big brother.

Sometimes I wish I didn't have to be alone.

I pull the blankets tighter around my head when someone knocks on my door. "What?" I grumble, my voice muffled. The door handle rattles before the light from the hall floods the room and through the thick material of my blanket.

"Is that any way to talk to your favourite soon-to-be sister?"

I rip the blanket off with flailing arms and launch myself at Ava. My squeal mutes her gentle laugh and I throw my arms around her shoulders.

"You reek like sweat." She sniffs me with a scrunched nose.

I roll my eyes and sit back down on my bed, running a hand over my hair in an attempt to diminish the static left behind from my duvet.

"I thought you would have been in Vegas with Oakley this weekend. When did you get here?" I'm nearly bouncing in place.

"Vegas isn't really my thing. I decided to pay a visit to you guys instead. You know how your brother gets at the Casino. There's only so many poker games this girl can watch before she falls asleep at the table." She drops a small bag down beside my door and sits down beside me. "I got here last night but Morgan insisted I stay with them."

We laugh together and I feel a smile touch my lips for the first time today. "How is the mama doing? She's gotta be ready to pop soon, right?" I'm sure we're all more than ready to meet baby Miller.

Ava nods. "A little over a month to go. Matt is about ready to pull his hair out."

"I don't blame him. The guy's a damn saint for being able to handle Morgan." We all love Morgan, but God she makes Regina George look like a saint when she's pregnant.

"Speaking of saints. How's Tyler?" she asks, brows dancing with excitement and a knowing curiosity. I shake my head before I let the guilt reach for me again.

"What's that look for? Did he do something? I swear! Between him and Adam I'm going to lose my damn mind," she growls, and with a huff, shoves her hand into her jacket pocket and pulls out her phone.

"No, Ava. Don't. He didn't do anything!" I nearly shriek, reaching into her lap to grab the phone.

"He didn't?" Her eyes widen and she stares at me without blinking. Sheesh, you would have thought I just told her the sky was falling.

I drop my head in my hands and shake my head a few times. "No. I did."

"You did?" she sputters. I still don't think that she's blinked.

"I finally started to make a dent in that fucking wall of his right before I helped glue it right back together," I groan and throw myself back on my bed.

I hear her sigh as I stare at the tiny lumps on the ceiling. She lies down beside me and links her hand with mine, giving it a squeeze.

"I'm sure it wasn't that bad."

Always the voice of reason, this one. "I met his family, Ava. And he opened up to me, about his feelings," I sigh.

She sucks in a sharp breath and turns her head to the side to stare at me again. Her eyes are nowhere as big now. "You did? Isn't that a good thing? What happened? What did you do?"

"They're awful, Ava. Absolutely awful. And I did nothing. That's the problem. I did absolutely nothing. I just stared at him —*silently*—for a good five minutes after he finally opened up to me."

Ava turns her head to the front again and gnaws on her lip. I groan and wipe my hands down my cheeks. "I'm an idiot."

"You're not an idiot," she scolds and pushes herself up into a sitting position. "Maybe a little slow, but not an idiot."

"What do I do? You know Tyler better than I do."

She flicks me in the arm. "We both know that isn't true anymore."

Okay, maybe that was a bit of a stretch.

"Just go talk to him. I'll even drive you on my way to Adam's," she offers, smiling warmly. "After you shower that is."

I push myself out of bed with a laugh. I hear the soft ding of Ava's phone when I stretch out all the tight muscles that have been extremely unused in the last day.

"I'm going to get rid of my stench. Just make yourself at home," I say, earning a nod in response.

"Always do." She winks. When she looks down at her phone, green eyes popping open with excitement as she presses it to her ear. "Hey, baby. "

I catch the muffled voice of my brother on the other end of the call before I turn and head to my bathroom, smiling wide.

"Tell me again why you need to go to Adam's?" I ask when we get inside Ava's brand-new Range Rover—a very extravagant gift from my brother. Apparently, her old car wasn't cutting it for Oakley, so like any twenty-three-year-old millionaire, he went out and bought her her dream car. Of course, in good Ava fashion, she insisted he bring it back that day, but the silly girl should have known that wouldn't work.

"It's a long story," she sighs over the soft murmurs coming from the fancy sound system.

"Too bad. Tell me."

Flipping on her blinker she moves into the far lane. "Oakley and I kept something from him that we shouldn't have."

Raising a brow, I wait for her to continue.

"Last time your brother and I were here, we went out to this new bar opening and saw Cora there. And she wasn't there with Adam," she sighs and furrows her brows, causing a few wrinkles to slide across her otherwise smooth forehead. My stomach swirls at the thought of Adam's girlfriend—of one seemingly solid year—out partying with another guy.

"Okay," I ask. "Who was she with? A guy?"

Ava nods. "No clue. I've never seen him before, but we're pretty positive that it wasn't just a friendly meeting. Unless making out with your friends is the new normal."

"For real? What a bitch." Poor Adam. He always ends up with the shit end of every damn stick.

"I should have told him, Gray. He's really hurt." She turns into Tyler's visibly unappealing neighbourhood with a frown so deep I'm afraid it could stay like that forever. My mom always said that if you frown for too long, your face would stay like that. Although it was just a scare tactic, I wouldn't want Ava never to smile again. She has a smile that could turn anyone's day from gloomy, to bright and sunny.

We stand out like a sore thumb as we continue driving down the pothole-infested street, our bodies jostling around with every bump. Would it kill the city to fill in some of these? It's clear the neighbourhood hasn't heard laughter in a while as the cracked concrete remains unscuffed, not a single soul braving to walk alone even underneath the sun's bright glow. We pass building after building, all of which are empty. The once well-loved store-fronts are now decorated with smashed glass and chipped paint, an eyesore to every set of curious eyes. At one time, this must have been a booming neighbourhood. A place people went to mingle and enjoy the light air. But now, it's a place people go when they don't want to be found.

"Adam always forgives you. Don't be too hard on yourself. You didn't mean to hurt him." I give her an encouraging smile before starting to twist the strings of my hoodie. A nervous habit.

"And Tyler will forgive you." She reaches across the centre console and gives my arm a squeeze. We pull over to the side of the road and Ava parks beside Tyler's truck.

The building gawks at us as my thighs remain glued to the seat and fear starts to creep up my spine. This could go terribly wrong. He could open the door just seconds before slamming it back in my face, not listening to a single word I try forcing from my lips.

"You got this, Gray. You're a boss-ass bitch. Now go get your man," Ava encourages me from her seat and nods toward the building.

Taking a much-needed breath, I nod a few times and smile at her. I can do this. "Thanks for coming, Ava. I missed you." I lean across the car and give her a quick side hug that she returns just as eagerly. Grabbing my purse from the floor, I open the door.

My sneakers hit the busted sidewalk cautiously as I send Ava a wave and watch her pull away from the curb. I turn to face the building and swallow the ball in my throat and force myself to start walking. It only takes a few seconds to reach the heavy glass door. The heater tucked in the corner of the entrance blows furiously as I step inside and the overbearing smell of cigarette smoke fills my lungs. As I reach forward to buzz his apartment, I notice the door is already held open by a ratty old phone book.

"Guess it's my lucky day," I mumble under my breath and push it open, placing my foot on the first step. I try not to gag when the dirty carpet squishes under my feet. I'm out of breath when I reach his door three floors later.

My fist hits the door three times before I take a step back and shove my hands in the pocket of my hoodie. I hear footsteps thump from in the apartment. The intimidating sound syncs perfectly with the thumping rhythm of my heart. I hear him curse under his breath before I hear the chain lock slide. The door is pulled open quickly and my mouth dries when I come face-to-face with the guy in front of me. All coherent thoughts dissipate as fast as the air from my lungs.

"What?" he grumbles.

"Hi." My voice raises awkwardly in some sort of embarrassing squeak as I stand awkwardly in the doorway. Tyler looks down at me, wearing nothing but a loose towel and an intimidating scowl.

"Do you need something?" he asks. His scowl twists up into a smirk when he notices where my attention has fallen. My eyes find the scattered water droplets that hang from his naked skin. The perfectly spaced indents that form his impressive six-pack yank the breath from my lungs. I itch to reach out and touch him, to feel the heat beneath my fingertips, to snake my hand beneath that freaking towel.

"Want me to just drop the damn thing?"

"What?" I nearly choke on a cough.

"Do you want me to drop the towel? It seems to be obstructing your view."

My eyes pop open quickly before I collect my composure and narrow them into slits. "Can I come in or not?"

Tyler moves aside, opening his arm as a silent invitation. I straighten my back and walk past him. A sharp breeze scrapes along the living room floor and nips at my thin sock-covered toes as I walk cautiously around the random clothing items strewn around. The patio door is slid open, exposing the bland cement balcony that looks onto the empty streets. Not much of a view if you ask me.

"Are you here to embarrass me again?" Tyler mutters behind me.

I turn with a sigh and fold my arms across my chest. He's no longer in only a towel. Now his chiselled chest is covered by a plain white t-shirt while a pair of grey sweats hang on his hips.

"Can we sit and talk or do you want us to fight instead?"

He rolls his eyes and walks past me to sit down on the couch. With a deep breath, I nod my head and follow, sitting on the cushion beside him.

"I didn't mean to embarrass you," I mumble and stare at the dark hair that covers his jaw while he keeps his gaze locked in front of him. I watch as he swallows harshly, throat bobbing before he runs his fingers through his onyx hair.

"I should have said something. I *wanted* to say something."

"Don't worry about it. I actually don't even know why I said anything. I wasn't thinking." He shrugs and finally brings his brown eyes to mine. The lack of any feeling in those dark chocolate orbs is like a stab to my chest. I know he doesn't mean that. This is what Tyler does, he's just trying to push me away.

"Don't try it, Ty. You're not fooling me."

"Then you're dumber than I thought."

I drop my eyes to the button on the couch cushion lying beside my thigh, half pulled from its stitches. His words hurt, regardless if they're true or not.

"Stop it. You know you can't push me away."

He keeps staring at the wall and leans his elbows on the loose pants that cover his thighs. He doesn't say anything as I continue to watch him. I can feel my anger rising while my patience drops.

"Just look at me. What good does fighting this do? Clearly, you care about me in one way or another. So stop being a damn pussy and admit it already!" I shout, fed up.

"Are you really calling me a pussy? After what happened?"

"If it hadn't taken you so long to finally admit you have feelings for me then maybe I wouldn't have been so damn shocked!"

"I never said I had feelings for you." He's retreating now, looking out toward the window.

"Fine. Then I'll leave. Is that what you want? Because I'm not going to keep doing this. If you don't want me, then I'll leave. Simple as that."

My words seem to spark a reaction from inside him because he whips his head to the side and lets out a string of curses before smashing our mouths together. Our groans intertwine as I throw my leg over his thighs and sit in his lap, straddling him. I grab his hair in a tight fist and pull him as close to me as possible, terrified that if I don't, he'll push me away. He takes me by surprise when he grabs my cheeks in his palms and deepens the kiss, keeping me in place.

I release his hair and take the opportunity to run my hands over his hard body, not stopping until the soft material of his shirt is bunched between my fingers. He unlatches his lips from mine for a brief second so he can tug the shirt over his head and throw it across the room before moulding our mouths together again.

His skin is hot under my touch, addicting almost as I continue to feel him with abandon. He's rough, yet somehow gentle as he places his hands on my hips, pushing the material of my sweater up until I feel his fingers sending shocks through my bones.

We should talk.

My core throbs as I grind down on the hardness beneath me, waves of pleasure shooting up my spine when he lets out a thick sound of approval. His thin sweatpants do little to hide his erection.

We need to talk.

I squeak in surprise when he pushes up from the couch, his hands tightening on my hips as he lifts me with him. I wrap my thighs around him on impulse. I drag my lips from his and move them down his neck, kissing every inch of the sensitive skin as he moves us out of the dimly lit living room.

Maybe we can wait to talk.

My back hits the bed seconds before Tyler's hands start roaming my body. His touch is greedy, frantic, and all too addicting. When he reaches for the band of my leggings, his eyes meet mine, filled to the brim with an emotion I can't decipher as he leans down to place an open-mouthed kiss on my collarbone. His fingers slide under my sweater, moving upward until my bra-covered breasts are held firmly in his hands.

"Relax," he coaxes, pushing my bra away and exposing my skin.

"Tyler," I sigh and he starts dragging my sweater up my chest, pushing it over my head and tossing it onto the floor. My back arches when he unclasps my bra and pulls it off. His eyes are stormy as they watch me writhe underneath him.

"Stop teasing me," I plead when he leans back and traces a finger over my wet panties.

"Patience *has* never been your thing, beautiful." He has a smirk stretched across his swollen lips that I want to suck off.

He's right, it never has. But I don't want to start being patient now. Not when the pulse between my legs is faster than the one in my chest.

No, I need him inside me right now.

"Can we talk now?" I murmur as we both fall from our highs. My chest rises rapidly and his warm breaths cause loose hairs to fall in my face. I have my head on his chest and he lays beneath me, hands resting at his sides as if he's suddenly afraid to touch me.

"We should."

I nod and reluctantly push off his chest, instantly missing his warmth. "Well, what are we? Because I don't usually do what we just did with all my other guy friends."

"I fucking hope not," he growls, wrapping an arm around my waist and pulling me back to him, much to my pleasure.

"There would be no need to be jealous if you just made me your girlfriend, you know?" I tease, throwing him a wink that I hope doesn't look as nervous as I feel. I don't know why I said that.

He scowls at my joke but keeps his arm wrapped tightly around me anyway. "I don't know if I can do the whole girl-friend thing, Gray. I'm a shitty person in case you forgot. I don't think I would treat you how you deserve to be treated."

"Shut up. You're not a shitty person," I scold him. "You have a shitty attitude, sometimes sure, but you're a great person. You just do a good job of hiding it."

"Someone thinks they're smart this morning."

"Don't be an ass hole." I swat his chest but wear a small smile.

"I can't promise that I'll be a good boyfriend," he sighs and shakes his head.

"Then we'll work on it together."

"You say that now," he laughs, the sound empty of all emotion. "What about when I inevitably fuck everything up? I'm not reliable, Gracie. Between having to take care of my mother, and everything that comes with playing professional hockey, I can't promise that you'll be my first priority, as hard as I try to make you be."

I know that this is hard for him. I understand that he must have enough emotional trauma to last far longer than a lifetime, but I want him to let me help him. I *need him* to let me help him.

I keep my voice quiet and my tone free of judgment. I'm terrified of spooking him with the pressure I'm dying to finally put on him to make a decision. I reach toward his face and turn it toward me, forcing him to look at me with guarded eyes. "How much longer are you going to fight this?"

He blinks slowly and his jaw tenses slightly in my hand before relaxing soon after. I grab the hand lying closest to me and bring it to my chest, pressing it flat against the bare skin between my breasts.

"Feel how hard my heart is beating," I mutter, almost begging. "That's for you. It's been like that for years, but you never gave me the chance to tell you."

There's a subtle flex of his fingers against my skin and the air he's been holding comes out in one big puff. His eyes are hooded, but for the first time in a year, I don't see a speck of regret in them before he gently kisses the top of my head, lingering there.

"Okay, Gray. Okay."

21

Tyler

"TELL ME WHY I HAVE TO COME TO THIS?" I ASK, WATCHING IN AWE as Gracie flips her curly hair behind her shoulder and shifts to give me a pointed look.

"Because I need to be there, and seeing as how you're my boyfriend now, it's also important that you're there." Her cheeky grin almost makes me forget about that damn label. *Boyfriend.* I'm sure it's pretty clear that I have no fucking clue what I'm doing here. Having to care about someone else's feelings is so out of my comfort zone. Sure, I'm used to caring for my mom, but this is not the same thing. No amount of practice could have ever taught me how to handle the blue-eyed demon in front of me.

"I'm sure Oakley would be fine without me there."

"Who cares? I wouldn't be fine without you." The statement was meant to be simple, but it hits me low in the gut and stays there, curling around my insides.

"It'll be nice to see Ava. It's been a few . . ." I trail off, my eyes getting stuck on Gracie's round ass as it dares to rip through the too-tight material of her pants when she bends over to tie her shoes. Blood rushes to my groin immediately, a full-grown hard-on ready to make its appearance as she rolls her body back up, teasing me. A knowing smirk rests on her lips when she turns around to face me again, seconds before her eyes flicker to my crotch. She knew I was watching. The little minx.

"Do you want to take care of that before we go? You wouldn't want my family seeing that you have a hard time controlling yourself," she teases, taking slow steps toward me.

I swallow greedily and grab hold of her hips, pulling her into me abruptly. A quiet moan slips from her lips and she looks up at me with wide, hungry eyes.

"You should know better than to tease me by now, baby." I nip at her ear before capturing her lips in a fleeting kiss. "We better be going, don't wanna be late, do we?" I taunt as I drop my hands from her waist. I'm heading out of the bedroom when I hear her grunt her displeasure. I slip my shoes on with a quick laugh and lean against the front door to wait for her. Seconds later, she's walking toward me like a woman on a mission.

"You can't beat the master at his own game, Gray." I open the door for her and step into the hallway. She swats me across the back with what feels like a purse full of rocks. "Shit!"

"Just wait. One of these days, I'm going to have you eating your words."

I roll my eyes and shove open the exit door. She intertwines our fingers as we walk in step to my truck. I don't doubt that you will, Gracie. In fact, I count on it.

"Oh, how I missed you, Gracie baby!" Anne Hutton squeals once we step foot inside the Hutton family home.

"I missed you too, Mom." Gracie's sporting a massive grin as she lets Anne wrap her up in a tight hug. I spot Oakley and Ava sitting on the loveseat, arms around each other and a large note-book between them.

"Don't think I forgot about you, Tyler," Anne says, snapping my attention back to the two girls that stare at me expectantly.

"How could you? We all know I'm your favourite, Anne." I grin at her and my chest swells when her cheeks darken in colour. They're thinner than they used to be, but I assume that's because of her past stint in the hospital when she had pneumonia. She was there for a couple of months, but as far as I know, she's made a full recovery since then.

It's been a while since I've been in this house, but every time I have been, I've left wishing I grew up with the kind of love that flows through every room. The Hutton's are the family that all families want to be: kind, caring, generous, and most importantly, loving, to everyone, regardless of who they are. It's why I admire Oakley so much. He has a heart the size of a mountain.

"Give me a hug, sweetheart," Anne demands before I feel her pull me into her warm embrace.

"Share him with the rest of us, Anne," Ava teases, and starts to make her way over. A soft chuckle shakes through Anne when she releases me and moves back so Ava can all but throw herself around me.

"Hey, Ava." I return the hug comfortably and almost laugh at myself. A few years ago, I wouldn't have let a single one of these people touch me, let alone hug me.

"Holy crap did I ever miss you," she sighs into my shoulder.

"I missed you, too."

I haven't seen Ava since the engagement disaster–which really wasn't all that long ago–but I can't count the number of times I've wanted to call and get her advice since then. We've always been really close. With our similar childhoods and lack of decent parental figures, she was always someone I felt comfortable talking to about my shitty problems. We both pull away a few seconds later and I'm grateful that my mind feels more lucid than it has been the past few days.

"Are you really not going to come hug me, Oakley?" Gracie

chides from beside me, her eyes narrowed at her brother when he remains seated in the living room.

"Well, I'm going to check on supper," Anne says before high-tailing her way into the kitchen, obviously not wanting to witness the wrath of her daughter. I can practically see the steam shooting from Gracie's ears as she places her hands on her hips and stalks over to her brother. My gaze flickers to Ava as she continues to stand mute, lip pulled between her teeth.

"What's going on?" I cock a brow.

She swallows nervously. "I'm not supposed to say anything."

I lean back against the front door with a snort. "Out with it."

"Oakley won't be playing in Seattle next season," she gushes, now staring back at me with a bright grin that takes up half her face. It's funny that she thinks I didn't already figure that out myself. I mean, come on? He had Vancouver eating out of the palm of his hand. He wasn't going to turn them down regardless of what they decided to offer him. He was never going to stay in Seattle.

I shake my head, laughing. "That's amazing, Ava. I'm guessing he's telling Gracie today?"

"Are you kidding me?" Gracie squeals and captures the attention of everyone in the room. I guess that answers my question. "So, you're coming home then?"

"Yes, you weirdo. Now stop screaming."

Oakley stands up from the couch and grabs his sister, pulling her into his chest as she starts to shake with sobs. I'm suddenly fully aware that I'm standing in front of them. My heart lurches as I back up and sit on the opposite couch. I want to be the one comforting her right now. Fuck, what is happening to me? Get a fucking grip.

"Why are you crying? This is good news, Gray," Oakley mumbles in her ear as his hand rubs slow circles on her back.

"Because I'm happy, you dumb ass!" she croaks.

"Then stop crying. You're freaking me out."

The cushion beside me sinks as Ava sits down beside me, mumbling, "You really like her."

Turning my head, I search for any sign of judgment. Unsurprisingly, I come up short of anything but pure happiness and a thick sense of approval.

"I do," I admit, knowing there's no point in trying to deny it anymore, especially when it comes to Ava. No matter how hard I try to pretend Gracie hasn't swung a sledgehammer at my defences, I always find myself helping her brush away the smashed pieces.

I look at Gracie when she pulls away from her brother and wipes a hand across her tear-stained cheeks and let myself stare at her without the fear of being caught.

"Good."

"Good?"

"Yes, good. Gracie might be the only girl on this planet that can put up with all of your bullshit. She's good for you."

I find myself nodding at her words, although my eyes are still locked on Gracie. My girl turns to me now, eyes red and starting to become swollen, but still somehow just as beautiful as she always is. The wide grin on her lips tugs at my heart, bringing a wave of foreign feelings to the surface. She flops down on my lap and wraps her arms around my neck, sticking her face in my neck. A soft kiss is placed on my exposed skin as she lets out a content sigh, blocking out the glare Oakley is currently hurling my way.

Ava stands up from beside me and moves quickly over to her fiancé before pulling him up by his arm. She sends me a wink and leads Oakley into the kitchen so that Gracie and I are alone.

"I guess this means that the gang will finally be back together," Gracie whispers against my neck, sending an electric zap down my spine.

"Back and better than ever, Gray."

"So, are we the first ones that know about your new team?" Gracie asks excitedly, using my lap as her own personal stool like she has been for the past half-hour. Not that I mind. I'm more comfortable now than I think I have been in a long time. Maybe *ever*. But I would never admit that to anyone, especially not her. I would never hear the end of it.

Her left cheek is flush to my chest and a slim arm is wrapped around my side. Gracie's fingernails are trailing along my rib cage as she keeps herself busy talking to her brother, seemingly oblivious to the fact that he hasn't taken his narrowed eyes off of me since she plopped down on my lap.

Long strands of blonde hair rub against my chin when she lifts her head, connecting our eyes just long enough for me to notice the annoyance in hers. I raise my brows and get ready to ask what crushed her mood when she glares at Oakley, snapping, "Oakley, for Pete's sake, what do you think he's going to do to me in front of everyone? Slip a hand up my shirt? Cool it and answer my question."

Oakley flinches, his eyes widening to resemble saucers as he fumbles with a response, finally choking on a few words. "No. We told Adam about the move yesterday."

"Wow. Fuck you too, then."

"Gracie Rose! Watch your language," Anne scolds her in a way that I could imagine her doing quite a few times in Gracie's teenage years before returning to us with her hands on her hips. All eyes fall on her intimidating posture—a sight that looks weird on someone so lighthearted and sweet.

"Sorry," Gracie mutters under her breath like a kid caught with their hand in the cookie jar. I drop my head and place a kiss on her shoulder, laughing lightly.

"Who wants to watch a movie?" Ava asks, bouncing off the

couch and moving toward the wide assortment of DVDs resting on the shelves under the T.V.

"Sure, baby. Something good this time, though." Oakley pokes fun at her with adoration beaming across his face.

"I would rather go upstairs and make our own," I whisper in Gracie's ear, nipping at the sensitive, smooth skin and loving the shiver that runs down her spine as she moves further into my body. "I vote for something scary." I address the entire room now while Gracie attempts to reel back in her scattered breaths.

"Scary works for me," Ava says while shuffling through the seemingly endless piles of movies. I had no clue the Huttons were such movie fanatics. *That's because you never asked,* I scold myself and tighten my grip on Gracie's waist.

"I hate you," Gracie mutters under her breath, wriggling in my grasp. I laugh under my breath, knowing full well the last thing she wants to do is pull away from me. I move my open palm down to her thigh–bare from the shorts that have ridden up–and squeeze the area I've learned is more than ticklish.

"We both know that isn't true, baby."

I grin when she jolts in surprise, a loud shriek flooding the room. I ignore Oakley's curious eyes as Gracie turns around, glaring at me. I tilt my head and smile innocently.

"You're the worst, you know?"

"That's not what you were saying earlier."

"Can you two knock it off? I'm going to barf," Oakley grunts, his gaze pin balling between Gracie and me and Ava by the T.V.

"Oh, I think it's adorable," Anne gushes, sighing contently with her hands clasped in front of her. The happiness in her wrinkled, tired features makes my own chest feel all warm and fuzzy. Anne Hutton may not be my blood, but she's been more of a mother figure to me than mine has been. Seeing her so happy is all I want for the woman who fed me on every holiday until my pants didn't fit over my gut and washed my laundry when she noticed I was wearing the same dirty clothes for three days in a row.

"Thank you!" Gracie turns back around and throws her hands up in appreciation of her mom.

In her own world, Ava shouts, "Got it!" while quickly slipping the disk into the player and running back toward Oakley.

"You watching too, Ma?" Oakley asks when the opening trailers start playing on the flat-screen hung between black-framed photos, all of which hold a picture of the Hutton family throughout the years.

"No, no. I have a new book calling my name. You guys have fun, though. Call me if you need anything." All four of us nod in agreement before she leaves the room, still smiling warm enough to comfort the most broken of men.

I can't help but grunt in disapproval when Gracie gets up from my lap and crosses the room. She stops in front of a pile of blankets shoved inside a brown wicker basket and begins digging through them.

"Jesus, dude," Oakley chuckles, shaking his head. I flip him the finger, keeping my eyes on Gracie as she grabs the fluffiest blanket, grips it right in two fists, and rushes back over to me. When she stops short, mere inches from moving between my open legs, I tilt my head with a silent question.

"Lay down," she orders while moving her hand in the air, down the length of the couch.

With a grin, I nod once. "Yes, ma'am."

I push myself down the couch and shove a small decorative pillow behind my head and lay on my side, pushed against the back cushion. With my brows raised, I drop my eyes to the empty space in front of me. She doesn't hesitate before joining me and throwing the beige blanket over our legs. She lays down and pushes herself back until our bodies are flush again and rests her head beside mine on the tiny throw pillow. I can smell the fruity smell of her shampoo–the same one she's used for at least the past year–as her hair sprawls across the pillow and tickles my nose.

"You good, princess?"

"Will be when you wrap your arm around me," she mumbles, and I would bet a hundred bucks she's grinning in the dark. The thought makes me aware of the smile I'm currently wearing, too. I'm suddenly remarkably grateful Oakley and Ava are lost in their old world again, whispering to each other under the T.V. light.

I pull the blankets up to our necks, reach under with my free arm and grab her waist with a tight grip. I relax my shoulders and run my fingers along her side, loving how my touch affects her when goosebumps cover her skin. The steady rise and fall of my chest moves in sync with Gracie's, and by the time I find myself staring at the television, the movie has already started.

The movie is long over by the time I manage to peel my eyes open again. When I look around the room, I spot Oakley and Ava curled up together, fast asleep on the long, three-seater couch across the room, making me feel less guilty about the fact I also fell asleep. Somehow, they've maneuvered themselves so that Oakley is lying on his back, with Ava now covering his body with hers. Her leg hangs off the side of the couch and Oakley's head is hanging off the arm of the couch, neck looking like it might just snap in half. It's quite a sight. One I wish I could grab my phone and snake a picture of.

Gracie's put my arm to sleep as she continues to lay utterly dead to the world against me. She's never been much of an active sleeper when it comes to sleeping beside me. I swear someone could shoot off fireworks standing no more than a foot from her and she wouldn't so much as stir. But as much as I would *love* to sleep on the couch tonight and wake up with the same kind of pain in my neck that Oakley will, there is a perfectly comfortable bed waiting for the both of us upstairs.

After shaking Gracie a few times–only to be rewarded with nothing but a subtle snore–I throw my head back with a groan. I decide to carry her instead and carefully move off of the couch. I tuck a hand under her thigh and upper back and gently lift her up. She weighs nearly nothing, and I feel the urge to shove an extra-large deep dish down her throat. Yeah, maybe not the best idea I've ever had.

By the time I reach the carpeted staircase, she's placed her head in the curve of my neck, giving me the feeling she's been awake the entire time and just wanted a free ride.

"If you wanted me to carry you, all you had to do was ask," I whisper, my words barely audible as I attempt to see if I'm right. I feel her body tense just as a soft giggle meets my ears. "You're ridiculous."

"It's about time you used these muscles for good," she says in a hushed tone and runs a hand slowly down my bicep, squeezing the hard-earned muscles with a content sigh.

I push her old bedroom door open with my foot. Thankfully it wasn't fully shut. I stumble through the darkness, not wanting to bother turning the light on and blinding my eyes with the god-awful pink walls sixteen-year-old Gracie thought were the best idea ever. I gently set her on the bed and yank my shirt over my head, discarding it with my sweatpants in a pile by the door. A smirk falls on my lips as I look over to see her pull my hoodie off, exposing the solid abdominal muscles crafted beautifully from years of dancing as the material bunches up under her sports bra.

"Want some help?"

"No," she scoffs, her usual response whenever I offer to help with something she finds ridiculous, and throws the black hoodie across the room. She pushes her thin tank top down her exposed skin before settling under the blankets.

"That's a shame," I mutter as I crawl in after her, lying on my side and pulling her back against my front on instinct. When her tank top meets my chest, I simply groan, not liking the annoying barrier.

"You have got to be the horniest guy I have ever met." She attempts to scold me, but the humour in her tone betrays her. I swallow my laugh and toy with the hem of her tank top before slipping my hand underneath. I'm relieved when my palm meets bare skin.

"Like you're any better," I say while tracing circles around her belly button. I pat my pillow as an invitation for her to settle herself as close to me as possible, and she does just that. In one swift, easy movement, she places her head on my pillow and floods my nose with the smell of her shampoo. She reaches for the hand I've got on her hip and laces our fingers together.

"Okay, you make a good point."

She kisses the top of my hand, over the scars I know cover my knuckles from years of fights caused by unresolved anger toward my stepdad and the life I wished I could escape.

"That's what I thought," I hum knowingly, feeling my eyes become heavy with sleep.

"Do you remember the day that Oakley found out about us?" she asks me a few seconds later, once I can nearly taste the sleep I crave on the tip of my tongue.

I manage to push my face into her hair and nod. "How could I forget?"

"I realized something that day."

"Oh yeah?" My nerves build with how vague she's being. Gracie is never vague. Not usually, anyway.

"I think I'm falling in love with you," she whispers, words so carefully mouthed and quiet.

Swallowing harshly, I nod again, unable to form a coherent response. I'm surprised, undeniably nervous, and so exhausted that I'm finding it hard to stay awake with her warm body pressed up against mine. Her breathing serves as the perfect lullaby.

"I just wanted you to know. So that, you know . . . " she trails off. "I just wanted you to know."

I nod again, but this time, I manage to scrape up a reply. "You've opened up a part of me that I didn't even know existed, Gray. I know that doesn't mean as much to you as what you said, but it does to me. It means everything."

22

Gracie

"So, you and Tyler are like a thing now?" Jess asks from across the room, her long, bubblegum pink painted fingernails tapping furiously against her phone screen. Sharp, steely blue eyes watch me carefully.

Are we a thing now? I think so. But Tyler is hardly an open book when it comes to anything personal, especially anything special enough to make him overly vulnerable.

Our moment at my mom's house last weekend took me by surprise. In a good way, of course. I'm still not sure what possessed me into saying that I was falling in love with him. The truth is that I am already way too close to actually *being* in love with him. How could I not be? The rugged, broken, shadow of a man only seems to light up for me, and my God, the beams are so bright that the sun wouldn't dare challenge him.

It's the way he always presses the tiniest bit harder on the thick flesh of my heels when I beg him to massage my feet because he knows I put too much pressure on them when I dance. It's that no matter how lame he might think it is, my phone will always light up with a text before he heads to the ice for practice, saying something blunt yet comforting, something *very* Tyler.

My heels hurt. Tonight's your turn. Gotta go, his text read when I received it an hour ago. It brought a smile the size of Texas to my face and I giggled like a schoolgirl while staring at the bright screen for an embarrassing amount of time.

"No need to sound so excited for me." I force out a tight-lipped laugh and try to hide my annoyance with her attitude. She's had a flagpole up her ass for the past few days now, and I am far from enjoying it.

"Sorry. It's just new."

I guess she has a point. After watching me pine after Tyler for so long, it has to be weird seeing us actually spending time together now—a lot of it at that. And I can't seem to get enough of him now that I finally have him at fingers length.

"I get it. It's weird for me too." I shrug and plop myself down on the couch beside her, sitting cross-legged. She drops the phone on her chest and pushes herself up from her lying position on the sofa. She sighs when her eyes meet mine again, this time full of enough judgment to fill the role of an entire jury.

"You don't think it's kind of, I don't know, sudden? I mean, he went from never even giving you a second look to grabbing all over you. It seems weird."

A pit starts to grow in my stomach as she stares over at me mockingly, her shoulders rising in a shrug before she returns her attention back to her phone.

Is it weird? Have I found myself too close to an open flame, waiting to get burned? "Are you okay? You seem different lately." My words come out as soft as I can make them, but it's not easy. Not when she's both pissing me off and making my chest ache.

"It's you that I would worry about. Tyler Bateman is nothing but trouble," she replies nonchalantly, as if she knows him better than I do.

"Jesus, Jess. Spit it out already. What is your problem with me lately? Is it really Tyler? Because you've never acted like this when it came to him before. You were so supportive of the entire thing. What gives?"

Throwing her phone back down, she rolls her eyes and folds her arms tightly across her chest. "I don't have a problem. You're making this into a fight because that's just what you do."

Excuse me? It's what *I* do? She's got to be kidding. I stand up and snort with squinted eyes. "You're kidding, right? You started this with your judgmental attitude lately! You barely even know Tyler. Where do you get off talking about him like that? About us?"

She mumbles something under her breath that I don't hear and stands up. She starts picking at her nails. I'm not sure why the small action pisses me off so much, but it does. Maybe it's the fact she stole my nail polish again and won't give it back. Or maybe, I'm just a really petty bitch. Either way, it doesn't matter.

"What was that? I couldn't quite hear what you mumbled under your breath like a child," I snap.

Pushing out a sarcastic laugh, she shakes her head once and pulls her top lip back. "I said that I know him better than you think I do."

I know my eyes have to be the size of soccer balls as I stare at her. My heart pounds away furiously in my chest, knocking against the bones like it's trying to burst through them. *Don't freak out. Keep calm,* I try to remind myself. My efforts are futile when her smirk sends a punch straight to my gut, nearly making me curl over and cover the floor with the chicken salad I had for lunch.

"Stop trying to get under my skin. We both know you're just going through something right now. Is it your brother? Is he okay?" Jess's brother has been deployed for the past two years, so it wouldn't surprise me if she was worried about him more lately. The selfish part of me hopes that's why she's more on edge, but the smart part of me knows that Jess has always had a problem with keeping her paws away from other people's property.

"God, Gracie, relax. Ashton is fine. Stop being dramatic." She waves me off carelessly, and her words hold me in place, frozen to the plush carpet under my curled toes.

"Oh," I reply while my heart sinks deeper into my chest.

"Yeah, *oh*. Just leave me alone for a while. You're driving me crazy with your hovering lately," she snarks before taking off toward the front door and slipping *my* white sneakers on.

"I'm sorry. I had no idea I was hovering. You don't have to leave, Jess." I feel embarrassed, ashamed that I've been acting in a way that has upset her as much as it has.

She throws her head back and groans. "Yeah, I do. I'll be home later." She's gone before I have a chance to respond, leaving my eyes glued on the welcome sign we picked out together last year hung beside the front door.

Tyler

I grunt, exhaustion from the last two hours spent training on the ice kicking my confidence down a few notches. My calves burn and my shoulders ache, the time spent running laps and getting shoved into the boards a mere lighthearted pastime compared to the actual game we're about to face this weekend.

The Calgary Steamrollers plan to do just that, steamroll us. And their confidence isn't unwarranted either. The aggressive pricks in the form of Anthony Meyers and Ryan Delaware wouldn't know a clean hit if it literally hit them in the face. The other defensemen simply follow the lead of their two starters when it comes to their own defensive play.

Suppose Ryan has a hard night keeping his stick out from between one or *five* of my teammates' feet, and Anthony throws his shoulders into a few too many sets of numbers. If that were the case, their crew would follow suit, making the game as dirty as Braden's sheets after a night out.

I've tried not to let myself get too worked up, but my teammates feel it too. It's not just another game against the Steamrollers that we're worried about. It's the fear of something happening to the league's favourite player. The guy who picked the worst possible game to make his Vancouver Warrior's debut after signing his new contract—Oakley fucking Hutton—and it's my job to protect him out there. No matter what.

Gracie's baby blues flash across my vision. The way they hold such adoration for Oakley only restates the importance of this game for me. She would be devastated if anything happened to him, and I would never forgive myself if I didn't do my job and keep him safe out there. I cough to clear my throat and give my head a shake when the locker room door opens. I'm the only one still here, thanks to my inability to stop pushing myself so damn hard, so I assume someone forgot their car keys or something when I shove my practice jersey in my bag and yell out, "Forget something?"

"Are you alone?" Jessica, Gracie's best friend, comes barreling over to my cubby, throwing herself against me as her knees give out. Sobs shake her short figure, the sound coming off more forced than I think she was expecting. I place my hands firmly on her shoulders and push her off of me.

"What are you doing?" My mouth becomes the Sahara as I stare at her with a tick in my jaw. Finally, I gather my thoughts and move past her to look out the door and make sure she wasn't followed. I turn back around. "You're not allowed back here."

"We need to talk."

"We don't. Now leave," I hiss, steel-jawed and waving toward the door. "We don't need to talk about anything." I feel my stomach tightening, a wave of nausea swirling, making me squeeze my eyes shut so tightly that I see stars on the back of my eyelids.

"Yeah, I think we do. I have to tell her about us. I just completely blew up on her. You should have seen her face," she cries, hugging her chest in a way that should make me feel sorry for her, but I don't feel anything but anger. If she really cared about Gracie at all, she wouldn't be here trying to climb me like a damn tree.

"You what? What did you do to her? And what do you mean, us? There never has and will never be an us," I growl, baring my teeth as images of an upset Gracie terrorize me. I know that I should probably be more worried about Gracie finding out about Jessica and me hooking up a couple years back, but that pales in comparison to the hurt Jessica could have caused by just being her self-absorbed, insecure, petty self.

"I hurt her. Really bad. I couldn't control what I was saying. It just spewed out of me!"

"Can you stop your fucking crying for five seconds? I don't have time for your bullshit, Jessica." I walk back to the door. If Gracie's upset then I need to be there, not here with her horrible excuse of a best friend.

"You can't just leave me! I need you right now," Jessica cries out again.

"You don't need anything from me. Just get out. I'm leaving." Footsteps echo behind me as I grip my duffle and fling open the door. I stalk down the empty hallway at an alarming rate. I can hear Jessica's quick footsteps as she likely has to run to keep up with me, but I only pick up my pace.

"We need to talk about this, Ty!" she yells, desperation so thick in her voice that I have to swallow back the bile that makes its way up my throat. The nickname makes my body freeze up in anger while my brain yells at me to keep moving, to just get away from her before I let myself become incensed. But it's my body that wins when I can't seem to move my feet.

"Don't call me that. Ever again," I spit, making sure to pronounce each word a bit harder than the next so she can't misinterpret me this time. "You were a mistake, one that I regretted as soon as it happened. I was too drunk to even know who you were when I fucked you, and I wish I never had to find out. We are not *ever* going to happen. And if you want to keep your friendship with Gracie, then I suggest you accept that and stop trying to fuck her boyfriend behind her back. Have some respect for yourself, Jessica."

She's silent as she takes slow steps away from me, refusing to blink so the unshod tears in her eyes don't fall. I take her silence as a sign that she's finally understood me. She straightens her back and glares at me. "Tell her, Tyler. Or I will."

I nod stiffly and spin on my heels, storming out of the arena. Once I reach my truck, I slam my hand against the body. Sharp twinges of pain radiate through my palms as I use them to support my body weight and hang my head, staring blankly at the pavement. Fucking Jessica was by far the dumbest thing I've ever done. Gracie's best friend or not.

23

Gracie

"YOU HAVE NO IDEA HOW EXCITED I AM!" I SQUEAL, PRACTICALLY vibrating in my seat. My left hand is grasped around Ava's, and my right squeezes Mom's. "It's packed!"

I trail my electric gaze over the arena, not failing to notice how there's not a single empty seat. We're on the lower level, five rows from right behind the empty, soon-to-be full Vancouver bench.

"I'm nervous," Ava mumbles, visibly swallowing and gripping her knee with her free hand, the fluorescent lights pulling a sparkle from the loonie-sized rock on her left hand.

Tyler was tight-lipped whenever I asked about the game today. I didn't force him to tell me anything he didn't want to, but Ava's visible fear makes me think that maybe I should have poked a little harder for information.

"Oakley's going to do great. He always does. Plus, this is his first game as Warrior! He's going to play his best." I try to reassure her, but the forced smile she sends my way makes my stomach swirl.

"I remember you arguing with your brother back when you were sixteen about wanting to wear Tyler's jersey to their games," Mom says, squeezing my hand weakly before letting it go and pointing to the white number three I know stands proudly on my back. "Now look at you!"

Looking down at the jersey I found wrapped in ugly brown paper on my bed this morning, I grin, beaming no doubt. It's honestly surprising that I didn't already have one of my own despite my brother's protests. I've never been one to listen to my brother if I didn't want to.

"We'll have to get a picture afterwards," Ava adds, participating in the conversation half-heartedly.

"Of course." I lean my head on her shoulder and the lights dim as players get ready to hit the ice. The cement beneath our feet begins to vibrate as the entrance music blares from the speakers. We're too close to the ice to have to watch the jumbotron, so we look straight ahead instead. I don't recognize most of the players that skate out first, a swagger in their step, but I recognize a few from T.V and the clubs.

I can almost feel my heart climb up my throat when I see the familiar coffee-coloured eyes, narrowed and intense, penetrate through the visor on his helmet. Tyler's jaw is clenched, lips stretched in a straight line, but he's never looked more beautiful. He's focused, but his gaze bounces from left to right. It looks like he's scanning the crowd for something. My face burns with the realization that he's looking for me. I can feel his eyes on me as clearly as I can see them, and I smile so wide I'm sure the cameraman is having a heyday catching our encounter on the jumbotron. My blood thumps in my throat, and I nearly choke on air when he pulls his helmet off and smiles that damn spine-chilling smile. Right. At. Me.

"Oh my God," Mom sighs. There's an unmissable smile in her voice.

It's obvious that people are looking at me, I can feel their eyes on my skin, thick with curiosity. But I don't care. The only eyes I care about are the ones that belong to the guy I'm so helplessly in love with. The realization of it all has my eyes blurring with unshed tears.

I tear my eyes from Tyler's and let out a short laugh, wiping at my face before anyone notices. When I look back up, Oakley's skating out onto the ice. Tyler's frowning when I meet his eyes again, but Oakley is stopping beside him and slapping the area between his shoulders quickly enough to distract him. Oakley says something to him that nobody but the two of them has a chance of hearing over the music. I can't see Tyler's reaction, but my brother's lazy smile says it all. He wants him to relax. He wants him to have fun.

I sneak a look over at Ava and nearly swoon at the affection pouring from her eyes as she watches Oakley like her life depends on it. Her lips lift into an even higher smile, one that makes the skin beside her eyes wrinkle and the gums above her top teeth show just the slightest bit.

"Your starting line-up for your Vancouver Warriors!" A deep, manly voice is shouted from the speakers and pulls my attention toward the ice again. Tyler stands tall beside my brother and three other players at the blue line, and there's only one I recognize. Logan Trinity, the other starting defensemen for the Warriors and Tyler's line mate.

"Tyler Bateman! Logan Trinity! Michael Heller! Jacob Yollan! And for the first time on this ice as a Vancouver Warrior, Oakley Hutton!"

The crowd hollers with excitement for our team. I don't hesitate to join in. I love the warm feeling that flows from my toes to the top of my head, left hand to right hand, when Tyler spots us sitting in our seats again and winks, a simple action that I doubt anybody saw but me. My cheeks throb with a fierce flush.

"Boo! Put Delaware in the box! What are you doing!?" I shout with my arm raised in the air, hand in a fist as I shake it furiously. The ref pays no attention to the outrageous number of angry voices in the crowd and continues to practically hand the game to the Steamrollers. He pushes Tyler into the penalty box again, completely carefree and unbothered before coming back to drop the puck at the face-off zone on the left of the Warriors net.

It's nearly the end of the game, with only five minutes left in the third period. The score is two to two, but it would have been a complete Warriors sweep had the referees not been playing favourites.

Tyler's currently in the penalty box for the third time tonight, and I know he's about one call away from getting himself sent to the dressing room. I'm not sure if he cares at this point, though. It hasn't mattered what he did all night, whether he delivered a completely solid, clean hit or skated full speed into a set of numbers, he was getting the brunt of the unfair calls. I've seen his plays get sloppier as the anger and frustration set in. But who can blame him? He sits hunched over, elbows on his knees and glares at the players that continue to skate past him, muttering things that have him baring his teeth.

"This is the dirtiest game that I've seen in a long time," Ava groans through the hand covering her face. She opens her fingers slightly and peeks through them before closing them again with a sigh.

"Tyler's going to lose it," I reply with a sigh. The idea of watching him start throwing punches should scare me, but I find my belly filling with heat instead. A beautiful mental picture of him, his jaw clenched, lips pulled tight as the muscles beneath his hockey gear cord with power and strength.

My fantasy comes to life as soon as Tyler's let back onto the ice. He skates straight over to Ryan Delaware and yanks on the back of his jersey, sending him flying back. Ryan stumbles briefly but expertly balances himself. Tyler spins to face Ryan and without hesitating, he throws an ungloved hand straight to his mouth. He hits him where Delaware had punched Tyler's line mate a period prior. Delaware deserves every punch that Tyler sends him after the illegal check he dealt to *another* one of the Warrior players that went unpunished earlier this period.

I feel the need to cheer Tyler on, so I do. I stand and throw my arms up, screaming things like, "Let's go Bateman!" and "Knock him down!"

I continue to scream words of encouragement even though I don't know if he can hear me. Who cares if he can? I'm just one voice in a choir of fans who adore him almost half as much as I do. The thought makes me beam with pride. I start to cheer even louder for him to continue beating the crap out of someone, as if it's the most casual of things. And it hits me full force that I'm the one that gets to help clean him up afterward.

I scream again, but for me this time.

24

Gracie

I'M THE JEALOUS TYPE. I'M SMART-MOUTHED AND SOMETIMES BRASH. I don't like to share. I can't cook anything that doesn't come from a microwavable container. I hate talking on the phone—texting works *just* as well without the awkward silences that come from a phone call. And I would do absolutely anything and *everything* for the people I love. That is why I'm sitting in a hospital room, missing my twelve-year-old dance students perform the routine I spent all summer creating, perfecting, and teaching, because my mom needed me.

The Vancouver game was two weeks ago. Our team won by a single goal, much to the referee's displeasure. Since then, everything had been fine, *great* even. I hadn't spent a single night at my own apartment, for which I am more than thankful since I'm still avoiding Jessica's hormonal ass. I slowly started sneaking some of my things into an already half-empty drawer in Tyler's dresser. He still hadn't mentioned anything about my few pairs of granny panties or my makeup bag before I was leaving for the hospital a few days ago, so I chose to take that as a good sign.

The pungent odour of disinfectant and sick people that blasts through the vents is what pushed me to go buy four dozen bouquets of daisies for Mom's room. I hoped that it would help her feel a bit more comfortable. I know that if I were stuck in one of these hideous ICU rooms with absolutely no decor or privacy and a T.V. the size of a lunch tray, that that's what I would want. And when I saw the grateful smile that greeted me when I had one of the nurses help me bring in the flowers, I knew I was right to assume she would appreciate the same thing.

"I think I'll go out tonight and pick up a bright bedspread or something, Momma. The amount of beige in this room should be illegal," I ramble and slide another coat of Ruby Rose nail polish on my thumbnail. The low rumbling of the television that hangs from the wall across the bed helps drone out the eerie silence that more often than not plagues this room.

As per usual, we're waiting on the doctor, and *Desperate Housewives* reruns are the only thing helping take Mom's mind off of her diagnosis. Or at least I hope they are. She hasn't said much lately.

"It's only for a few more days, baby," she replies, voice harsh and sounding more unsure than I think she knows she's letting on. It's been the same way for the past three days.

"Oakley should be here soon. Tyler told me that they got back to town this morning." I change the subject and tighten the cap on my nail polish, setting it back inside my overnight bag. It's around three in the afternoon now so Oakley should be here any minute.

She smiles at the mention of my brother and nods before a wet cough pushes up her throat. It causes her to grasp awkwardly at her chest in a way that makes my eyes water as I rush toward her. I grip her shoulder and push her into a sitting position and rub her back like the nurses told me to. I squeeze my eyes shut and envelope the hand held against her chest in mine, pulling it toward me.

The coughing subsides a couple of minutes later, and I let go of her hand so that I can grab the full glass of water from her bedside. I bring it to her lips and urge her to take a sip. When she does without arguing, I finally release some of the tension in my shoulders and breathe.

"I'm sorry," she croaks, avoiding my eyes and staring at one of the scratchy hospital blankets wrapped around her thinning legs. "You shouldn't still be here taking care of me, sweet pea. Go home and have a shower or sleep in your own bed."

Yeah, I could go for a shower and a night in a bed that didn't have springs shooting into my back and wouldn't creak whenever I so much as breathed, but I wouldn't be able to sleep. Not without knowing if she was okay or not.

"Maybe when Oakley gets here," I reply. "I don't want you to be alone. Not here."

She knows she won't be able to convince me to leave. She hasn't been able to since I got here, so she nods and turns back to her show. When her door is pushed open a few minutes later, I nearly burst into tears. Bringing a finger up to my lips, I shush Oakley. He nods and quietly sets a bag down on the floor by the bathroom and joins me on the couch.

As soon as he sits down, I'm tucked into his side. His arms move to shield me from the empty room as I cry, soaking his black hoodie. I keep quiet, only letting silent sobs shake my body as he rubs my arm. He sighs heavily, "She'll be okay, Gray. Go home. I got this. I'll let you know what the doctor says later. I promise." My sobs have now transitioned into pitiful after-thoughts, my cheeks still wet.

"I'll text Tyler and ask him to pick me up. I don't have my car here." Tyler dropped me off before the team left for Carolina. I was too busy crying to bring myself. Crying seems to be the only thing I'm doing lately. I suddenly feel more pathetic than sad.

"He's already outside. He followed me here, swearing up and down that he wasn't letting you stay in the hospital another night without recharging at home."

I pull back, surprised. I use the sleeve of my sweatshirt to wipe my face. "He is? He did?"

"Yeah. I would go before the guy storms the place," he snorts before silently cursing himself for being loud.

"Are you sure? I'm scared that something. . ." I trail off, not wanting to speak the words into reality. If I keep them to myself, it'll be like they were never said. Right?

"She'll be fine. I'll have my phone on me the whole time."

I swallow the lump in my throat and force myself to nod, stretching my arms above my head. My muscles constrict with immediate relief. I've been hunched over for way too long.

Oakley is already up and reaching for my bag and pillow by the time I stand up and move over to Mom. I place a gentle kiss on the crown of her head and let myself soak in her sweet honey scent. I turn back after a few seconds and grab my bag from Oakley, throwing it up over my shoulder and clutching my pillow.

"Text me every hour. I'm serious."

"Yeah, yeah." He pulls me into his chest and I sigh when I return the hug. The dread I've been feeling is coming to a head, and I know that if I don't leave now I probably never will. So when we pull back a few heartbeats later, I nod, more to myself than to him, and push myself out of the room before I have the chance to change my mind.

I feel instant relief when I see the beaten-down Ford parked in the hospital's drop-off zone. Tyler leans against the passenger door. He has his left hand in the pocket of his ripped jeans and thick black eyebrows scrunched as he stares down at the phone resting in his hand. He has a pink lip held between his teeth and a leg bouncing anxiously, his foot tapping the pavement.

The corners of my mouth twitch and a small smile fills the space between my cheeks. He notices me a few feet away and instantly puts away his phone. He opens his arms for me to walk straight into and I do without hesitation. It isn't even a breath later that I feel a wave of exhaustion and anguish blow me back onto my ass. I'm sure that if it weren't for the two solid, thick arms wrapped around me, I would have collapsed on the curb.

"Are you okay?" Tyler asks softly, his words brushing through the knotted strands of hair blanketing my ear. I nod, too tired to respond verbally. He doesn't believe me, I can tell by the stiffness in his shoulders, but he doesn't push me to tell him otherwise. I think I give him another piece of me right then and there.

He keeps our bodies connected, not daring to let go of me yet and spins us around so he can open the passenger door behind me. He helps me into my seat, does up my seatbelt, and places a soft kiss on my cheek while hot, fat tears begin to cascade down my cheeks. He uses his thumb to wipe them away as they fall, but there's no use. I reach up and grab his wrist, moving it away with a shake of my head. I lift the neck of my sweatshirt over my face instead to dry the tears, hoping that they'll stop sooner rather than later. At this point, I'm not even sure how I have any tears left to shed.

Of all the things it could have been, it *would* be something so *simple* that threatens to take down the strongest woman I have ever known. Bacterial pneumonia. An illness that she should have made a full recovery from—and she did, for a few weeks. At least we thought she did. But now I don't even know if she'll ever recover from it.

I need to puke.

"I just want to crawl into bed with you. Can we go now?"

The brown in his eyes is darker today, moving from the hazelnut colour I'm used to to a dark chocolate one, but I shake it off. He presses his lips to my jaw, then the corner of my mouth before he speaks again. "Yeah, baby. Let's go home."

25

Tyler

FLY AWAY BLONDE HAIRS FROM GRACIE'S MESSY PONYTAIL BRUSH MY chin every time the tall white fan does another lap around the room. I'm watching the steady rise and fall of her chest as she lays beside me, head tucked where my neck and shoulder meet, bare leg tangled with mine. Her arm stretches across my torso and then she's asleep, so exhausted from this week to bother attempting to stay awake. She's breathing much calmer now, not so ragged and forced. I'm grateful. I was beginning to think that I would have to take her back to the hospital for her own health this time.

The movie playing in front of us has been long forgotten. The fan makes a loud humming noise that makes it near impossible to hear a word that's being said anyway. My eyes haven't moved from Gracie for about an hour now. Her eyelids are puffy and swollen, her button nose resembles Rudolph's, and her fingers haven't released their python-like grip on my bicep since I made her crawl into bed with me. She looks like a beautiful disaster. But for some ungodly reason, she's *my* beautiful disaster.

I'm worried about her. Anne is sick. Not in the easy sense of the word either, if there was one. But *really* sick. Sick enough that I know Oakley won't be leaving her side again but will insist

Gracie stay home, and sick enough that Gracie will tell him to shove it up his ass. But Oakley will have already known that, and I'll be the one driving Gracie to the hospital every damn day just to make sure she gets there okay.

Anne is their everything. She always has been. They love her with a ferocity that used to intimate me beyond belief. It was too confusing to understand as a kid who grew up taking care of himself before he knew how to and with no parents who actually gave enough of shit to teach him.

It wasn't until the fifth time I was invited over for one of Anne's phenomenal home-cooked meals that I began to feel the warmth behind their "hello's," the concern behind every frown, and the happiness it brought Anne to serve her kids like it was her sole purpose in life. Hell, I still have a hard time wrapping my head around it. But I admire it more than I am confused or intimated, and I suppose that's how I know Gracie *will* survive this.

Their intense, unrequited love stretches far beyond this cruel, selfish world. It's so deeply ingrained in that family, beaten into them with soft words and warm hugs, homemade chicken noodle soup on cold days and random phone calls twice a week just to catch up. A love like theirs doesn't just die with someone. It stays forever, lingering in the nipping wind and chirping with the birds.

A long, shuttered breath fans across my chest when Gracie's grip on me tightens, turning the skin of my bicep white under her fingertips. My brow arches and I watch with a growing smile as she pulls herself closer, turning me into her own personal body pillow.

If only Braden could see me now. He'd laugh in my face and call me a pussy for letting myself get wrapped up in the hurricane that is Gracie Hutton, falling for her along the way. I wouldn't want to agree with him; I've always hated allowing people to see my weak spots. But he'd be right and I hate lying even more.

It's still such an odd concept to me—caring for someone so intensely that your stomach bounces around, picking fights and throwing rough punches at the rest of your organs whenever you so much as lay eyes on them. I would do anything for Gracie, even lock myself in a glass box full of Anaconda's if it made her lips so much as twitch upward. That fact scares the shit out of me.

"Penny for your thoughts?"

I swallow past the boulder in my throat and peer down at a now semi-conscious Gracie. Her eyelashes flutter as she struggles to keep her eyes open and lets out a squeaky yawn.

"Go back to sleep, Gray," I mumble and rub the dip in her back. She shakes her head in response and lazily drags her leg along mine.

"What were you thinking about?"

"You," I answer honestly. There's no point in lying. She'd call me out on it instantly.

"Me?" Her eyes close again, and warm lips meet the underside of my jaw. "Good or bad?"

I can hear the sleep coating her soft whispers and nod once, letting my own eyelids slide shut. I find myself focusing on the steady rise and fall of her chest against my side and barely manage to mumble a response before falling asleep beside her. "Good, baby. Always good."

My eyes open with an unforgiving burn as the phone on my nightstand vibrates. There's still no light attempting to peek through my curtains, so I must not have been asleep very long. I tighten my jaw and swipe the fucker away from the hard surface. I grunt, relieved as the room is swallowed in silence again.

"What?" I hiss into the speaker, voice heavy with exhaustion. I can barely make out Gracie's silhouette in the dark, but from the fact she hasn't moved, the call must not have woken her.

"Have you told her yet?" Jessica's nagging, high-pitched voice makes me kiss my teeth. I carefully slide from the bed and open the door just enough for my broad torso to push through the doorway. I shut it with a soft click.

I should have looked at the damn caller ID.

"You're kidding, right?" I head barefoot to the kitchen and slip on the light before tossing myself into a dining chair with a soft *thud*.

"Do I sound like I'm kidding?" Jessica retorts, annoyance thick in her words.

"No, but you do sound fucking nuts. I'm not telling her something like that right now. Her mom is in the goddamn hospital, Jessica." I spit her name through the phone with the hope that she'll hang up out of anger. She doesn't.

I can almost hear her eyes roll when she sighs dramatically into her phone. Jessica has always been overly dramatic. It's driven me fucking nuts since the moment Gracie introduced her to everyone two years ago.

I was sitting at one of the large, teal booths at Lucy's, my ears burning from listening to Oakley drone on and on about the cost of new skates—as if he hadn't just signed a three-million-dollar starter contract with the Seattle Seals– when the two girls walked in. One seventeen and the other twenty, they were both bright-eyed and bushy-tailed and reeked of *naivety*. Gracie thought she had found the best friend she hadn't had growing up–an older sister of sorts– and even *I* was happy for her. But what none of us were expecting was for the older girl Gracie was so proud to have befriended to turn out to be a venomous serpent disguised as a five-foot-nothing, sapphire-eyed girl with a habit of touching things that don't belong to her.

I've always known that sticking my dick in crazy was a bad idea. Still, twenty-two-year-old, drunk Tyler didn't give a shit about consequences that night, and now sober Tyler has to deal with those mistakes. As awful as they may be.

"She'll be fine."

My pulse picks up and thumps against my throat. I shut my eyes and my teeth make an unnerving sound when they grind together. "We both know that you don't want her to be fine. You want her to leave me so I'll come running to you and it won't happen. So in the worst way possible, Jessica, fuck off."

I don't give her a chance to reply before I hang up and toss my phone on the table, moving a hand up to yank my hair out of sheer frustration before I stiffen. I hear ragged, shuddered breaths coming from the entrance to the kitchen and I turn to see Gracie leaning on her left foot. My black comforter is wrapped around her figure and she has unshed tears in her eyes. She looks at me with a slightly jutted bottom lip and a crease above her brows. If betrayal had an expression, she would be wearing it right now.

Fuck.

Gracie

I shoot up in bed with a sheen of sweat coating my entire body. I place a hand on my chest and attempt to focus on steadying my racing heart. The nightmares haven't left me alone since I left the hospital, my fear of losing Mom clutching them in a strong fist, keeping them locked inside my head. My cheeks are damp, and when I lift my hand to wipe away the sweat on them, I find fresh tears and the lines they left behind instead.

I'm eager to check my phone to see if Oakley has texted me to give me an update on Ma, but an unnerving feeling of worry keeps me from reaching over and looking. I'm too terrified of what I might see.

As soon as I left the hospital, I knew I shouldn't have. Yeah, Oakley and I have already lost one parent, but it hit him differently than it did me. I barely had a chance to know what it felt like to have more than one parent. To have a dad. Oakley felt the loss of Dad deeper. It changed him. And I'm terrified of what losing Mom will do to him. I guess he's older now and has seen more of the darkness the world holds, but losing someone you love never gets any easier, and our mom is everything to the both of us. We would be lost without her.

The doctors say that we should keep a middle ground and not get our hopes up too high or too low either. There's a chance they can kill the infection and that Mom will be able to recover. But it's not looking good. I can tell by the way her smile doesn't make it to her eyes anymore, and her eyes—the ones she gave me—are dull, the once subtle hint of grey now washing away the ocean blue that I love so much. Her hugs are weak too. The strong medication sucks her strength faster than the infection itself. I want to comfort her, to heal her. And knowing that I can't is killing me a bit more every day that my hands remain tied behind my back.

Reaching to the side of the bed, I prepare myself to feel Tyler's warm body but instead feel the spot beside me cold, with only a hint of his warmth left radiating there. Knowing that he couldn't have been up for long, I swing my legs out of bed, snatch the comforter and wrap it around me before opening the bedroom door. Tyler's strong voice flows from the kitchen and I tighten my grip on the blanket before heading toward him. I can tell that he's on the phone but by the harsh words being spit toward the person on the receiving end, I know he doesn't want to be.

"We both know that you don't want Gracie to be fine. You want her to leave me so I'll come running to you and it won't happen. So in the worst way possible, Jessica, fuck off."

My face drains of colour and my breath catches halfway up my throat. My airway has become so small that it hurts to breathe. My legs itch to move, but I don't. I can't. I stand frozen in the dark of the hallway, staring with wide eyes as Tyler reaches into his dark hair and yanks on the strands that have been stuck up from how he slept.

I can't hear anything over the pulsing in my eardrums and when he notices that I'm there he lifts his head. Tyler watches me with wide eyes the colour of coffee grounds for a few raced heartbeats. Then he pushes off the chair and steps toward me. I can see his lips moving, what looks like my name forming on them, but I just shake my head and lift my hands in front of me, silencing him.

There are only a handful of reasons why Jessica should be calling Tyler. None of them involve me leaving him. *None.* The brutally quick realization of what's going on has the fracture in my heart spreading through whatever parts of it were left untouched by the events of the past few days. My throat keeps tightening to the point I'm not sure how I'm still managing to breathe as I gulp for air, desperate to fill my burning lungs.

"What's going on? What won't you tell me?" I croak. I don't know why I bother asking, although I'm sure it's because a big chunk of me hopes this is just a big misunderstanding. My eyesight is blurring from another round of unwanted tears waiting to be shed. I blink them back this time. I refuse to cry over this.

"Gray, baby. Calm down," Tyler begs in a hushed voice. He reaches where I stand and places his hands on my shoulders in an attempt to pull me to his chest. His grip tightens, but I keep my arms by my side and chew on my quivering lip.

"You slept with her." It isn't a question because I already know the answer. Every petty dig, all of the unsupportive pieces of advice and angry looks make sense now. Jessica was jealous. She was jealous because she wanted what I had—what she *already* had. I push at his chest and step away from him when I feel vomit burn my throat.

"It was way before we ever—"

"Before or after Mexico?" I meet his desperate gaze and shudder at the deep-rooted regret looking back at me. I don't know what I want to accomplish from asking him that. I don't even know which answer I'm hoping for. Either way the result is still the same. Tyler slept with my best friend. My best friend slept with Tyler. They slept together knowing how I felt.

They both *knew*.

They both didn't *care*.

"Before," he replies without hesitation, as if sleeping with her *before* somehow makes it better–makes it hurt less. Maybe it would have been better had he not known about my crush on him since the moment he met me. But he knew. Jessica knew. *Everybody* knew. They just decided to do it anyway. Damn me and my feelings, right?

Tyler drags a frantic hand through his air and pulls. "Fuck, I never knew that I would feel this way about you back then. If I did, I wouldn't have even entertained the idea of Jessica. Shit, Gracie. I know it's not an excuse, but I was so drunk off my ass when it happened and as soon as I sobered up, I knew it wouldn't happen again. She has never, and will never mean anything to me."

I offer him a simple nod in response but avert my eyes and play with the frayed edge of the blanket still wrapped around my shoulders. I do believe what he's saying. He didn't owe me anything back then. He had every right to sleep with whomever he wanted. But it feels like such a cruel twist of fate that it happened to be with her.

"Of any girl, it had to be her?" I ask, but don't give him a chance to answer before I speak again. "I spent *years* pining after you, Tyler. I didn't expect anything when we first met. I wasn't looking to send you to jail for fucking a minor that was wasting her time with a different guy that she didn't love. But after all of the time we spent together in Mexico, I thought you finally felt the same way that I did. But then we got back and you disregarded me like I was nothing. *Again*."

He flinches. I stand up straighter. "Can I jus—"

"You told me you weren't in the right place to give me what I deserved and I respected that even though it made me feel awful. Even after two years, I was still willing to wait for you. I'm not hurt that you didn't think of me as anything but Oakley's little sister when you fucked around with other girls. I'm hurt that you could have slept with *anyone*, but you chose to sleep with my best friend knowing full well how I felt about you. You didn't respect me the same way that I respected you and that fucking hurts, Tyler."

I exhale and let my shoulders sag. My head drops forward as I stare at my toes. Tyler swallows so loudly I can hear it, but I don't look at him. I keep my head down, grip the blanket until my fingers turn white and walk to the bathroom as fast as possible, desperate to get out of the situation I literally walked into.

26

Gracie

MY STOMACH IS IN KNOTS AS I FIDDLE WITH THE COLD DOORKNOB. I've never been one to hold back my feelings, especially when I'm angry. But this is different. I've never felt such extreme betrayal from someone who I trusted before. This is way too close to home. I never expected that I would have to confront my best friend about sleeping with my boyfriend. Granted, Tyler wasn't exactly my boyfriend at the time, but the details aren't important right now. Regardless of whether he cared about me or didn't, and if we were together or not, Jessica knew that I cared for him—*deeply* so.

Jessica has always been the guy magnet between the two of us. Whether it be for her perfect body that she's spent way too many hours moulding to perfection in the gym or if her outrageously bubbly personality was what reeled them in, she has always been the centre of attention. Regardless of what lured Tyler into her ravaging claws, she broke the number one rule of being a best friend. *Never* fall for your best friend's crush. And more importantly, don't have *sex* with him. It sounds like a pretty simple rule to follow for most girls, myself included. Yet somehow, it's always the simplest rules that become broken–

snapped in half like a brittle piece of tree bark when you least expect them to.

I've been scratching my head for hours now, trying to come up with some sort of reasonable explanation, but I keep coming up short of anything other than utter and complete selfishness. It just doesn't add up, and as much as I want to believe it was some sort of ill-mannered mistake, I know it wasn't. And I just have to accept that. Jessica has always been this way. I've just been too blind to see it.

There was only one solution to the problem that I could ponder on my drive back from Tyler's house—eyes raw from the embarrassing amount of tears I've shed the past two days and a hole slowly carving itself in my chest—and as much as I wish it was a pleasant solution, it isn't. I don't even think there *is* a positive solution when it comes to such a heartbreaking betrayal.

The flat screen is blaring through the apartment as I suck in a sharp breath and push open the door. My teeth clamp down on my tongue and I quietly slip out of my shoes and walk into the main room. I spot the snake camouflaged as my ex-best friend spread out on *my* expensive faux leather couch. I let out a cough and roll my eyes when she continues to scroll through her phone, not even paying attention to the loud show that's making the space between my brows ache.

"Jessica," I say, raising my voice over the T.V. She jumps in surprise and whips around to stare at me with a wide grin. *This is going to be a lot harder than I thought.* "Can you turn it down?"

"What?" she calls back.

Pointing at the T.V., I lift my brows. "Turn down the volume!"

She nods slowly and reaches across the coffee table to grab the remote and turn the show-off. "Where were you? You didn't let me know where you were going," she scolds like she cares, dropping her gaze back to her phone.

"I didn't know I had to report to you whenever I left my apartment," I snap.

"Woah, calm down. I was just saying." She drops her phone and lifts her hands in the air in a sarcastic act of surrender.

"We need to talk."

"Now? I promised my mom I would go over and help her with a few things."

"Yes. *Now.*" I manage to hold back the growl growing in my throat and give myself a mental pat on the back.

"Okay. So talk." She sighs carelessly as if talking to me right now could make her drop dead from boredom. Spinning her body around, she crosses her legs on the couch.

"There's no easy way to say this, b-"

"You're pregnant, aren't you?" she asks, jumping straight to it with her eyes narrowing in on me sharp enough that they would have chilled me to the bone if I wasn't as pissed off as I am. "Jesus Gracie, how could you be such an idiot? And with Tyler's baby at that."

The way she says Tyler's name– like he's the dirt under her shoe–has my nerves frayed and anger starting to pulse deep in my chest. How could that be her first thought? She knows I'm always careful and even if it was Tyler's baby, it's not like she knows enough about him to make any kind of rude assumption.

"What's that supposed to mean? Tyler's baby at that?" I ask, taken aback by her casual insult.

She scoffs and fiddles with the large, tacky gold hoop hanging from her ear. "Exactly what you think it means. He's a deadbeat."

"Stop it, Jessica. Don't talk about him like you know him any more than a random hookup," I hiss, not missing the shock that flashes across her features at my not-so-hidden accusation. She opens her mouth in an attempt to defend herself but I raise my hand, silencing her. "Please, don't bother denying it. I know you've slept together."

"It didn't mean anything, I promi-"

"Don't try to take it back. I know you've slept with *my* boyfriend and loved it. But what I don't understand is why you did it. Why the guy I liked?" Each word becomes more bitter than the last as I hurl them toward her. An unmissable ache radiates throughout my entire body. It starts in my chest and spreads like a parasite, eating at every inch of me until there's nothing but that intense, unforgiving hurt left for me to taste. "You've been my best friend for two years, Jessica. Was it worth it? Sleeping with a guy who never was going to give you more than a good fuck? Did it make it any better knowing that I was in love with him? Did it make it more exciting? You knew how I felt! You always have. I would have never slept with a guy you wanted because that's *not* something best friends do. But I guess we weren't really best friends, right?"

My eyes burn as my voice continues to rise until it bounces off the walls. Tears stream down her cheeks, tugging further at my frayed heartstrings as I stay rooted in my spot, rigid. "I want you out of my apartment. Now."

Her jaw drops at my harsh command. She shakes her head just enough to show how badly she's hoping this isn't really happening. "What? Where am I supposed to go?"

I shrug and force my lips to stay in a tight line. "That stopped being my problem the minute you stabbed me in the back. I wish I knew how much of a shitty friend you were before I welcomed you into my life with open arms." She continues to stare at me, awestruck as I raise my brows at her. "I would start making arrangements. I want you gone by the time I'm back." I force the strongly pronounced words through clenched teeth and turn my back to her, heading back for the door. I don't have anywhere to go either, but I sure as hell am not staying here any longer than I need to.

27

Tyler

My shoulder hits the boards again and a sharp pain radiates throughout my entire side, starting in my shoulder blade and not easing up until it reaches the top of my ass crack. I adjust my right glove and grip the black tape on my stick harder in an attempt to collect myself from the hit I just received. I inhale, push the blades of my skates into the ice, and continue playing the most energy-consuming game of fucking chase ever.

The Winnipeg ThunderJackets are kicking our ass with their mediocre-at-best roster. We've only lost to these pricks a handful of times but we're a broken team right now. We haven't been able to recognize our sticks from our skates for almost an entire three periods and the scoreboard shows it.

Eight to nothing.

Zilch.

Nada.

Fucking zero.

I had a feeling our game would be off tonight and probably for the next few games but I was still way off. We're missing Oakley—which honestly shouldn't have been such a big deal considering we were playing alright without him last season—but it goes further than that. I haven't been myself either. I haven't been able to keep my hits clean—when I can even finish one—and I've tripped up enough players that our coach threatened to bench me the rest of the third if I didn't get my head out of my ass.

The threat did nothing.

The hit I just received was payment for the dirty one I laid on their first-line centreman earlier before I spent the last two minutes in the penalty box—my fourth time tonight warming that damn seat. I guess having my ass handed to me during a fight that I could have easily won wasn't sufficient enough for the ThunderJ's defence.

I barely even made it to the game tonight. I spent last night with Braden at some dingy bar watching him suck tequila shots out of some girl's belly button before he ditched me to get laid. I knew that going out was the last thing I needed but alcohol always helped me forget, and I needed to forget about Gracie for one fucking night. But no matter how many glasses of whiskey I drank or cigarettes I smoked, I couldn't erase the image of the shattered look in her eyes when she left me standing frozen in my kitchen yesterday. I hadn't even had a chance to form a reply before she grabbed her stuff from my room and bolted out the front door. My comforter was even still wrapped around her shoulders.

"Bateman!" The rugged voice of our royally pissed-off coach hits me when I swing my leg up and over the boards and join the rest of my team on the bench. I ignore him, grab my water bottle, and squeeze it to send the cold water all over my face instead.

A hand grips my shoulder and roughly spins me around. The move has the somewhat dormant pain in my side roaring back to life and my top lip peels back. I narrow my eyes at Coach and snarl, "Don't fucking touch me, Jack. If you want to bench me, then bench me. I'm fucking done out there anyway. The deeply etched frown lines in Jackson Talon's face sink deeper into his forehead as he digests my blatant disrespect. I shove past him and head toward the dressing room before he has a chance to tell me to get the fuck off his bench. I don't trust myself enough not to say anything else without risking getting myself thrown from the team.

My hair's still damp, and I haven't changed from my ironed slacks and white button-down when I step out of the elevator just footsteps from Gracie's apartment. I can only assume she's alone now. Honestly, it wouldn't surprise me if I found Jessica's cold corpse hanging from their balcony. Death by ruthless insults and a criminal death stare, anyone? I shake my head and clear my throat before knocking on the door and almost shitting myself with the fear of really losing the only person who ever really gave a damn about me, and who I found myself caring for just as much.

My heart stills in my chest when I hear the only laugh to ever give me an annoying tickle in my stomach. I hear it a second time as it slides under the door and slithers up my body. My curiosity becomes laced with a strong feeling of jealousy. Maybe Ava came over to comfort her? Fuck, it better be Ava.

The door is pulled open and electric blue eyes meet mine, making me swallow and my Adam's apple bob. My skin flares and my fingers itch to reach across the threshold and touch her, to remind her that she's mine and that won't be changing anytime soon. But I shove my hand in the pocket of my dress pants and offer her a small smile. "Hey," I say, not a hint of confidence in my voice.

"What are you doing here?" she sighs, shoulders sagging like there's a fifty-pound weight on them that she can't hold up anymore. One hand rests on her hip while the other doesn't let go of its iron-tight grip on the door. I bite my tongue to keep my groan behind my teeth when I drag my gaze along her body, my eyes becoming hooded.

There's nothing more than a baggy Vancouver Warriors t-shirt hanging off her shoulder and a pair of tiny boxer shorts riding high on her hip bones. I suddenly remember the laughter from when I arrived and my eyes narrow, pinning her in place. "Who else is here?" My voice is strong, unwavering, making it clear that she shouldn't try to lie to me. "Who's seen you dressed like this? You're half-naked."

My hands form fists at my sides and I shove my way past her into the grossly extravagant apartment. She scoffs loudly behind me, clearly pissed off, but I don't give a shit. I round the corner separating the entrance from the massive living room and kitchen before my vision goes red. My knuckles burn with the urge to use them when a lanky, less than six-foot, blonde polo-wearing fuckboy looks at me with wide eyes tainted with under-wear-wetting fear.

"Who. The fuck. Are you?" I snarl, straightening my back and tilting my head. I slowly inch to where he stands by the fridge like a lion who just caught the scent of his prey. A lion who hasn't eaten in days, starving for the taste of blood.

The trust fund daddy's boy blinks in response, his eyes saucers and his mouth gaping open. My brow arches and I take a few more steps toward him, the muscles in my biceps tighten, getting ready for a fight.

"That's Cody," Gracie rushes, trying to save his ass. I whip my head in her direction and attempt to wipe the sheer aggres-sion from my features because I don't want to scare her. "He's my neighbour."

"That's cool. Why is he here? In your kitchen? When you're wearing the same amount of clothes you do when you make coffee every morning after I fuck your brains out?"

A soft gasp falls from her lips. The accusation behind her eyes is as clear as day and I only shrug carelessly in response.

Tyler," she growls, a flush crawling up her face.

"Yes?"

"Uh, I think I'm going to go, Gracie." Cody fumbles for his words and fear flashes across his face. He attempts to rush past me but I shoot my arm out and place my palm firmly on his chest. He halts in place, frozen.

My neck cords as I tighten my jaw and tower over him. I let him writhe in my anger as it wraps around us in a tense bubble, daring to suffocate us both. His shaky breaths make my lips twitch at the corners as they beg to lift in an arrogant smirk. My next words have him gaping up at me.

"I never want to see you near her again," I snarl just loud enough for him to hear me. A familiar throb appears in my temple—the telltale sign that I'm struggling to hold back my anger. My fingernails poke holes in my palms and stain the tanned skin with red as I click my tongue. "If you see her in the lobby, turn around. If she's in the elevator when the doors open, wait for the next one. If you can see her wherever you are, close your fucking eyes. But I don't want to find you so much as breathing the same air as her again unless you want to spend the remainder of your days in a fucking wheelchair. Got it, Cody?"

He gulps and nods his head a few too many times before blinking at the hand that's still shoved against his chest.

"Tyler," Gracie chastises me again and I look at her, instantly letting my glare subside and my hand drop back to my side. She watches me smile as it slaps my thigh.

Cody uses my distracted state to slip past me, running toward the front door. I hear it shut with a slam a few seconds later.

"Jesus, Tyler. You didn't have to be such an alpha male. Cody's not a bad guy." I watch Gracie use the thin black elastic around her wrist to tie her hair back. She huffs with an unmistakable sense of annoyance.

"You still haven't told me why he was here," I state bluntly, ignoring her attempt at a scolding. Telling me not to go all "alpha male" on a guy who just saw half of my girlfriend's ass cheeks, while doing something that made her laugh that fucking laugh is like telling a dog not to piss on a tree. It's a waste of time.

She rolls her eyes, cocking her head. "What is it to you, anyway?"

She's poking the bear, begging for him to come out and play. The brief dilation of her pupils when I grind my teeth confirms my suspicion. She wants to see how jealous I can really get— how far she can push me. This is payback for Jessica and she loves the control she has over me far too much.

I force myself to clear all signs of emotion from my face and stare at her blankly, forcing a yawn. "He's a little bit of a down-grade, is all. I expected better from you, Gray."

She doesn't buy my words at all. Instead, they make her eyes light up like this is the most fun she's had in a long time. She sends me a coy smile that lets me know how royally fucked I am.

"Really? So it wouldn't bother you if I said we spent the night together? That I only put these clothes on before I answered the door?"

I clench my jaw until it hurts but keep my lips pressed firmly in a straight line.

"You wouldn't care that I was screaming someone else's n—"

I have her shoved back against the living room wall before she can finish her sentence. My lip curls and nostrils flare as I lean into her, letting my heavy breath blow across her pink skin. She's boxed in between my arms, chest pressed flush against mine as it rises and falls quickly. Her eyelashes flutter while she watches me, waiting for my next move.

"Is this what you wanted?" I grumble the question against her lips and she shivers against me. I can feel her nipples pucker through her shirt when they rub against the silk fabric of mine. "Did you want me to lose control? To fuck the attitude out of you?" I grind my aching cock between her legs and her soft sounds of encouragement play in my ears like the most beautiful symphony.

She doesn't answer my questions so I reach down and cup the heat between her legs. I use my middle finger to follow the seam of her thin pyjama shorts and bite my bottom lip hard enough that I draw blood when I feel how slick they are with her arousal.

Holy fuck.

"Oh," she coos, mouth open against my shirt.

"Who made you this wet, baby? Because I know it wasn't him."

Her eyes close as she leans her forehead against my shoulder, panting with desire. I pull the shorts to the side and expose her pussy to the cool air before I rub my palm across the smooth skin. I groan when my index finger nearly slips between her folds.

"Tell me, Gracie. Who made you this fucking wet?"

I still my movements, keeping my middle finger just inches above where I know she wants it. She pushes against my hand, attempting to create some friction. "You! Fuck, Ty. Please."

I grin into her cheek and nip at her earlobe. "Please, what?" I move my finger along the outside of her slit before I stop again, this time with her clit pressed beneath it. She whimpers and clutches at my shirt, bundling it up in a tight fist and pulling until I wonder if she'll actually rip it open. She does, and the buttons go flying around us, scattering around the apartment.

"Touch me. Please just touch me."

28

Gracie

I BEG FOR HIM TO GIVE ME WHAT I NEED AND PULL AWAY FROM HIS shoulder so I can look at him. His lips are parted, pupils blown, and there's a carnal hunger etched deep in his furrowed brows that makes me clench around him, needy for the orgasm I can feel building in my belly. He's beautiful. So beautiful that it makes my chest ache with the fear that one day I won't be enough for him. I hate that I think that, especially when I know worrying about the future won't do anything but throw a wrench in the present. He's here with me, touching me in a way that I had only fantasized about, thinking would never happen. He's here and he's mine. Or he was, at least.

Tyler pulls me out of my thoughts with a pinch to my clit that has me gasping his name. He rolls it between his finger and thumb and tugs on it as I struggle to hold myself up on wobbly legs. My knees buckle when he slips a finger inside of me and I hear the deep rasp of a groan in my ear. He pushes another finger inside of me, stretching me while I whimper under his touch.

"Tell me what he was doing here," he growls, shoving a third finger in my wetness and moving his lips to suck and nip on my neck, no doubt in an attempt to mark me as his. It's such a possessive action, one that has me tightening around him in approval.

"Our mail got mixed up," I mumble subconsciously, obeying Tyler's order without a second thought. It's like he's found my control panel, flicking at the switches and revelling in the different responses he gets from me. It turns him on to boss me around—to pull my strings with his greedy fingers. But I think I like it. *A lot.* "He was just giving me mine."

My words only anger him more and I'm crying out from the beautifully sinful mix of pleasure and pain when he tugs sharply on my clit and bends his fingers to reach the spot that has me seeing stars. *"Oh* shit. I'm going to come. Please, Ty. Make me come." I'm begging him, but I can't find it in me to be embarrassed. It's no more than an afterthought as I grind against his hand, starved for the orgasm I can almost taste on my tongue.

"Well, he won't be giving you anything anymore. You have no idea how badly I wanted to end him, baby. Seeing him next to you, looking at all of your bare skin." He uses the hand not knuckle deep inside me to shove my shirt up to my collarbone and roughly grab my breast, palming it. "Just the thought of him touching this pretty pussy had me seeing red. I didn't like it." His tongue slides along my jawbone before he's staring at me, eyes bursting with so much raw emotion that I come right there, unable to hold back any longer.

The ruthlessness of his rough touch and the sinful, guttural sounds of his approval make me tug on my bottom lip, ripping it apart as continuous waves of pleasure shoots through me, frying every nerve ending in my body until I'm jerking from the aftershock. I only see him, even with my eyes closed. My heart thumps so hard against my bones that I fear it might jump right through me and fall into his hands. I wonder for a brief second what he would do with it if it did, but the thought is washed away quickly when I fall forward, unable to hold myself upright.

I fear that I might smack onto the floor but a strong, hard thigh is shoved between my legs and Tyler grabs at my waist to hold me up. The pressure on my clit doesn't stop regardless of the fact I've already come and I know that he'll make me orgasm again if I don't stop him.

"I need you," I sigh through burning lungs. My arousal begins to drip down the inside of my thighs and soaks into Tyler's perfectly hemmed dress pants. God, those pants. The way they stretch around his perfectly round, muscular ass is sinful and I'm incredibly jealous.

Tyler doesn't say anything when he pulls his fingers from between my legs and slides into my mouth. He grabs my chin with his other hand and spins me around by the waist so I face the wall. My naked chest rubs along the cold wall and acts as a temporary cure for the ache in my hard nipples. His breath is on my neck, making the baby hairs rise as a shiver of anticipation travels up my spine. I can taste myself on his fingers—a taste that doesn't gross me out as much as I thought it would—and when I suck bravely on them, his mouth touches my neck and the groan that hits my skin lets me know that that's what he wanted me to do.

He pulls away too soon for my liking and the sound of a zipper being pulled down and the ruffling of fabric makes me rub my thighs together, hoping to tame down the heartbeat between them. A warm, sweaty palm makes contact with my back, the touch gentle and steady as it moves along my skin. Fingers spread and explore, moving down to the waistband of my shorts and sliding inside, pulling them down my legs. I gasp when a hand makes sudden contact with my right ass cheek, sending a loud clap through the air. A burst of pain travels down my legs before Tyler's gripping onto the sensitive skin, palming and massaging it until the pain is replaced with a quick wave of relief—pleasure almost.

He does it again, this time to the left cheek, palming and massaging it just the same as he did to the right one. But when his hand comes down again, it's my pussy that gets his touch, gentle this time. He slides two fingers inside but pulls them out a second later. I don't hesitate to look at him over my shoulder, my eyes wide with a silent plea.

"Face the wall like a good girl and I'll give you what you want," he grunts. It's then that I notice his cock is pointing toward the ceiling, so hard that it curves ever so slightly, the head glistening with his own arousal.

"Face the wall," he orders again. A strong hand grips his length while the other touches my back, pushing me roughly against the wall, making me arch inwards and forcing me to follow his orders. I whimper in satisfaction when his cock touches my entrance for a mere second before he's sliding it along my slit, coating himself in my juices.

"Oh my God. *Yes*." My whole body shudders the moment he enters me. The sheer thickness of him still takes me by surprise, regardless of how many times I've had him between my legs.

"This pussy is mine." He snakes a hand between my legs and swirls circles around my clit, making my walls clench around him as his dominant words turn me into putty. "And this cock . . . " he trails off and pulls out completely, teasing my dripping hole with his fat tip before he's thrusting back in. He repeats the movement over and over again while grunting, "This cock is yours, baby. Not Jessica's. *Yours*."

I nearly come a second time from his words alone. The small part of me that hates him bringing her up while he's what feels like a mile deep inside of me is shoved to the back of my consciousness as I only focus on the most important part of what he said. He's *mine*. I always knew he was, but fuck does it feel good to hear.

A delicious pain radiates from my scalp when he wraps my tangled hair around his fist and pulls, yanking my head back so his lips can place wet kisses along my pulse point. I reach back and grab his neck so I can keep him close when I feel my high building, my second orgasm of the night coming to a head.

"That's right, Gray. Come for me," he groans, his warm breath tickling my ear. He thrusts himself into me harder and quicker, forcing the fire in my belly to explode. Sparks whip around in my veins as I burn from the inside out with a heavy satisfaction. I feel him twitch inside me the same second a throaty groan vibrates against my neck. His grip on my hair tightens and the finger working my clit halts in place as his hips jerk, sloppy thrusts following his own release.

A smile threatens to light up my face and I don't bother trying to hold it back. As Tyler slips out of me and peels our spent bodies apart, I spin around and meet his warm, melted chocolate eyes.

Jessica didn't mean anything to him when they slept together and means even less to him now. And I know he didn't do it to hurt me. I don't even think he cared enough about me back then to have a reason to go out of his way to hurt me. I can't hold the things he did before we had any sort of relationship against him unless I want him to do the same. I'm no saint. I know that Oakley probably told him about me, Grant and the houseboat. Honestly, I'm surprised Tyler's never brought it up before. We've both done things—or people, I guess—that we regret. I'm no better than he is. So I'm willing to let it go and move forward. As long as we do so *together*.

"Gray?" He whispers my name and his Adam's apple bobs when he gulps.

"Yeah?" *Please don't say something that will tear me to shreds while I'm standing naked as the day I was born with cum dripping down my thighs.*

"When you told me you were falling in love with me, did you mean it?"

I almost laugh at his question, but I know that would only send warning bells through his head, forcing him to lock himself up again. Instead, I give my head a light shake and stand on my tiptoes to place a kiss on his right cheek.

"I would never lie to you about something like that." My words are painfully sincere, and I'm about to tell him that I've moved on from the state of falling and have tumbled down the terrifying, intimidating, yet thrilling hole of loving all that Tyler Bateman is when he greedily sucks every last molecule of air from my lungs.

"Good."

"Good?" I repeat the word as if I have a personal vendetta toward it.

"Yeah. Or else telling you that I'm in love with you would have been incredibly awkward."

I suddenly can't breathe.

What even *is* air right now? All I know is my lungs are empty, and it seems impossible to fill them in the bubble of surprise surrounding me. He stands so confidently, so unfazed by the heavy words he just let fly from his tongue as if they were the most natural ones in the world. Yet I can see the slight flicker of nerves as they tug on the left corner of his lips and cause his cheeks to take on a subtle shade of pink.

"You what?" My mouth feels like I've spent the past few months in the desert. I slap my tongue against the back of my teeth to keep from repeating myself when my brain tries convincing me he's taken too long to answer.

His lips spread in a toothy grin and my heart skips more than a few too many beats. God, he's beautiful. So fucking beautiful. I want to reach out and touch him, so I do. And it feels like I'm touching him for the first time all over again. Like I'm sitting beside him on the edge of that hourglass-shaped pool watching the sunset in Mexico, trying to keep my infatuation for the stereotypical bad boy under wraps but failing miserably.

But now, I don't have to keep my feelings under wraps. Now I can place my palm softly against his left pec and push myself on my tiptoes. I don't have to wait for him to bend his neck and meet me halfway. Now I can use my other hand to do it for him and press our lips together in a kiss that makes lips burst into flames. I get to feel him hold me like it would cause him pain– both physical and emotional–to ever let me go again.

This moment right here, in the middle of my living room,

both of us still butt-fuck naked and reeling from what we did just minutes ago, is one I wouldn't dare change for anything. This is a moment that I will remember in five, ten, or fifty years as if it were yesterday. As if I were right here again, feeling the flutters deep in my belly and Tyler's smile against my lips. And I can't help but feel like that makes me the luckiest damn girl in the world.

29

Tyler

"You're sure you don't want me to stay? I don't really want you to go through this alone," I mutter under my breath and grip Gracie's thigh in an attempt to keep myself from getting out of the small sedan and walking into the airport. Gracie only shrugs me off and places her hand on mine.

"You can't put a pause on your career for me, Ty. I'll be fine."

I'm not sure if she believes her own words but I sure as shit don't. Even if I did, they wouldn't take away the guilt eating away at me. The thought of leaving her here alone, worried sick about her mom for the next three days makes me want to throw up. Anything can happen in three days.

This is the first time I've left her side since I told her I loved her and fuck do I wish I never had to be without her again. I had denied myself the ability to accept my feelings and act on them for so long that I think I'm trying to make up for the lost time. And leaving for an away game and doing the exact opposite of that isn't exactly what I had in mind.

"Don't lie to me."

"I'm not," she sighs. "Ava is coming to stay with me for a couple of days. We'll keep each other company."

That makes me feel a bit better. If there was anyone I would choose to be there for her right now, Ava would be my top choice. Not only does she love Anne like a second mother, but she also loves Gracie like she's the little sister she never got.

"I'm only going to be gone for a couple of days. Call me whenever you need me. I don't care what I'm doing. I'll answer."

Her lips form a smile and she nods, squeezing my hand before using it as leverage to push herself off her seat so she can kiss me. I return the kiss instantly but she pulls away too soon, nodding toward the passenger window to where the airport stands. With a grunt, I grab her hips and pull her back to me. I kiss her hard and long and try to get a big enough fix to last me the next couple of days. I don't think I could ever collect enough of them to last me, though.

When she giggles into my mouth, I pull back and say, "I love you."

Her eyes warm with what I assume to be adoration as she looks at me through a thick blanket of black eyelashes. "And I love you." My heart lurches as I grin. "Now go before you miss the plane and have to fly commercial like the rest of us."

I nod and with a chuckle, let go of her waist. She sits back behind the steering wheel and sends me another smile, reassuring me that she'll be okay. It's only for a few days. Nothing's going to happen in three days.

"You know, I always thought she was a bitch." Ava shrugs beside me while dragging a finger along the rim of her half-full wine glass.

"Thanks for telling me that now," I scoff and continue to blow warm air on my wet, neon-pink nails.

"What was I supposed to say? Oh hey, your best friend is a total bitch? Yeah, right."

She makes a good point. Not only is Ava not the kind of person to say that in the first place, but I would have just shrugged her off anyway. Jessica had me wrapped around her finger, playing me like her very own personal puppet.

"Okay, I get it." I give my hand a shake and grab the bottle of nail polish, screwing on the lid. "Is it bad that I feel guilty for kicking her out? I know she has nowhere to go."

"It's not bad. You're human, Gray. You can't just forget about everything you two have gone through, no matter how badly you want to coochie kick her."

I lift a brow, snorting. "Coochie kick?"

She grins. "Yeah. Coochie kick. It's my new favourite way to thank a bitch. Feel free to use it anytime." It's at this moment that I know I couldn't have asked for a better person to keep me company for the next few days.

"I feel like that's been the worst part, though. I just keep replaying memories in my head. I feel like I'm going through a bad breakup. It's getting tiring," I sigh, leaning my head back against the couch.

Ava nods knowingly and turns to face me. "I guess in a way, you kind of did. I mean, you even lived together."

Yeah, it's just a shame she had to go and ruin everything.

"You can't spend all of your time worrying about her, though. She made her bed and now she has to lay in it," Ava adds firmly. I nod slowly, letting out a tired groan.

"Now that we're on the topic of living with someone." She switches topics with ease. "What are you going to do now that you have the place to yourself? It's going to be pretty lonely, no?"

"What exactly are you hinting at, Ava?" I tease, snorting when she bats her eyes innocently.

"I just think it'll be too empty with just you, that's all."

"As much as I would love to have Tyler out of that shit box apartment, he wouldn't go for it."

She scoffs harshly and green eyes buzz with excitement. "Why not? He loves you, doesn't he?"

"It's not that easy." Not with Tyler, at least.

"Make it that easy. You two are my ultimate ship."

I choke out a laugh and eye her curiously. "Did you just say ship?"

"Yes. What about it? That's what it's called, right?" she asks, clearly flustered and maybe even a little embarrassed. Ava has never been one to keep up with the social media lingo. It's cute to see her try and be hip.

"You're adorable."

"And tired." She yawns right on cue, eyes watering when they meet mine again. "You okay if I go to bed? I still have to call your brother."

"Yeah." I nod to reassure her when she looks at me warily. "Go. I'll see you in the morning."

"Okay. Night night, Gray." She gives me a half-hug over the cream-coloured armrest and starts walking toward Oakley's old room. She turns around a few steps away with a mischievous grin. "Call your man. I hear he's missing you." She turns back around and walks away without another word.

I move through the darkness with ease and make it to my room without so much as stubbing my toe. After Ava went to bed, I watched T.V. until I knew Tyler would be back in his hotel room. It's now after ten and I want nothing more than to slip into one of his shirts, crawl under the pink bedding that still covers my double bed, and call him.

I don't bother to turn my bedroom light on. The barbie pink walls will no doubt burn my eyes if I do. I just strip from my baggy clothes and slide under the duvet, swarmed in a wave of nostalgia in an instant. A hint of laundry soap crawls up my nose when I pull it under my chin and close my eyes, wishing Mom were here with me and Ava tonight. Instead, she's held up in a hospital room alone again. I offered to stay with her, not wanting her to be alone, but she was adamant I not stay. Her dismissal burned me to the core, but I tried to remind myself that she didn't mean anything by it.

My mom has never been one to let others see her at anything but her best. Sometimes, though, I would be able to catch the hidden sniffles when she was sick with a cold or the grimace on her face when a knife would slip while cooking dinner. But I never said anything. I knew that she felt like she had to be strong for us. She didn't realize that by not giving up after the love of her life was taken from her, we already saw her as the strongest woman in the world. I have always wanted to be just like her. I just wish she would realize that. Especially if the end is as close as I fear it is.

I'm happy when my thoughts are interrupted by the ringing of my phone. The last thing I need to clog my mind tonight are questions I'm too scared to come up with answers to.

"You didn't call me when you got to your brothers." Tyler's gravelly voice makes my stomach flip flop

"Hello to you, too. Miss me already?"

He ignores me, grumbling, "You're doing okay?"

"I'm good, Ty. Relax." I laugh lightly. "How was practice?" Running a hand through thin strands of blonde hair, I scrunch my face in pain when I tug a little too hard a knot, ripping a clump of hair from my scalp.

"It was good," he hums, and I can almost see the light in his eyes that grows whenever he talks about playing hockey. His passion for the sport is one of the things I love most about him. "It's fun watching your brother taking orders from someone with half his skill."

"Yeah?" I snort. "Did he do that pulsing neck thing?"

"Course he did. I was worried his carotid was going to burst."

"Keep giving him a hard time for me, kay?"

"Wasn't planning on stopping, Gray." His chuckle is washed out by a loud rustling sound that irritates my eardrums before a low rasp tickles them instead. "I do miss you, by the way. The bed is cold."

My heart lurches at his words, nearly coming to a complete halt. Now that I think about it, we haven't spent a night apart since . . . I can't even remember when. Tonight will be different without him, that's for sure.

"How are you ever going to be able to sleep? Do you need me to sing to you?" I half-tease. I'm almost positive that I really would if he wanted me to.

"Depends on what kind of singing you had in mind." His voice is like silk, flowing through the phone, teasing me when tendrils of excitement slither up my spine.

"Singing, not shouting," I giggle, feeling my cheeks turn hot.

"Same thing, I'm not picky as long as it's my name I hear."

"You'll be home in a couple of days," I mutter, suddenly breathless. "Think you can survive that long?"

"No." His bluntness has me rubbing my thighs together, heat starting to pool between them. I've had plenty of sex in my life, but I'm unapologetically a phone sex virgin. There's something about not seeing the other person to gauge their reaction to what you say and what you're doing while you hide behind the phone that's always made me too nervous. But with Tyler, I think I would do just about anything. Nerves or no nerves.

"Fuck, I wish you were here. I want to be running my hands along your body and pulling you against me."

I focus on his words and shut my eyes softly. My skin starts to buzz, my insides becoming a flaming liquid of desire.

"Is that what you want, Gracie? For me to touch you?"

I nod my head, sighing. I'm too encased in a bubble of lust to form words.

"Use your words, baby," he coaxes and I find my fingers toying with the hem of my panties.

"Yes." I choke on my tongue, gasping for air. "I want you to touch me. I always do."

"Can you touch yourself for me?"

"Yes," I whisper as my fingers slide inside the silk between my legs, forcing a gentle moan up my throat when they slide along the smooth, wet skin. "You too."

"That's it, sweetheart. I already am," is his husky reply. My back arches slightly, pulling away from the bed when my fingers find my clit, swirling around the bud and continuing their assault while I push my other hand up my shirt and grip my breast.

"I'm going to have you face down on this bed the minute you get home, begging for me to fuck you like the good girl you are," he groans in my ear, sounding winded—a sound that only intensifies the growing burn in my abdomen. "My perfect, dirty girl."

Knowing that he's pleasuring himself with me, using nothing more than my voice is enough to push me over the edge. "Tyler," I whimper as my legs spread across the sides of the bed, feet hanging off the sides. My phone drops to my chest as I fist the bed sheets until my knuckles are white. My fingers keep stroking my clit, soaked in my arousal and intensifying the shudders that shake through me.

"That's it, baby. Come for me," he groans. The sound of slapping skin makes my eyes roll into the back of my head as the image of him lying on the hotel bed, hand wrapped around himself, stroking furiously and bringing himself to a climax paints my vision. His moans cut through the phone, mixing with mine as we both ride our highs.

"I love you. You know that right?" he asks a few seconds later, sounding breathy and tired.

"I know. And I love you."

"Get some sleep now, Gray. Call me in the morning," he says and I can hear him moving around.

"Okay," I mumble as my chest begins to rise and fall at a steady rate again. I can feel my eyes fluttering shut as my mind begins to shut off, sudden exhaustion taking over.

Tyler's quiet, raspy voice is the last thing I hear before I fall asleep. "Sweet dreams, my love."

30

Tyler

As soon as my foot moves through the threshold, a boulder grows in my throat. I know that I have to hurry. She needs me. I can't hesitate.

Lingering cigarette smoke nearly suffocates me as I stand rigid, frozen in place. My boots stick to the beer-stained carpet that I'm sure hasn't been washed since I watched Allen soak it with a freshly opened Corona when I was fourteen, face held in a tight sneer that I'll never forget. He did it in front of Mom and she flinched back, covering her arms around herself, wearing that flimsy diner outfit. I don't remember why he was upset with her, but I remember the fear etched deep into the stress lines that covered her face. I've tried to forget what her fear looks like, but it seems like an impossible task. I see it in my nightmares far too often.

The familiar recliner is still shoved against the wall across from me, hiding the several fist-sized holes in the cracking drywall with its torn fabric. An old coffee tin rests on the ground beside it, packed to the metal brim with ashes, chewed tobacco, and what looks to be a crushed white powder. It's made abundantly clear to me that both my mom and Allen still haven't learned to clean up after themselves. I wish I could say I was surprised. Our house was always a fucking mess.

It's been a long time since I've been here, in this disrespectful attempt at a childhood home. And for what? What could possibly be so important that I would drag myself through these shattered walls and shrill silence?

My mom. That's who's so important.

Like every time I bring myself to relive all of my childhood trauma, it's for her. The woman who would have sold me for a new crack pipe if given the chance. Come to think of it, I'm surprised she never tried to trade me off for a quick fix. But who knows? Maybe she did try. Maybe I just wasn't a good enough offering.

I was halfway home from the airport, buzzing with anticipation, ready to see Gray when I picked up my phone and heard Mom crying for help. I knew that I shouldn't have said I would be right there. I knew that it would only continue to enable her destructive behaviour knowing I would always come rescue her. But dammit, she's my mom. And no matter how many times she tosses me to the side like a used tissue, I have to keep trying to save her from herself and this life she continues to live. She can't keep going on like this.

I can feel my blood pump in my eardrums, my body's harsh reminder that I need to move quicker. This isn't the time to relive my childhood memories and feel sorry for myself. There's plenty of time for that later. When I know Mom is okay.

"Mom?" I call into the silence, hoping to God my nerves aren't making my voice shake. My fear turns to full-blown panic when there's no reply. I pick up my pace, pushing myself up the rotted old staircase as I take each step two at a time.

Please be okay.

I push her bedroom door open, rushing inside as I look in every nook and cranny. My throat closes up, strangling me with my fear when I don't find her hidden in the small room. "Mom?"

I call out again, and this time I know my voice shakes. I can hear it.

A subtle thump catches my attention, the sound coming from down the hall. My feet move quickly, dragging my newly numb limbs to the closed bathroom door. My fist slams against the cracked wood and echoes down the hallway.

"Mom? It's Tyler. Open the door." I hear a small groan as I rattle the locked doorknob. "I need you to unlock the door for me." I focus on the sound of a body sliding across the stained tiles that I know lay right behind this door. The sound makes my muscles tighten. My breath catches in my throat.

For the first time in my life, I hope that she's just high.

"Tyler. I can't. . ." Her voice is placid as she manages to slam what I assume to be a hand against the thick wood. My pulse lurches and my stomach dips as I run a shaky hand down my face. Think, Tyler. *Fucking think.* I need to get this door open.

"Mom, I need you to move away from the door, okay? I have to kick it open." Once again, her body moves slowly across the floor. A painful cough tears through her as a loud bang rings from the side of the bathtub. I take a step back before raising my leg and pushing every inch of my terror into the kick. My boot makes contact with the door, sending the now shattered wood slamming back against the bathroom wall. My jaw drops when I finally lay eyes on her. I can feel the bile rise in my throat as my wide eyes move over her beaten, broken body.

"Mom," I choke, my chest closing in on itself.

"Tyler." She forces the words through her bloody lips, a few stray tears sliding from underneath her swollen, purple eye. Her head rests against the red-stained bathtub, providing the strength for her to keep herself from sliding to the floor. She coughs again, sending a wave of fury through my veins when my eyes wander to the prominent finger marks wrapped around her neck. I drop to my knees in front of her and grab her bruised cheek in my hand. Trailing my fingers along the fresh bruises, I squeeze my eyes shut.

"Did you take anything?" I nearly choke on the question as I grab hold of the bathtub with my free hand to steady myself. She doesn't reply as her normal coloured eye starts to slowly shut. "Fuck, Mom. Stay awake. Did you take anything? Are you high? I need to take you to the hospital." My vision becomes hazy as my anger starts to morph into a fury that terrifies me to my very core. It's in my chest, my mouth, my veins. Fuck, it feels like it's crawled under my skin, rippling underneath it like a worm in fresh mud.

"I don't know."

My head drops as I take a shuddered breath. "What happened? I need to call an ambulance."

That gets a reaction from her as her eye pops open and she shakes her head furiously. "No. No hospitals. No cops."

Narrowing my eyes at her, I growl my next words. "You're high, beaten, and you might have a concussion. You need to go to the hospital."

"Hospital means cops," she replies slowly, playing with each word.

"And? That bastard deserves to be locked up. Look at what he did to you!"

"I made him mad. My fault."

Not believing what I'm hearing, I shoot up and away from her. My jaw slacks as I shake my head incredulously. "You're kidding me."

When she doesn't reply, I pull out my phone.

"Who are you calling?"

"The only people who won't ask questions," I mutter, standing up and turning to the sink. "Please tell me you have a first-aid kit." She doesn't meet my gaze. "Right. Of course not."

I pull the front door open quickly, letting Braden and his dad come inside. Brooks places a steady hand on my shoulder and gives it a firm squeeze before heading upstairs, not saying a word. He doesn't have to.

"He'll take care of her," Braden says a few seconds later. I don't know if he's trying to convince me or himself.

"I know." I push out a harsh breath and nod to the kitchen. Braden follows after me and we walk to the table, sitting down.

"I'm sorry, man." There's genuine concern in his eyes. I appreciate it but don't bother telling me that. I rest my head in my hands when I feel my eyes start burning. I have no idea what I'm doing anymore. I just want her safe. Is that such a bad thing? Allen has another thing coming if he thinks I'll let him lay a fucking finger on her and get away with it. He's a dead man.

"He has her so brainwashed. She thinks it's her fault that he hurt her. Not to mention she's still using. I think it's the worst it's ever been."

"Have you ever thought about looking into rehab centres for her?" His voice is void of any sort of judgment. "Kill two birds with one stone kind of thing?"

"She won't go. She won't listen to me."

"We can help, Tyler. Me, dad, Gracie, Oakley. You're not alone in this."

My thumb swipes across the damp skin under my eye before I look at him. "Nobody is helping me take care of my addict mother." I brush him off more aggressively than I meant to.

"I don't think Gracie would give you much of an option."

"I'm not going to tell her about this. And neither are you."

Braden raises his brows and stares at me like I just told him I had a third eye. "That seems like a stupid idea."

I shrug. "Gracie has enough going on in her life. She doesn't need to worry about my fucked-up problems."

With everything going on with her mom, the last thing she needs is to worry about this. I never should have even introduced her to my problems in the first place. It was incredibly selfish of me.

"I'm not trying to tell you how to act in your relation-"

"Then don't. Just leave it alone," I snap, cutting him off.

He looks like he wants to push me further on the topic but doesn't. Instead, he just nods, leaning back against his chair. "Okay. I'm sorry."

"Tyler?" Brooks is standing in the doorway now, a piece of wet paper towel squeezed tightly in his clenched hands. "Where is that sack of shit?"

"I don't know," I reply grimly. If I knew where that son of a bitch was, I wouldn't be here sitting around talking about my feelings. I would be out there with my fist through his skull and my foot so far up his ass he would be able to taste my leather boots.

"What are we going to do with her? She can't stay here." Brooks' voice has an edge to it that I've never heard before. It manages to send a chill down my spine.

"She could stay with us?" Braden offers, standing from his chair and offering me a look of support.

"What? I'm not dropping my mom on you two. You've already helped more than enough."

"No, that's a good idea. She's probably safer with the both of us. At least until we can convince her to go to the police," Brooks adds while dropping the paper towel in the garbage. "You don't want Gracie to be involved if Allen shows up at your house and she happens to be there, Tyler."

My fists clench at the thought of Allen getting within an inch of Gracie.

"Okay. That's that then," Braden chuckles with his eyes stuck on my fists with a knowing smile.

"I don't know how to thank you both. For coming here and everything," I mumble, unable to make eye contact with either one of them. I don't know what I did to deserve the kind of support they're offering me, but I'll take it. No questions asked.

"You don't have to thank us. You're family."

I move my gaze to Brooks when he smiles, exposing his several missing teeth and smile lines that look as if they've been there since he was a kid. His words hit a nerve deep in my chest. Family? I don't think I'll ever be used to that word.

31

Gracie

THERE'S SOMETHING DIFFERENT ABOUT TYLER. EVER SINCE HE GOT back in town it's like the past few months never happened. He's cold again, barely sparing the time of day to even speak two sentences to me, and doesn't stay over for longer than a couple hours at a time. It's scaring me. Actually, I think it's far beyond that now. I'm terrified and confused—two emotions that mix as well together as tanning oil and pale skin under the scorching sun. I've been here, done this whole too cold to show emotion bullshit with Tyler before, for way too damn long. I don't plan on doing it again. I don't even know if I can do it again.

Not now.

Not ever.

"Wanna watch a movie?" I drag my tired eyes over to the stone-faced man beside me, a familiar burn bringing tears to them when he ignores me again. Something must have happened when I was gone, something severe enough to bring back the vacant look in his eyes and the icy touch to his skin. I've tried asking—only to be answered with an eye roll or a wave of his hand. I'm frustrated, anxious, and angry. We've come too far to let something come between us. He's crawled too far under my skin. His name is too deeply engraved into my heart—my *soul*.

"Okay. We don't have to watch a movie. What about we get some dinner instead?" My voice is full of fake cheer and I force a smile and blink away the wetness that's threatening to drip down my cheeks.

"I'm good," he grumbles, not tearing his attention away from one of the home improvement shows that I know for a fact he hates.

"Are you sure? It's past dinner, and we didn't e-"

"I said I'm good, Gracie. Leave it alone. I just want to sit here." He narrows his eyes at me. "Quietly."

Alright then, asshole. I give my head a quick nod and stand up off the couch. I square my shoulders and tilt my chin, attempting to pull forward every molecule of confidence and self-worth that lives inside me regardless of the overwhelming ache in my chest.

"You can enjoy your quiet night then. Alone." I speak the words harshly, equally as cold as his were.

My footsteps are heavy and loud as I throw as much pressure down as possible with each step I take. Yes, I might be stomping away. And no, I don't care if it makes me look childish because he is being a giant man-baby right now.

He sighs, loud and sharp, and I can hear him cursing under his breath from the kitchen. "Don't go."

I turn back around to face him and see a brief flash of worry in his eyes before it's quickly masked once again by the same damn vacant stare that is sure to haunt me in my dreams tonight. Throwing my hands on my hips, I raise my brow. "And why not? It's obvious that you want nothing to do with me, so why am I even here? Why bother even asking me to come over tonight? I could have gone out with my friends instead of being ignored by you all damn night."

"I missed you. I don't know. I didn't think it would be such an inconvenience for you to come see me," he scoffs as if I'm the one that should be under attack. He's shifting the blame to me to try and hide whatever's been eating at him the past couple of days. But he should really know that I wouldn't fall for it by now.

"You must have a really fucked up way of showing that you miss someone if you think that ignoring me and treating me like a fly that won't stop buzzing in your ear is the way to go. What is up with you lately? What happened?"

Tyler avoids eye contact and keeps his attention on the wall behind me, a striking tension building in his shoulders, causing him to hunch forward. I want to run back and knead at the tight muscles, but I would only end up smacking myself in the face if I did.

"You know you can tell me anything, Ty. We're not supposed to keep secrets from each other," I plead, my tone softer now. Moving back toward him, I let out a soft, defeated sigh. All I want is to help him carry half of what haunts him. Half of what keeps dragging him back into his mind, shackling him to his past whenever he finally gets to a better place. A *happy* place. But I can't do it unless he lets me. And right now, it's clear that he has no intention of letting me help.

"The last thing you need right now is any more of my drama, Gray," he groans and rubs his hands down his jaw, scratching at the stubble that he's been too preoccupied to shave. He's always had some sort of facial hair, but as he's grown older and more mature it's taken on a whole new look. Now every time I see him, instead of just wanting to jump on him and smother his cheeks with kisses, I want him to return the favour somewhere else. Somewhere that a few years ago would have landed the both of us in a whole universe of trouble.

"That's not your call to make. It's mine." I sit down beside him, grabbing his left hand in mine and slowly pulling it away from his face. I notice the slight shake in his hand but decide not to say anything. When he gives me an inch, I know better than to take a mile.

"I want to make your world better, Ty. You've gone through enough already without me adding anything else to it." I lean my head on his shoulder and let my eyes flutter shut. "You've already made my world as bright as it can possibly be. There isn't anything that you and I could go through now that could possibly dull its glow. And that's a promise."

"Fuck, I love you," he murmurs, his tone as sharp and definite as ever. His arm moves around my shoulder and he pulls me close, tucking me into his side and holding me so tightly that I couldn't move if I tried.

I grin and lift my chin so I can meet his hooded gaze. "If I say I love you back, will you finally tell me what's going on in that big handsome head of yours?"

"Maybe." He shrugs and the corners of his mouth twitch.

"I love you," I sing, hoping to God that the emotion I feel building in my rooted stare is as apparent to him right now as it is to me. He presses a gentle kiss on my cheek. I feel his laughter echo in my chest. It bounces around and claims my body as his.

I have to admit, this was far easier than I thought it would be. I guess a few months ago, I probably would have had to fight tooth and nail, maybe even had to have really walked out of his front door before he would finally tell me what was wrong. But that was then and this is now. We really have come so much farther than I could have ever imagined a few months ago. Come to think of it, I can only imagine what a younger version of myself would have done if she were here right now, what she would have thought.

"Something happened with my mom. Well, *to* my mom, I guess," he mumbles, suddenly very still. "She called me when I was on my way home from the airport."

My stomach dips. "What happened?"

The hand that's wrapped around me tenses up as he registers my question. "I know you don't want to talk about it, but I want to help. Please let me help."

He sucks in a long breath of air before answering me, his

words sharp as a whip. "I found her drugged-up, beaten body on her bathroom floor the day I got back to town."

I watch, chilled to the bone as his lips peel back and his jaw ticks so harshly my fingers itch to reach out and touch it, hoping to calm him.

"It was Allen." He spits his stepfather's name with a thick venom that has my skin crawling. I swallow nothing but air but feel as though it could choke me with how thick with rage it is. Goosebumps rise on my arms and spread quickly as the temperature suddenly dips and feels a few dozen degrees cooler than a couple of minutes ago.

"He's always loved throwing his fists around at people smaller than him. It wasn't uncommon for him to do it at home when I was growing up. It didn't matter why he was pissed off that day or who picked a fight with him. The only way a guy like Allen knows how to deal with any problem in his life is to hurt something or someone. I grew to expect it. Fuck, I was too young when Mom first brought his drunk ass home to know any better. I never had a dad. I didn't know that how Allen behaved wasn't normal. It wasn't until I got a few years older that I start to realize that the other dads at school didn't drag their kids by the ear when they picked them up at school or offer them a smoke before they could ride a fucking bike."

My eyes burn as I try to hold back my tears. This isn't my time to cry. I don't have the right to pull Tyler's attention away from himself and toward me because I can't keep it together for him. He deserves to have somebody listen to him for once. To have someone *want* to hear him. No matter how badly I want to let my building sob rip up my throat and cry for the childhood he lost and for all the pain he has inside, I can't. Instead, I reach for the hand clenched on my thigh, spread it open, and grip it so tight that mine goes numb and continue to listen.

"River didn't use to be the way he is now. There was a time when he would shove me behind him and take a hit that was meant for me. I remember a twelve-year-old River cooking soggy pasta and making me watered-down hot chocolate before bed on the nights that Mom never came home. Allen would be passed out on the couch after finishing a two-six of vodka most nights, so at least we had that going for us. River would tell me to wait for him in the small room we shared before making sure the kitchen was clean and meeting me there. Our bunk bed took up most of the room and was barely holding on. It got to the point where every time he had to go to the top bunk, he would have to move from my bed to the dresser before hopping up onto his mattress because the ladder was broken. We knew better than to ask anyone to fix it, so we never did. It was easier during the nights when he was with me. I knew that I wasn't alone. But when he turned sixteen, it was like Allen flipped the lights off in his head."

Again, I don't say anything when Tyler stops and sucks in uneven, scattered breaths that ring the alarm bells in the back of my head. I bite my tongue until the taste of metal attacks my taste buds and squeeze his hand harder, nearly passing out with relief when he squeezes back.

"I couldn't tell you the day or even the month that I lost my brother. But I know it was Allen. It was the little clear baggy of coke Allen pulled from his pocket after we got home from school and the used, traded-off pussy that I found River fucking in our living room while Allen and four of his pin-pupil buddies sat back and watched. It was like a bomb went off, mutilating every single human emotion and feeling that lived inside of River, turning him into a puppet that only Allen held the strings to," Tyler's voice cracks and when the first tear falls from behind his closed eyelids, I let his pain slaughter me from the inside out.

"Ty," I whisper, broken. I'm ready to throw myself into his lap and wrap myself around him like a protective coating but he sucks the air from my lungs, startling me. He turns toward me and pushes his face into my neck, letting his sobs become muffled in my skin. His chest shakes as his cries intensify, building to a peak that has his arms squeezing around me so tight that my chest has trouble expanding. I know that I should probably tell him he's holding me too tightly, but I can't find it in me to do so. Who knows how long it's been since he's had someone to hold, someone to open up to and confide in? If he ever has at all. I'm not about to shatter that. As long as I can manage to breathe, I won't complain. I know that he would do the same for me without so much as blinking from the discomfort. So, I press my palms to his shaking chest and rest them there. I allow my fingertips to rub calming circles against him and lean my cheek against his fluffed hair.

Tyler doesn't deserve this. Hell, nobody does. My insides burn with a fit of stormy hatred toward the people who call themselves his family. I can't imagine the agony that has to be living inside him, following him through his entire life. All of his success, and his happiness, will all be overshadowed by his history. His past taints his present and future, but I will do everything that I can to help him get past this. To help him heal.

What feels like a few minutes later, his cries start to slow. I feel him tense under my fingertips for a brief second before he relaxes again and pulls his head out of my neck. He keeps it down though, out of view.

"Now the only person left in that fucking house is our mom. She's the only one left that Allen beats on, using her as a personal fucking punching bag. And the worst part is that most of the time she's too drunk to realize that anything has even happened. She won't let me take her away from him—someplace safe. She's too fucked up to realize that he doesn't care about her any more than he cares about a prostitute on the fucking street corner. When I got her call and went to find her. . ." he trails off, running a thumb along his jaw as it tightens, "she refused to let me bring her to the damn Hospital—too afraid of what would happen if the cops were called. I don't know what I would have done if Brooks hadn't come when I called. He's taken care of enough wounds in his lifetime that patching her up was just a typical night for him."

He uses the back of his hand to roughly swipe across his face before looking up. A broken gaze stares back at me with an intensity that makes me gulp.

"Where is she now? Is she okay?"

"She's at Braden's. Brooks can take care of her better than I can right now. I don't even know what to say to her. She didn't look like herself, Gray. She looks like a zombie." His eyes are squeezed shut like he's trapped in a cage of emotional disarray.

She's at Brook's? Better safe than sorry, I suppose. The only danger she's in there is having to listen to Braden's sex jokes all the time. The Lowry's will take good care of her. I'm just glad to know that there are other people in Tyler's life that he trusts enough to help him. He's going to need as much support as possible to get through this.

"Hey." I reach up and grab his jaw, holding him in place as our eyes stay locked, unwavering. "You saved her. She's okay now. She's safe. We can help her." I know my words probably don't do much. Not with everything that he must be feeling. But Tyler isn't the type of guy to let these things go, especially not with everything Allen has done to him and his family. And I think that's what terrifies me the most. I don't know what he's going to do. I can only hope he won't try to do it alone.

32

Tyler

"ARE YOU SURE EVERYONE STILL HAS TO COME? I HAVE NO PROBLEM with having our own party instead, preferably in the comfort of your bed."

An overplayed pop song is floating through Gracie's huge apartment as I throw another rippled chip in my mouth. I've lost track of the number of times I've tried to change this awful music only for Gracie to stop me with an impressively terrifying glare. She throws a piece of curled hair over her bare shoulder. She knows that she's teasing me with the smooth skin peeking out of her dangerously deep-cut sweater thing and leans forward on the island, ocean-blue eyes locked on mine.

"This is important to Oakley. You know that."

"I know," I groan. "You can't blame me for not wanting your brother's beady eyes on my back every time that I get near you, though. It's been months since we got together. He should be over it by now. You should see the stink-eye he gives me in the locker room."

"Don't worry about him. Just ignore it." She shrugs me off and walks around the giant, marble-topped island, stopping in front of me and placing both her palms on my thighs. My eyebrows jump as her warm touch burns through my jeans. I place my hands on hers and lace our fingers together, desperate to touch her. I pull her forward and grin proudly when she lands in my lap, straddling me. A surprised squeak escapes her before she wears a grin nearly as wide as mine.

"Don't even start," she giggles.

"Start what?"

Leaning forward slightly, she rolls her eyes and grabs the back of my neck. She scratches her nails along my arms, my neck, until her fingers become tangled in my hair. She pulls me so close that I can feel her warm breath spread across my cheeks. My eyes watch her carefully, dangerously even, as her tongue wets her lower lip, the slow movement making my dick form a thick ridge in my jeans.

"You can't stop this party from happening, baby. But if you behave, I promise it'll be worth it for you in the end," she purrs, her cheeks flushed.

"Is that so?" I grab her hips tightly and pull her against me, letting out a grunt of approval. She nods slightly, eyelashes starting to flutter. Trailing my hand up her side, I don't miss the roll of her body when I trail my hand up her side. Her chest slacks against mine and she rests her forehead on mine, blowing on my mouth.

Flickering my gaze to the clock behind her, I groan, "We don't have time."

She nods but stays rooted in my lap. I chuckle under my breath and push the stray, curly blonde hairs out of her face as they fall in a small halo around her flushed skin. "Unless you want your brother to walk in on me eight inches deep inside of you, I suggest we get up." My words must strike a chord because she jumps away from me, nose wrinkled up in disgust.

"You're the worst."

I throw my head back and burst out in a fit of laughter. "I've been told."

She turns her back to me and heads toward the bathroom with a confident sway in her hips. Groaning lightly, I watch her teasing display while reaching down and readjusting my aching cock.

Oh, Gracie. You little minx.

Ava and Gracie are in what looks to be a very serious conversation in the kitchen as Oakley and I sit on the couch, a hockey game playing on the television in front of us. It feels almost surreal to sit here with him, hanging out as we used to years ago. Our lives are so drastically different from back then; so much more complicated, yet somehow better beyond words.

"How's your mom doing?" he asks, turning his attention to me with a raised brow.

After busting open like a walnut and explaining my past to Gracie and what happened to my mom, we both decided that it was a good idea to tell Oakley. It's not like he has any right to know, but if I'm going to get through this, I will need his support.

"Sober since she left with Brooks, not like that means anything."

"It's something at least. Have you seen her?"

I push out my breath and lean my head against the couch. "No."

"Are you going to? Soon at least?"

Am I? I have no clue. The sooner I see her, the sooner I'm going to want to find Allen. And if I find Allen— "Not sure," I grumble, forcing myself to stop thinking of that bastard and the thousands of ways I want to hurt him. I've been dreaming about all the ways I want to have him screaming for me to stop hitting him, the way Mom did when he was beating the lights out of her without so much as a flicker of remorse. "I don't know what to expect."

Oakley doesn't respond for a few seconds so we sit in silence, both of us reeling in our own feelings. I'm not sure what I expect from these people, honestly. Some sense of clarity? An overwhelming feeling of support? This is still so new to me. My head can't get a handle on it. I don't know how to act, let alone how to show my appreciation for things that I've never received before. I'm seriously fucked up.

"Brooks will take care of her until you *are* sure. Don't rush," he says a few moments later, nodding reassuringly. I look over and send him a silent thank you just as our two energetic girls come walking into the room. They steal our attention without so much as a word.

Gracie happily plops herself in my lap and places a soft kiss on my jaw. "What are you boys talking about so seriously over here?"

"Just guy stuff." I wrap my arms around her waist, pulling her into me and resting my forehead against her side as I greedily breathe her in. I've never been so grateful for someone before Gracie. She's brought out parts of me that I never thought I would be able to see. Made me feel things that I never thought I was able to feel.

She's my light—my guide as I walk through the darkest parts of myself, always leading me back home.

Back to her.

Where I should have been a long time ago.

A few minutes later, Gracie and I have migrated back to the kitchen. *Alone.* Her ass is on my thighs as we sit together on a black leather bar stool. The same pop music keeps playing around us but as I continue sitting here beside her with my head in her neck, it seems to bother me less and less. That seems to be a common theme when I'm around Gracie. The things that used to bother me just *don't* anymore when she's with me.

"You're doing good so far. I'm proud of you," Gracie mumbles while leaning back further against my chest. Although I would be lying if I said her subtle praise doesn't fuel a rise in my pride, I can't help but let my eyes roll when I feel a grin grow on my lips.

"Anything for you."

Her fingers crawl up my forearm in a soft motion and she sighs, "Can I ask you something?"

I tighten my grip on her waist, plant an open-mouthed kiss on her collarbone, and nod.

"Promise you won't just run off? This is important to me." Her body is tense as she anxiously awaits my answer. Although I can't help but feel confused, I don't hesitate to calm her mind.

"I promise."

"Pinky promise?"

"Yeah, yeah, yeah. What's up, baby?"

"I was just thinking about something with everything that's happened recently and I don't know, I just thought that maybe. . ." she cuts off her nervous rambling with a sharp inhale.

"Holy shit, Gray. Out with it," I groan.

"Move in with me."

The words are tossed from her lips quickly that she spins around in my lap, her eyes wide with what I can only assume to be shock that she actually asked me to move in with her. My mouth drops now, my own surprise obvious before I feel her hands on my face. Her touch is gentle, almost non-existent as she rubs her thumbs along my jawline.

"That's not a question." I swallow nervously.

Her silence is a clear enough sign that she's hurt by my all-so-awkward response to her, but come on. Living together? That's a serious step. One that I don't know that I'm ready for. I don't even know if she's ready either. Feeling Gracie jump from my arms, I desperately start to clutch at my thoughts, as if maybe they would choose now to save me before they end up getting me locked in the dog house for whoever knows how long. I'm let down like usual.

"Adam!" she shouts with forced happiness when the front door opens. I curse myself out and groan while running my hand through my hair.

Way to go, you fucking asshole.

My scowl is obvious as I stand and follow after her. I have to bite back my possessive growl when Adam wraps his arms around her in an obviously friendly hug. I know that acting out will only fuel Gracie's anger toward me. It doesn't take long for Adam to sense my annoyance, though. He chuckles and backs away from her, but not without seizing the golden opportunity to piss me off even more with a teasing wink.

"Nice of you to join us, Tyler," he teases half-heartedly. I brush him off and wrap my arm tightly against Gracie and pull her into me possessively. The conversation that happened a couple of minutes prior won't stop me from touching her and staking an invisible claim over her that isn't even necessary. Everyone already knows she's mine.

"Hey, man." I nod.

"Can I talk to you a bit later?" he asks, sounding oddly nervous for such a confident guy. I don't hesitate to nod with a lifted brow. Adam doesn't give me details or an explanation, he only sends me a look that says, *leave it alone for now.* So I do.

When Oakley joins us and starts explaining the specifics of his team switch to Adam, I tune out the conversation and grab onto my girl's hip instead, pulling her back into me with a scowl. Her body is still tense under my touch but I don't care. She doesn't get to be the one running away without giving me a chance to fix the mess I've made. She's supposed to be the better half of me. She's not supposed to sink to the level I've been trying so hard to stay away from. That's not who she is and I won't let her follow my shit example.

"Is Braden here?" Adam asks.

I pop myself back into the conversation and shake my head. "Not yet, should be here soon," I say and adjust my grip on Gracie so I can wrap an arm around her waist. I can almost hear how fast my heart starts pumping when finally she lets her body relax again, sinking into mine.

A few beats later, there's a knock on the front door. Ava pulls it open and Braden's confidence fills the apartment. "Hey, little H. Nice pad, can't believe you've never invited me over before." He clicks his tongue while setting two cases of beer down on the floor. "Looking as good as ever, Ava baby."

"And you're just as flirty as ever," Gracie snorts, moving away from me and toward Ava who simply flips Braden the bird with a dimpled grin. They both pick up a case of the foamy alcohol before heading off to discard them in the kitchen.

"It's about time you showed up, you fucker," I grin and slap my hand in Braden's open one.

"What can I say?" He smirks. "I was a little tied up."

"I always knew you were into some kinky shit," Oakley says before bursting out in a fit of laughter.

"I'm the only one who does the tying in the bedroom, Lee," Braden throws back, not missing a beat.

Before we all get a play-by-play of Braden's adventures in bed, our attention is pulled elsewhere. Ava's uncomfortable gag makes me cringe as she places a hand over her mouth and rushes past the four of us, heading to what I can only assume would be the bathroom. I watch Oakley's eyes pop open before he's taking off after her in long strides while reaching into his pocket to grab his phone when it begins to ring.

"Tell Ava how bad Tyler is in the sack, little H?" Braden asks, looking between us with a grin. He must pick up on the tension that has morphed around the both of us in an uncomfortable second skin when his eyebrows jump. "Or not?"

"Not," Gracie grumbles before I can answer, crossing her arms and narrowing her eyes at me from her place beside the fridge, a few too many feet away.

"Trouble in paradise?" he prods, unable to help himself. I shove him with my shoulder and send him a steely glare that effectively shuts him up.

"Gray?" The quivering sound of Oakley's usual confident voice makes ice form in my gut, sharp edges tearing me to pieces. I'm moving toward Gracie without missing a beat. I watch her head shake furiously seconds before her knees buckle, her body folding in on itself as she collapses, falling right into my open arms.

An agonizing, soul-tearing cry rips through the room and her body begins to shake with ruthless sobs, leaving my jaw unhinged as I look over at Oakley, phone resting unlocked in his hand. The pure anguish flaring in his watery eyes says everything so he doesn't have to.

Anne.

She's gone.

33

Gracie

I DIDN'T GET TO SAY GOODBYE.

Out of every emotion clanging around in my head, feasting on me like a family of leeches, guilt is the most prominent. It's in my veins, turning my blood into lead, weighing me down until I'm sure I would sink to the bottom of the ocean if I took a swim. I haven't left my room in days. Weeks, maybe.

Yeah, I think it's been a week.

Tyler's been here every chance he gets. Holding me, trying to have as much of a conversation with me as he can, bringing me strawberry milkshakes.

Guilt swallows me again.

Oakley and Ava haven't gone back to Seattle at all since Mom died. A sob crashes through my chest. It makes my throat burn and my hand rises to cover my mouth as I try to calm myself down. It doesn't work and before I know it, I have myself hunched forward, fists gripping my blanket as I throw my head back and scream.

I scream because the ache in my chest is becoming unbearable. Because I've lost my best friend—the woman who loved so profoundly that it consumed her. I scream because Oakley's too young to have lost both of his parents. So am I. There was so much left for her to see. So much left to do. I scream because it isn't fair. Nothing about this is fair. It's so incredibly unfair that I'm not even sure why any of us try. We're all going to die eventually—ripped away from our loved ones, leaving them to grieve us, hoping it was all just a nightmare.

My bedroom door pounds. Two deep, angry voices clash behind it but I can't stop crying long enough to ask who's there or to tell them to go away. I move my hands to my face instead and my palms push against my eyes until I see static. I don't move when hands grip my shoulders, pulling me toward a strong chest. I don't move until I smell Tide laundry detergent and a mixture of spices that I've never been able to pinpoint. My brother pulls me into him and holds me tight, letting me soak his shirt with my tears.

His arms envelop me, forming a human shield around me like he's trying to keep me safe from the air surrounding us, rippling with misery. I cling to him, terrified that if I let go, he'll disappear too, leaving me completely alone. My heart is torn, battered and bruised. As far back as I remember, Mom would tell me I stole her beating heart the first time our eyes met. But the hollow in my chest tells me that she not only took hers back, but she took half of mine too.

Oakley softly shushes me while pressing down the hair on the top of my head. His own chest shakes and a wild, raw cry of agony tears through the silence, shredding my insides to bits. My eyes squeeze shut and I clutch his back, keeping him close to me and wanting nothing more than to take away his suffering.

"I'm here," I whimper, sniffling a few times. I'm pushing myself to the end of my rope, using the rest of my strength to comfort my brother. He deserves to have somebody take care of him this time around. I know Ava will do what she can, but I'm his sister. It's different for us. He took care of me when Dad died and now, I'm going to return the favour. "It will be okay. I promise."

Will it? I choose not to focus on that heavy question and

focus on the relief of having my brother beside me. We can lose everything and everyone but we'll always have each other. That has to count for something.

It has to.

After what feels like an eternity, our eyes have dried up and we've both become still. With a deep, weighted sigh, Oakley pulls away and looks at me through swollen eyes. "I'm sorry."

My eyebrows furrow. "Why? For crying? I won't tell."

"No." His head shakes. "For having to go through this sort of loss again. You're so fucking young."

"Don't you dare apologize to me. This wasn't your fault. This wasn't Mom's fault. This wasn't anybody's fault."

His face remains void of anything but grief. The only sign that lets me know he heard what I said is the slight flinch when I mention Mom. I swallow.

"Ava's pregnant, Gray."

"What?" I recoil, my lips parted in surprise. My stomach churns, bringing forward a wave of nausea.

"We went to see her the day . . ." His words drop, eyes watering before he blinks furiously and pushes away the threat of crying again. "We saw her on her last day. Ava had convinced me we shouldn't wait any longer to tell her. She was already eight weeks along, Gracie." A tiny flicker of light in his eyes makes the corners of my mouth lift in a sad smile.

"Mom could barely stay awake, but fuck did she ever try. The way her eyes had life again and her smile beamed—I'll never forget it. We showed her the ultrasound pictures and she cried for what seemed like forever. She made me promise her that I would marry Ava in Hawaii like she's always dreamed. That I would walk you down the aisle and be the one that gave you away. That if presented the chance, I should bail you out of jail, no questions asked."

He licks his lips and covers my hands with his, squeezing them tight. "She knew it was coming. I knew it too. I just thought you would have had a chance to say goodbye. I didn't know it would be so soon. And for that, I'm so sorry."

I pull our hands to my chest and shake my head. "Stop apologizing. I could never blame you for that. One of us got to say goodbye and I'm glad it was you." There's not a hint of a lie in my words. No jealousy or anger. Just a warm sense of relief that Mom went knowing how deeply we loved her and that her kids would take care of each other.

"You're going to be okay. You know that, right?" he asks after a minute of silence. I nod, barely.

"I know. So are you."

"I know. We're not alone in this." There's a knowing look in his eye and I sigh. "Tyler wants to be there for you. As much as it nauseates me to say it, he loves you. And right now, the people who love you are the only people that matter. Let them carry some of your pain."

"He's here, isn't he?" I ask knowingly. I definitely heard two voices outside my door earlier.

"Hasn't left for anything all week."

"I'm surprised he hasn't kicked down the door yet." I choke out a rough laugh and my eyes widen in shock at the unfamiliar noise. It feels good to laugh.

"Want me to get him?"

"Please." I slip my bottom lip between my teeth and chew on it. With a quick nod, he stands up from the bed, places a soft kiss on the top of my head, and walks to the door. He straightens his back when he opens it, and in less than a second, I watch Tyler bust through the threshold, bee-lining it to my bed.

I let out a shocked gasp when he reaches down toward the bed and picks me up. He grips my thighs in a tight grip and wraps them around his waist. He holds me like I could disappear into thin air at any moment. He sighs deeply when his nose finds my hair and I smile, wrapping my arms around his neck and letting the stiffness fade from my limbs.

"When I heard you scream, I—" I fist his shirt and shake my head, cutting him off.

"Lay with me?"

His chest rumbles against mine. "You don't even have to ask."

The funeral was last week. And if I'm honest, I only remember small fragments of that day. Something I think I did subconsciously. A way to protect myself from the agony that filled me to the brim, threatening to bubble up and explode like a shaken pop bottle with the lid half twisted.

I remember the fat raindrops pelting down on the smooth mahogany wood as they lowered it into the wet hole in the ground. I remember the weight that rested on my shoulders as I fought to keep my knees from buckling when Oakley read the eulogy with streams of tears staining his wind-bitten cheeks. I remember our grandma—Dad's mom—as she showed up with tears in her eyes, pretending that she hadn't abandoned us when her son passed away sixteen years ago. And I remember holding the hands of the only other people who, like myself, wore white to the funeral.

Mom hated wearing black. The last time she wore it was for Dad's funeral. So we wore white. We honoured her that day: Oakley, Ava, Adam, Braden, Tyler, and myself. We didn't say goodbye to her. Why say goodbye when it wasn't goodbye? Not forever, anyway. We said, *see you later*, instead.

"I've been wanting to talk to you about something," Tyler mumbles against the bare skin beneath my breasts. His head lies on my stomach, my fingers laced through his hair. And the longer I play with his hair, the more I want to run to the bathroom and grab a pair of scissors so I can snip a few inches off.

He's been too distracted—between playoffs and taking care of me—to get it trimmed and he's looking a bit scraggly. My lips twitch into a smile.

"Okay," I hum and soak in this moment of comfort.

"I never gave you an answer when you asked me to move in with you."

The strands of black silk fall from my fingers. "What?"

He laughs a deep, content laugh that makes my skin break out in goosebumps. That beautiful sound is equal parts adrenaline pumping and heart lurching. I become addicted to this feeling almost instantly.

"Would we be living here or at your place? Because I don't fit in your castle, and you sure as shit don't fit in mine, princess."

I fumble for a reply, opening and closing my mouth as my tongue dries up. "Uh."

He tilts his head until our eyes meet, a mix between humour and curiosity consuming his. I swallow the nerves knotting together in my throat. "How about neither?"

"Really?" His eyebrows jump as if he expected me to push for him to live somewhere he wouldn't be completely comfortable.

"Really," I giggle. "The only reason Oakley got me that fancy apartment was because he wanted to make sure that I was safe. But I don't need anything like that anymore. Not if I'm with you, Ty. Nothing makes me feel safer than you do."

I watch a sliver of vulnerability flicker across his milk chocolate gaze as he stares at me, not daring to speak a single word. I trail my fingers down the sharp grooves of his cheekbones and grip his chin, pulling him closer so it's easier to place my lips on his.

"Then let's do it." His words have a strong sense of finality to them that makes my stomach flutter as they blow across my wet mouth.

"Yeah? You think you can handle being around me that much?"

He snorts. "I already am around you that much, Gray. And I've only almost jumped from your penthouse window a couple of dozen times."

I scoff and flick him in the ear. "Asshole."

"Too late to leave me now. My return policy is long expired."

"Shit. What do I do now?" I bat my eyelashes and push out my bottom lip.

"I can think of a few ideas," he mumbles slyly before I gasp, my breast becoming swarmed with the warmth of his mouth. Gripping his hair again, I decide that this is exactly where I want to spend every single one of my future days.

With him.

34

Tyler

"You have way too much shit," I grumble and drop the tenth box labelled Gracie's clothes in hot pink Sharpie in front of our new closet.

Yeah. *Our* closet.

"And you don't have nearly enough." She throws me a teasing look over her shoulder while dragging a tied garbage bag behind her. She drops it beside her with an over-exaggerated sigh.

She has a point. I threw away almost everything from my old place, leaving only two garbage bags of clothes and Gracie's favourite coffee mug. I figured if this is my chance at a fresh start then I want to do it right, with as little baggage as possible. Both mentally and physically,

"I already have everything that I need right here."

She doesn't miss the double meaning behind my words because the corners of her lips twitch and a flush crawls up her neck. She turns and scurries back through to the living room. I give my head a shake and look around our semi-furnished bedroom. It's clear that our new apartment is smaller than Gracie's old one, but I was happily surprised when she was the one to insist that this was the place for us. There's still enough room for our friends and family with the two bedrooms and two bathrooms, without us feeling like we were surrounding ourselves with empty space. That was a huge bonus.

It wasn't an easy decision in the beginning, however. When Oakley had first caught wind of his sister's sudden move, he insisted on helping her financially again, being even more protective of her than before. And it's safe to say that that was a huge no-go for me. It took hours of shouted words and angry jabs before he finally agreed to step back and let me be the one to take care of her. Not like she isn't capable of doing so herself. She has always made that abundantly clear. But I would fail as her boyfriend if I didn't at least try. God knows I can afford to give her whatever kind of life she wants. I think that the fact she still chooses to live a middle-class life when she has every option and resource not to is one thing that makes me love her as much as I do.

"Get your lazy ass out here and help me carry this!"

I choke back my laugh when I see her grunting by the front door. Crouched down in a squat with her ass an inch from the floor, she tries to lift our heavy-as-hell wooden dresser on her own.

"I don't know. I have quite the view from here," I tease with my eyes glued on the stretched, see-through leggings that barely cover her perfectly round, squeeze-worthy ass.

Her head turns, eyes narrowing into a glare. "I will choke you in your sleep."

The dangerous glint in her eyes pushes me to move toward her and with a sigh, I easily grab the opposite side of the dresser and lift it. "Do you want to walk backward, or should I?" I ask, wearing a slight smirk.

She huffs, frustrated. "Does it matter? Just start moving!"

I get a kick out of her frustration and lean on my left leg in an attempt to stall us. "Well, it's harder to walk backward, babe. I think I should do it."

Her cheeks turn red as she glances down at her shaky grip on the wood. "Okay! Go before I drop this damn thing on the ground."

"You sure?"

"Dammitt, Tyler! Just start walking before I break the damn thing!"

I burst out in a fit of laughter but turn myself around and lead us into the bedroom. She drops the dresser as soon as it's in place with a loud groan.

"You're such a prick." She runs her sweaty hands down her legs.

"You didn't already know that?"

Rolling her eyes, she throws herself back on the queen-sized bed. "I hate you."

"We both know that's not true," I say. My voice drops in volume as I walk over to her. I stop when my knees hit the mattress. I feel her dangling feet lightly hitting the outside of my thighs and wrap my hands around her calves. Tugging on them, she lets out a surprised sound while sliding down the bed. She rests on the edge of the bed now, feet touching the floor and my hardening cock pressing against the warmth between her legs. "Right?"

She swallows slowly and nods once, watching me lean down and press my palms to the mattress, eyes darkening. My breath fans her lips and her pupils dilate. "Cat got your tongue?" My words seem to spark the fire living inside of her because a jolt of unsuspected pleasure jolts through my groin. Dropping my gaze, I nearly come in my pants.

"Cat got your tongue?" Her lips are parted, a sharp breath puffing out and warming mine when she wets her lips. She grips my cock through my sweatpants.

"Fuck. I love you."

She pushes her hair out of her face and opens her legs for me, grabbing my neck as I move my body between them. "I love you," she breathes against my lips before kissing me, the roughness behind it making my mouth burn with a delicious throb.

I bite down on her bottom lip and slide my tongue in her mouth when her lips separate with a groan. My hands slip under her tank top and run over her bare tits. I roll her nipples between my fingertips and pull gently on them every few seconds.

A light breath runs against my lips as she arches her back off of the bed. I lean back and yank her shirt over her head, throwing it off to the side before doing the same with mine. She leans forward, eyes burning with desire. Gracie pushes me back and flips us so she can rest straddle me and let her breasts hang above me. The two rosy buds are puckered, begging to be kissed.

Silky blonde hair falls in a glowing halo around her face as she grins wickedly, leans forward, and trails her fingers slowly down my chest. They follow every deep line and rigid indent I've worked so hard to mould. She chews on her bottom lip and toys with the strings on my sweatpants. My breath catches in my throat when she slips her hand under the waistband and wraps a small palm around me. Her crystal blue eyes glaze over when she looks down to watch her hand slide along my cock. The slow, teasing strokes have me groaning, the sound rich with approval. She yanks on my waistband with her free hand and I lift my hips so she can remove the remaining obstacle easier.

"You don't have to," I choke out.

She simply shakes her head and I nearly blow my load at the sight of her opening her mouth and letting a long trail of spit drip onto the tip. She repeats the action a second time, this time allowing her hand to become coated.

Holy fuck.

Her eyes shine with a playful glimmer as her warm mouth wraps around me. My hands fist around her hair on instinct, pulling it into a makeshift ponytail. I push my hips up, forcing my cock further down her throat while she drags her tongue along the head. She moans, letting the sound vibrate around me as she looks up through batted eyelashes. The sight is criminal, lethal. And I have to squeeze my eyes shut when I feel the pressure in my balls build.

"Baby," I moan. "If you don't stop, I'm going to fill your mouth."

She releases me with a loud pop and I pull her to me by the hair still wrapped around my fist. The pain has her groaning in my ear; the sound adding to the aching pulse in my groin. I nearly rip her pants off as I push them down her legs and throw them away.

I waste no time in pushing Gracie onto her back and crawling back on top of her. My large body is completely swallowing hers. I run my hands over every inch of her smooth skin, feeling the goosebumps rise under my touch before I finally press my lips against hers, swallowing a whimper.

With one hand resting in her hair, I move the other between her legs and let the wetness waiting for me guide my finger into her tight pussy. "You're always dripping for me," I grunt, twisting my hand so I can use my thumb to press down on her clit, relishing in the way she grinds against my hand.

"Please, just fuck me already," she pleads, twisting her hips into my touch like she'll die if she doesn't get me inside of her.

"Always so impatient," I tease, letting another finger dip inside. "So needy." I do the same with a third finger.

"Tyler." It's a beg, a plea. My head falls forward slightly, lips parting when she moans out my name. I pull out my fingers and press a soft kiss to her lips. I grab my cock and coat the tip in her arousal before slamming the entire thing inside of her, grunting when she grabs onto my biceps and sinks her nails into my skin. My mind fogs over when our bodies rub together, our tempos syncing with every rough, unforgiving thrust.

"That's a good girl. Take all of me." She squeezes around me. Gracie's grip moves from my arms to my back and she yanks me toward her so she can latch her mouth to my neck, sucking and nipping until I have her mark etched on my skin as proudly as I wear it in my chest. Her body starts quivering around me as I pull out, only leaving the tip inside before slamming back in.

"Come for me, baby," I groan in her ear. She squeezes me

tighter, teeth pulling at my neck harder before she unhinges altogether, cooing my name and shoving her face against my skin.

"I'm right behind you, Gray." I pull out when my balls tighten, cock pulsing as my orgasm takes over. I coat her stomach in strings of white and let her name drip from my tongue over and over again.

I didn't realize my eyes were shut until I open them and see a lazy grin on Gracie's lips. She stares up at me, eyes half-lidded, utterly spent. My expression matches hers as I roll off the bed and pick up my discarded shirt off the floor.

"Ew, Ty." She scrunches her nose but makes no effort to stop me when I use it to wipe the cum off of her stomach.

"What? All of our towels are still in boxes." I grin and slide back into bed. She's taken into my arms the second I turn on my side.

"It's too early for bed," she giggles, but snuggles into me further, head tucked beneath my chin.

"It's never too early for a nap, though. And I'm pretty tired. Your pussy is an energy sucker, baby."

My eyes close but I can feel her shaking her head. I wait for her to say something else but she stays silent, and I take that as my sign to let myself fall into what I hope will be a very restorative sleep.

35

Tyler

A soft shove pulls me from what could have been a pretty decent sleep. I have to blink profusely to make out Gracie's anxious figure through the dark room as she leans over me from her side of the bed, panic clear in her tightened features.

"What time is it?" I croak. The sleep in my voice is heavy.

"Three in the morning," she answers and softly pushes the hair off of my damp forehead. "Braden called, baby."

I shoot into a sitting position and reach over to turn on the lamp beside me. As soon as the dull light washes over her, I see my phone clenched tightly in her fist.

"What happened?" I rush, throwing my legs over the side of the bed. "And how did we sleep until three?"

"Your brother showed up." She avoids eye contact and ignores my second question. "With Allen."

Fuck no. I'm slipping clothes on before she can throw the covers off of her naked body.

"Please tell me you're not planning on doing what I think you are," she sighs. There's a silent plea in her glassy eyes. I'm not sure if it's fear or sleep that's creating such a shine over her baby blues, but I don't have time to find out. I hold out my hand in front of her, eyeing my cell phone.

"I will not stand by and let River of all people drag our mom back into Allen's infected claws, Gracie. I can't do that."

Pushing herself up, she reluctantly hands me my phone. "At least let me come with you," she pleads out loud this time with a quiver in her voice that makes my heart pound painfully against my chest.

"No." I shake my head. "Just stay here and go back to sleep. I'll be back before you wake up again."

"You can't be serious," she scoffs while throwing up a hand. "You think I'll be able to go back to bed after this?"

"I'm dead serious, Gray. You're safer here. Away from them." *Away from me*, I want to say.

Her face drops and she looks down at the bare toes poking out from under the blankets. Stop making me feel guilty, beautiful.

"Okay," she mumbles, nodding once.

"Hey, look at me." I take a step toward her and place a finger under her chin, lifting it up. "I promise that as soon as I get back, we'll lay in bed and watch your cheesy vampire show all day. Sound good?"

Gracie's eyes light up when they move to mine. Her lips spread in a small smile and she nods in reluctant agree-ment. "No backing out halfway through an episode this time."

I let out a low chuckle before pulling her in for a deep kiss. "I'll be back soon."

She grabs hold of my hand and spins me around, pulling me back to her. Lifting herself onto her knees, she places a hand behind my neck and pulls me down so she can place her lips on mine again. The passion behind the kiss makes it hard for me to back away, which I think must have been her plan. I run a hand over her messy bed head while rubbing my thumb along her cheek.

"Be safe," she breathes out as she pulls away, hesitant to let me go.

"Always." It's the heaviest promise that I've ever made, but one I have every intention of keeping.

"I love you."

I ignore the twinge in my gut that urges me to run back into bed with her and press my lips to her cheek instead. "I love you." I drag my eyes off of her and push myself to get dressed and walk away, not stopping until I reach my truck.

Braden opens the door for me before I even make it up the front steps. "Hey."

I clench my fists at my sides knowing that my nails will leave pink crescent moons in my palms. I nod subtly and walk past him. River's voice slashes at my spine, bringing a flash of red through my vision as I stalk down the familiar hallway.

I hear Brooks growl, "You need to leave. Now."

Braden walks quietly behind me, keeping quiet to avoid pissing me off even more than I already am. As if that's a possibility. She was supposed to be safe here. But nowhere will ever be safe for her as long as that sack of human filth is walking around. I stop inches away from the living room archway and lean back against the wall. Braden's shoulder knocks against mine as he follows suit, his face pulled into a tight scowl.

"When did they get here?" I keep my voice low.

"Twenty minutes ago. River showed up first claiming that he needed to talk to her. We wouldn't have let him in if we knew he brought Allen."

"I know." I nod. "Do they have anything on them?" It might sound like a stupid question, but I wouldn't put it past Allen to turn this into a dirty fight in order to get mom back in his grasp.

"Not that I saw."

"Okay. Let me go first. If things go bad, beat them over the head with a fucking frying pan for all I care. Just get my mom out of here."

Braden's body shakes with a silent, humourless laugh before he nods and places a hand on my shoulder. I push away from the wall and walk through the arch.

"Now, I really hope you didn't plan a family get-together without your favourite son." I almost let a contorted laugh slip past my lips when River turns to me. An expensive, tailored suit clings to his built body like a second skin. I guess he has steroids to thank for that. A guy who sniffs as much snow as he does shouldn't be thicker than a tree branch. His pupils are blown and I know that he's high.

"You wore a suit? What are you, a mafia leader or some-thing?" I snort, tilting my head when Allen tries to take a step toward me. River shoves him back with his arm.

"Ah, perfect. The entire family's here, Mom." River scowls at me before turning to Mom and watching her expectantly as her eyes dart between her two sons. Two men who couldn't be more different if they tried. When she doesn't speak, he turns back to me, deciding to hit a nerve he knows will provoke a reaction from me. "Where's that tight piece of ass you had with you last time? Gracie, right?"

My nostrils flare and anger licks my spine like a tongue swirling an ice cream cone. The thumping in my ears is deaf-ening as my blood bubbles. I make out the pompous smirk resting on River's lips through the thick red mist painting my vision and stalk toward him, my lip curled back. My knuckles ache from how tightly my fists are clenched, my biceps hard and rigid as I force them to stay by my sides.

"Oh," he sighs, shoulders shrugging. Amusement dances in his dark eyes as he watches my face turn red. Our chests are only a few feet apart. "She left you, didn't she? Went to find a real man to fuck her the way you couldn't. Huh, maybe she's at my door, waiting for my co—"

An animalistic snarl escapes me as I pull my arm back and

swing. My knuckles burn and pain surges up my arm when I hit his mouth. River fumbles back, cursing under his breath before he's spitting a bloodied tooth at my feet.

He reaches up and wipes at his mouth. The urge to snort becomes nearly overwhelming when he runs his tongue over the bare gum where his front tooth used to be.

He clicks his tongue. "Well, now look what you've done."

"Don't talk about her. You don't deserve so much as to say her name," I growl, my fist still curled at my side as if it's waiting for another order. I almost give one before I hear Mom speak from behind me.

"Tyler."

I spin around instantly and narrow my eyes on Mom's hunched figure. She struggles to speak and Brooks places a hand on her shoulder. My brows raise as confusion washes over me for a fleeting second before Allen opens his vile mouth.

"There's no need for any more bloodshed. We're just here to get your mom back, ain't that right, Riv?"

Scoffing, I tighten my sights on my brother. "You've got to be kidding, me. You can't seriously think that she's safe with him? Are you fucking blind? He hits her! She needs help!" I yell, turning to look back at Mom. "Tell him, Mom. Tell him how I found you laying on the bathroom floor bleeding and blown out your mind!"

My eyes pour into hers. They're begging her to say something, to finally stand up for herself. To stand up for me. But she stays quiet, dropping her eyes to the floor and letting her tears splatter against the floor in unbearably loud silence. My throat closes, making me choke on the thin air around me as a heavy, unbearable weight pulverizes my chest. This can't be how her life is supposed to go. This isn't right. I need her. For the first fucking time in my life, I really need her. She's supposed to want to go to my wedding and change my kid's shitty diapers. I finally have a damn reason to think of my future with a feeling other than disgust and hatred. And she doesn't want to see it.

She doesn't fucking care. She's supposed to want me. For once in her life, she's supposed to choose me, the one who's always been there to take care of her. But again, she's choosing the wrong people. The only difference this time is that I won't be there to fix her mistakes. Not anymore.

"Mom, please," I plead. Brooks looks at me with defeat in his eyes and drops my mom's arm to give her the chance to choose. A pained, unfamiliar noise escapes me when she moves to stand beside Allen. I can feel my heart shattering again as I watch her choose them over me for the last time.

"If that's all, then you need to get the fuck out of my house." Brooks' tone is brutally rough and distant as he moves toward me and paces a heavy hand on my shoulder. I want to shrug him off but I can't find the strength in me to do so. I just stand in place, numb.

"Gladly." River grins, ever-so-proud of himself, regardless of the hole in his smile. I drop my eyes, not being able to watch any longer when I see Allen pull Mom into his slimy grip and drag her with him.

"Tyler," she chokes. I feel a light pressure on my arm. I fight hard to keep my gaze locked on my shoes and push out a shaky breath when her hand drops to her side again. Allen spits something at me before leaving, but I can't make out the words as my mind goes blank. Brooks tries to rub my shoulder and talk to me but I block him out too and let my body slide down the wall behind me. I place my elbows on my knees and drop my head in my hands before the tears fall.

"Fuck!" I hear Braden shout and the familiar sound of a punch meeting drywall. The noise reminds me that he's still here.

"Go to their apartment and tell Gracie what happened. I need to talk to Tyler alone." It's Brook's that speaks now, I'm pretty sure.

"You sure? I can stay, dad."

"Go." The door slams shut a second later.

"Tyler." A hand rubs my back.

"It's just me. It's Brooks. Can you look at me?"

I pull my head up and turn to him. My vision is so blurred with tears that I can only vaguely make out the large shape of a man.

"You need to breathe, Tyler. In for three, out for three."

I nod. In for three, out for three. My head clears but I continue to struggle to focus on my breathing.

"That's it," he encourages while handing me a dry tissue. My face is dry a few seconds later and I crumple the wet tissue in my fist.

"I really need to talk to you about something. It's important."

"Now?" My brows furrow. I swallow nervously.

He just nods and watches me with a deep intensity that worms its way into my gut and yanks, making me curl into myself.

"About what?" I croak and cringe when I realize that I sound as mangled as I feel.

"Did your mom ever talk to you about your father? Your birth father?"

"No. She never brought it up. I assumed she didn't know who it was." I've come to peace with that.

He nods again, slower this time.

"Brooks? Why are you asking about him?"

"There's something that you should know, but I need you to promise me you won't react until I finish speaking."

I nearly spew chunks all over his living room. The silence is deafening, so much so that I fight the urge to place my hands over my ears and squeeze my eyes shut so hard a deep ache pulses behind them.

"Do you know him or something? Don't fucking lie to me, Brooks."

He swallows so harshly his Adam's apple nearly bursts through his throat. He nods so subtly that I would have missed it had I not been staring so hard at him.

"Tell me what you know," I demand. There's a silent dare in my tone that makes it clear I won't tolerate being lied to. Not right now.

"I need you to know that I didn't know," he pleads, voice wavering. "Not until a few hours ago."

I move my hands to my bent knees and squeeze so hard my fingertips turn white and the bones beneath them whimper. "Spit it out."

His mouth opens only to close again before a proper sentence can be spoken. The silence is strangling me with no type of restraint as I stare at him, my eyes full of a deep-rooted emotion that I can't quite pinpoint.

"Before I met my ex-wife, your mom and I . . . we dated for a while." He nearly chokes on the words and a familiar coldness forms in his eyes. "I had no idea that Nora was your mom until the night that you called me for help. When I saw her in that state, I thought it was God's cruel way of punishing me for something that I've done in the past. As if losing her all those years ago wasn't punishment enough."

"I'm confused," I mumble. Brooks dated my mom? I'm surprised, yeah, but I don't get why it matters. Does he know my father? Did he meet him back then?

"I loved her," he coughs like he's choking. "Your mom. I loved her more than I've ever loved another woman. But back then I was just a stupid kid. I didn't know how to be there the way that I should have been. She was still upset about River's dad leaving, and I knew I wasn't ready to raise that shit-disturbed kid with her." Brooks clears his throat before continuing, "I assumed that was why she left. She ran out of town without a goodbye or an explanation. Not even a damn note. She was just gone. I never heard from her again. Until a month ago when I saw her battered and bloody in that broken shell of a house."

"What the fuck are you talking about?" I growl and push myself off of the floor so quickly that I nearly fall back on my ass.

I need to put some space between us. Betrayal makes an ugly, unwanted appearance as I narrow my eyes and tighten my jaw.

"I thought it was just a coincidence! Maybe even the second chance that I always wanted. But she's not the same as she used to be. She wouldn't let me help her." He follows me. My face scrunches up as I reel back at his words.

There's no fucking way. Is there? Mom met none of my friends because she was never around or sober enough to. So how would she have known that I knew Brooks? Fuck.

"She told me something before she called your brother tonight."

"She fucking called him? She brought them both here?"

I see red. My knuckles burn with the urge to throw them into the wall behind me. But I suck in a sharp breath and clench my fists at my sides instead.

"She left me twenty-four years ago because she was pregnant with another son. With my son."

His words paralyze me. They blow through my mind and rattle against the sides of my skull. They make my head throb to the point that my eyes water from the pain beating behind them.

"But . . ." I blubber. "Braden and I . . . we're the same age," is the only coherent string of words that I can wrangle together.

"You're six months older than him, Tyler."

"Is this some sick fucking joke?" I hiss before clenching my fists and throwing one straight through the living room drywall, unable to hold myself back any longer. "Fuck!"

The sound vibrates through the room as broken pieces fall to the floor, covering the wood in a thick layer of dust and leaving the beam that I punched exposed as I grunt in pain. I don't have time to feel a blimp of regret or guilt about the mess before I'm shaking my busted, bloody hand in the air to help ease some of the pain.

"Do you really think that I would joke about this? I've known you for years—treated you like a son without knowing that you've been my blood the entire time. That's the sick joke!"

The force behind his shouted words smacks me in the face and brings me back down to earth. Brooks has always been a father figure to me—teaching me more about the world than I would have been able to learn from any book or movie and disciplining me when I let my anger and hatred for the world get out of control. This all feels like some sort of heartless joke. Lord knows I deserve to feel this knife twisting in my gut. But there's also a tiny shard of hope flickering in the anger and betrayal that this is real. That I wasn't always alone as I thought I was.

"I don't know what to say," I sputter, and I mean it.

"She knew you deserved better than her, Tyler. I think that's why she told me after all these years. In her fucked up way, she loves you enough to let you be happy without her. She trusted me to take care of you."

I shake my head at him and slam my open palms into my forehead before sliding them behind my head. "She didn't just willingly give me up. She wouldn't do that to me." I hate that I don't know if I'm trying to convince him or myself. I feel a hand squeeze my shoulder tightly, grabbing my attention as I steal a quick glance in his direction.

"She didn't give you up. She's letting you start over."

"What if I didn't want to start over? Huh? Why does she get to make that decision for me? It's not fair!"

"She had her chance, Tyler. You can't force someone to change who doesn't want to change."

"But she's my mom." I can hear my heart being thrown through a grinder by the crack in my whimpered words.

"Maybe she'll find her way back to you when she's ready. She'll always be your mom. But right now, she's no good for you. You know that."

He's right. I know he is. But that doesn't make it any easier. "What now? What are we supposed to do now?" I ask as I push myself away from the wall and wipe a hand down my wet face.

"I have no fucking clue," he laughs. There's only a fleck of humour in the rough sound. "I guess we take it one day at a time."

"Does Braden know?"

He nods his head. "Yes. He has an awful habit of eavesdropping." A loud rumble sounds outside, followed by the slam of a car door.

My eyebrow cocks as I stare at Brooks, silently asking him if he's expecting anyone when the front door is swung open with enough force for the door handle to dig into the wall behind it.

"Tyler?"

A weight lifts from my chest as soon as I see Gracie come running into the room. My sweatshirt covers most of her body and her messy hair hangs out of the ponytail flopping against her back. She's jumping into my arms without a second thought to the watchful eyes around us and I grab her thighs with ease, holding her in place. I close my eyes and press my forehead to hers, letting her familiar scent calm me down.

She smells like home.

"I was so worried," she whispers, warm breath hitting my lips as she uses her thighs to squeeze my waist.

"I told you I would be okay."

"Braden told me everything." Her words are soft as she runs her hands through my hair. I meet Braden's eyes over Gracie's shoulder and roll my eyes when his fingers form a V around his mouth before he flicks his tongue between them. His childish behaviour makes it hard to be upset with him for telling Gracie, but lord knows that I probably wouldn't have been able to do it on my own. It's hard to stay mad at that fucker, that's for sure.

Gracie slides back down a few seconds later before wrapping herself around my arm and eyeing up the other two men. "So, what now?" A choir of mixed laughter floats around the room as we all shake our heads at the beautiful blonde.

One day at a time, baby. One day at a time.

EPILOGUE

Tyler

THE HOUSE SMELLS LIKE A MIX BETWEEN THE FIRE BURNING IN THE circular, brick-walled fire pit in the backyard and baby puke? The combination of the two is enough to make my nose scrunch.

"Where's my nephew?" Gracie squeals when we get inside Oakley and Ava's home. She takes off right away, leaving me standing in the doorway wearing an all-too-knowing look.

The happy couple moved from their old house in Seattle two months before their son, Maddox, was born, and Oakley's contract with the Warriors was signed, but they settled in almost instantly.

The elaborate six-bedroom acreage sits on four acres of green land, next to a man-made lake and an old, wooden treehouse built at least ten years ago. The driveway is long and twisty, leading from the gravel road off the highway, through their tall, locked gate and up to the four-car, double-level garage connected to the side of the house. I can't say what style the place is, other than it has tall, sharp peaks and a white, wrap-around porch that Gracie coos at every time we stop by.

It won't be long before the huge yard is taken up by a jungle gym and cluttered with scattered toys. Hell, I wouldn't doubt that before their baby boy can even walk that there will be an outdoor rink rooted somewhere in the grass as well. Poor kid is going to have skates laced around his tiny feet before he knows it.

"That was fast," Oakley laughs and beckons me inside before shutting the door.

"She's obsessed with that kid of yours," I reply with a subtle smile and walk in step with Oakley as he leads us toward the half-open patio door at the back of the house. From the high-pitched baby talk coming from the backyard, I can only assume that's where Ava and Gracie went.

"I think we all are."

I sneak a quick glance beside me and sigh when a blanket of happiness falls over my shoulders. I see the deep, dimpled grin he wears while saying those words. Pride floods his features, sinking into the slight smile-lines that have formed beside his lips and flaming like an uncontrolled forest fire in his squinted eyes.

Slapping a hand on his shoulder, I give it a tight squeeze and sigh, "Look at you. Getting all ooey-gooey."

"Fuck off," he snorts and shrugs off my hand. "How's Brooks doing?"

I swallow past the ball in my throat and reply, "He's good. We're still trying really hard to get used to the whole thing. It's weird, you know?"

He nods. "At least he's trying."

"Yeah," I mutter in agreement. I think that's the only reason why I've been able to handle the whole thing as well as I have been. If it wasn't because I knew Brooks actually gave a shit about having a genuine relationship with me, I'm sure I would have high-tailed it out of his house that night and never looked back. His willingness to make right what my mother made wrong means more to me than I think he'll ever know.

I haven't seen my mom since that night and as much as I hate not knowing whether she's lying dead in a ditch somewhere or making something of her life, I feel free too. I feel free not staying up for countless hours in the night worrying about whether she's going to show up on my doorstep half-conscious. I'm still not sure if that makes me as bad of a person as I think it does, though.

"I still can't wrap my head around the fact that Braden is your blood. I mean this in the best way, but he's such an arrogant fucker."

I bite back my laugh and slide the patio door fully open. Oakley's not wrong. Braden is what I consider an acquired taste. But he's my brother so I guess I have to suck it up.

The early September evening air has a bit of a nip to it tonight as we join the girls by the fire pit. Gracie sits on one of the four wicker patio chairs holding Maddox as he rests his tiny head against her chest, eyes closed, while Ava sits down on another and watches Oakley move toward her with a soft smile.

"Don't I look amazing with a baby in my arms?" Gracie asks when I sit down in the chair beside her, voice gentle in hopes of not waking the baby but not quiet enough that I miss the hint thick in her words. A somewhat terrifying noise—something like a cry from a wounded animal—tries to climb up my throat but I swallow it. I know my eyes are wide, mouth partially open from the serious question so I laugh, hoping to cover up my shock.

"You always look amazing," I reply, hoping I've been convincing enough to hide my nerves.

Her eyes move over my face, eyebrows slightly furrowed as she examines me, searching for something—fear, most likely. I wouldn't be surprised if she found it. The idea of kids terrifies me. It makes my knees wobble and my forehead clammy. But it isn't because I don't want them. I think I do. I want everything that I can get with Gray, but I'm pretty sure that I would be an awful dad. How would I even know how to raise a kid when I had nobody worth a shit raising me? The last thing I want is to raise another me, or worse, another River.

My knee shakes as I look across the fire pit at Oakley. He's a fucking great dad. With the patience of a saint, heart the size of a dinner plate, and an uncanny ability to fear nothing, it doesn't surprise me even in the slightest. He was born to be a husband and father. God knows he's already had enough practice being the man of the house. But me? That's another story.

I'm an arrogant, short-tempered hot-head with more baggage stacked inside my head than at an airport. I don't know what a normal childhood is even supposed to look like, how it's supposed to feel. How would I be able to raise a kid not knowing if what I was doing was right or wrong?

A pain throbs behind my eyes. Giving my head a quick shake, I look at Gracie again. I watch silently as she hums a soft lullaby, cheek resting against Maddox's' dark brown, peach-fuzz-covered head. Happiness radiates off of her in thick, chest-constricting waves and I try to look away but find my gaze locked on the fat, princess-cut diamond wrapped around her ring finger instead. There's a pinch in my chest as my heart throws itself around in my ribcage.

With one knee in soft, white sand on the same Mexico beach where Gracie began chipping away at what I assumed was an indestructible wall around my heart, I proposed to her—the love of my fucking life. In front of her brother and mine—the half-brother who isn't nose deep in cocaine—and my dad. She said yes and made me the happiest fucker in the whole damn world.

I nearly throw my palm against my forehead as I sharply realize that I wouldn't be the only one raising our babies. Gray was born to be a mom. I see it in the way her grins dimple and eyes warm when she teaches a dance class; how she bounces in her seat, excitement shooting in her veins every time she leaves to go babysit her nephew. She's still so young and I know that there's no rush, so why am I getting myself worked up over something that I'm sure I'll be ready for when the time comes?

Because I'm an idiot. That's why.

"Are you okay, Ty?" I hear her ask, the question breaking me out of the mental cage I've thrown myself in.

I nod and meet her curious gaze. "Come here."

She raises a brow before I pat my lap and understanding floods her features. Carefully standing up from the chair, she tightens her grip on Maddox and walks over to me, slow and steady in hopes of not waking him. Soon she's in front of me, turning around so she can sit down. I reach forward and wrap my arms tightly around her waist and pull her toward me, sucking in a greedy breath when her back rests against my chest.

I feel Oakley's beady eyes on me and turn to him, the left side of my mouth lifting. It doesn't take long for Ava to reach over and smack him on the arm.

"Leave them alone," she chides, swatting at a spark that flies from the fire toward her newly dyed, long auburn hair. It's a new look for her, compared to the short chestnut brown we're used to seeing but it looks good.

Oakley throws his hands up in front of him. "I didn't say anything!"

"You forget how well I know you," Ava teases, smiling deviantly. Oakley rolls his eyes dramatically before copying me and patting his own lap.

"Well?"

"Well, what?" Ava feigns ignorance, shrugging.

"Oh, you know what. Don't make me put you here myself."

"Was that supposed to be a threat?"

Oakley's Adam's apple bobs as he leans over the side of his chair and mutters something under his breath that I'm thankful I'm too far away to hear.

I rest my chin on Gracie's shoulder and shove my face in her neck, laughing against the warm skin. "What an idiot."

"Oakley or Ava?" She shivers against me.

"Your brother."

"You're just figuring that out?"

I pull away from her neck and look down at the button-nosed boy wrapped up in a Vancouver Warriors blanket, laying in Gracie's arms, dead to the world around him. I can hear his steady breaths falling from his tiny mouth and I feel the corners of mine tugging.

"How many kids do you want?" I whisper, knowing I took her by surprise when she gasps, turning her head to look at me.

"Since when do you want to talk about kids?"

That's a good question, baby. I shrug. "Since now, I guess."

She nods once. "I think two. Both boys. I know how much trouble girls are."

I half-expected the idea of having two mini-versions of myself running around to make me want to throw up. But the warmth whipping around in my veins makes my smile spread far enough that I wonder if it could rip my cheeks.

"Then two boys it is."

She giggles. "That's not how it works, babe. You don't get to pick."

"Too fucking bad," I scoff and my connected hands break apart as I slide one under her baggy sweatshirt and place it against her stomach, palm warm against the soft skin.

"What's up with you tonight?" she asks and leans her cheek against the side of my head.

"Nothing. I just love you."

She blows out a slow breath. "I love you too."

"Good," I reply before tilting my head and placing a soft kiss under her jawbone. "Because you can't get rid of me now."

"Is that a threat or a promise?"

"A promise," I mutter. I know my tone is pin-straight and determined. "Definitely a promise."

The sound of the patio door sliding open captures our attention as four heads snap in the direction of the house. I can nearly feel the tension rising like air in a hot-air-balloon when Adam steps outside, a miniature version of himself gripping his hand for dear life. It doesn't take long for Adam to speak just one word that falls as heavy as a bed of bricks, cutting through the cool night air.

"Surprise?"

Find Out What Happens Next In The Final Instalment Of The Swift Hat-Trick Trilogy, Vital Blindside, Out Now!

Read Now!

BONUS CHAPTER

Gracie

"Ready, Princess? The others are going to be here in a few minutes," Tyler calls from the living room.

I ignore him and continue to wrap his gift. The black ribbon is silky between my fingertips as I loop it the final time over the matching black package and smile down at it.

His birthday party tonight will be more than he bargained for, and while he might not love being the centre of attention, I don't think he'll mind it once I give him his gift.

Tucking said gift beneath my arm, I shimmy my dress down my legs and open the bedroom door, stepping right into his chest.

"I thought you got lost in there," he rumbles, immediately wrapping his arms around me and pulling me close.

I roll my eyes but return the embrace. "You make it seem like I was in there for hours. It was twenty minutes. That's got to be a record for me."

"It felt longer."

"That's because you can't go a minute without missing me," I tease, stepping back with a kiss to his jaw.

"You're not wrong."

"I never am. Now come, I need to make sure everything is ready."

He follows close behind, keeping at my heels until I shoo him away with a bottle of beer and a hockey game on the flatscreen. I make quick trips around the house, making sure I haven't forgotten anything. Food, check. Alcohol, check. Surprise, check.

By the time the doorbell rings, I'm glowing with anticipation. I beat Tyler to the door, and as I spin to stick my tongue out at him, he backs me up against the door, forearms resting beside my head.

"You haven't kissed me this afternoon," he says.

I trail my hand up his back, feeling the muscles ripple beneath my touch. "Oops. I haven't?"

He scowls. "Oops?"

"I guess that's not really fair to the birthday boy, huh?"

Pushing up on my toes, I kiss him softly, more so than usual. It may be his birthday, but I wouldn't be myself if I didn't tease him just a bit.

A groan escapes him as he kisses back, one hand cupping my jaw while the other grips my waist. His lips are demanding, and when I don't tease him any longer, he smiles into the kiss.

"I have plans for you tonight," he breathes, fingers skimming over my stomach before dipping beneath my skirt and cupping me between my legs.

I press into his touch, whimpering when he rubs my clit over my panties. "What a coincidence. I have plans for you, too."

The doorbell rings again, and I fight off a silly grin knowing time hasn't stinted our sex life. I still want him anywhere, anytime, and thankfully, he wants me like that too. We're insatiable. I think we always will be.

"Be a busy night then," he rasps, and with a final stroke along my centre, steps back.

You have no idea, baby.

I run my hands over my hair and down my body to make sure I'm not opening the door with my dress stuck inside the band of my panties, and then greet our guests with a grin, my broody man doing the same behind me.

An hour later, I'm watching my brother chase his oldest son around the kitchen island while his wife bounces their youngest on her thighs on the floor close by. Maddox screams happily when Oakley catches him around the waist and twirls him in the air, and my smile grows.

"Kids are both the world's greatest blessing and biggest pains in the ass," Brooks says, coming up beside me.

I look at him and take in the sparkle in his eyes and the hint of a smile creasing his face. He takes a sip of the beer in his hands and leans toward me.

"You have the look, sweetheart. My boy hasn't figured it out yet, but I would recognize it anywhere."

Surprised that he picked up on something I haven't told a single soul about yet, I point my finger at him. "You better zip those lips, Gramps. I have it all planned out."

He belts out a laugh, nodding. "I wouldn't dream of ruining such a well-planned surprise. Your secret is safe with me. But I gotta say congratulations to you now, so give me a hug."

I do, and as he gives me one final squeeze, I blurt out, "I don't think I've ever told you how thankful I am for what you've done for Tyler. He would never admit it to anyone, even me, but you mean the world to him. Taking him in and accepting him regardless of the circumstances . . . it fixed something broken inside of him.

"I know that he's ready to be a dad and that he will love our baby with everything inside of him, but I think we owe some of that to you. God knows the other parental figures in his life never taught him how to do that." Pulling back, I offer him a soft smile and a quick kiss on the cheek.

He blinks repeatedly before saying, "I would say that he's lucky to have you in his life, but I think that goes for all of us as well. Thank you."

"You're welcome. Now, what do you say we let the birthday boy know that he's about to be a dad?"

"Go get him, Gray," he says, ushering me out of the room.

I feel lighthearted as I search for my husband, finding him a few moments later in the living room. His eyes find me the second I enter the room, like he was waiting for me. I wiggle my fingers in a wave and pick the black box from the table of gifts, bringing it toward him.

"Do you want to open your gift in private, or should I call everyone in here with us?" I ask, already knowing the answer to my question.

He lowers the volume on the TV, silencing the sportscaster before patting his lap. "Private."

"I think I know you a little too well by now," I say, taking the offered seat and handing him the box.

"As you should, Wife. Because I know you just as well."

"Is that so?"

He kisses my hair, draping his arm around me. "It is."

"I guarantee you don't know what's in this box."

Giving it a slight shake, he curves a brow. "I have a guess."

"You're probably wrong."

"We'll see."

He carefully pulls the ribbon, and the bow falls free. Then, he peels off the top of the box, dropping it on the floor before pinching the tissue paper beneath, eyes lifting to me.

A coy smile curves my mouth as I nod, giving him the go-ahead.

The barked laugh of surprise that falls from his lips as he reveals what's inside is everything I was hoping for. He ever so carefully picks up the ultrasound picture and looks at me with the question in his eyes.

"I know it doesn't look like much now, but with your genes, it won't be lo—" I squeal when he bursts from the couch, pulling me up with him and spinning us around.

"I fucking love you," he breathes against my ear. "The both of you. Is this for real?"

I smile from ear to ear as I reply, "So real. And we love you, too."

And later that night, after everyone has gone home after saying a million congratulations, we hang the picture on the wall of our spare room and start making plans for how we'll transform the space into a nursery. Tyler rambles off idea after idea, seeming to have a million things already planned in his head, and it isn't until I distract him with kisses that he carries me off and lets me give him his second birthday gift.

How did I get so lucky?

Thank you for reading Blissful Hook! If you enjoyed it, please leave a review on Amazon and Goodreads.

This is far from the end of the Swift Hat-Trick series! Adam and Scarlett's story takes place next, followed by the second generation series!

To be kept up to date on all my releases, check out my website! www.hannahcowanauthor.com

If you have not read the previous books in the series, now is the time to do so!

Lucky Hit — Oakley and Ava
Between Periods (Novella and BH prequel)

VITAL BLINDSIDE

Adam White is many things, but a single dad was one he never saw himself becoming. He was twenty-three when the plan he had for his life crumbled at his feet. In the blink of an eye, he went from a flirtatious playboy just getting his new business up and off the ground to a struggling father of a two-year-old boy he never knew existed.

Yet somehow, Adam still accomplished what he thought was impossible. And ten years later, he doesn't think his life can get any better. His son is his world, and his business, White Ice Training, is one of the most popular hockey training facilities in Vancouver. But in the chaos of hiring a new trainer, he stumbles upon the name of a woman he would recognize anywhere. A woman he decides right then and there he'll do anything to convince to take the job.

One terrible game was all it took for Scarlett Carter to lose everything. After a career-ending injury destroys her chances of ever playing professional hockey again, she finds herself lost in a mess of guilt-stricken "what-ifs" and broken dreams. Moving back home to Vancouver was never in the playbook, but either was letting herself get tricked into taking a job working for a man who seems to want to stop at nothing to see her forgive the sport that broke her.

Scarlett wants to forget the hockey world, but the single dad refuses to let her move on. And the more time she spends with Adam, the harder she's finding it to resist him and the sly grins he seems to only give her. She can't help but wonder why he cares so much about her. And more importantly, why she can't bring herself to make him leave her alone.

CHAPTER 1

Adam

The lumpy clouds above Vancouver, British Columbia, groan into the sky before opening up to drown us beneath a heavy pour of rain. It wets my hair, making it stick to my forehead as I continue my morning run.

I'm on my seventh mile, and even though the weather just gave me the middle finger, my house is only a couple of blocks away. I can't exactly stop now, even if that means I'll have to listen to my twelve-year-old son scold me for bringing wet clothes into the house as soon as I walk through the front door.

Cooper loves to poke at the bear, as long as that bear is me. I can't help but take complete responsibility for that. He learned at a young age that the majority of the time, I'm all bark and no bite, which only makes him enjoy picking on me like a little shit even more.

Our two-story craftsman-style house pokes its head around the eyesore of a spruce tree planted dead smack in front of Mrs. Yollard's house. It's almost the size of her entire front yard and looks like it hasn't been trimmed once in its lifetime. I've tried convincing the widow to have it cut down, even going as far as to offer her my assistance, but she's shut me down each time.

My persistence has no limit, however. I'll get her to agree one of these days.

I jog past the neighbouring yard and toward my house, noticing the open garage door. Cooper's bike is leaning up against my workbench inside, his Marvel-sticker-decorated helmet dangling from the handlebars.

Neither my son nor dog are anywhere to be seen, but I can only assume they're close by. My kid wouldn't dare leave his precious bike out in the open without protection, and Easton doesn't move from his best friend's side for a second longer than necessary.

Slowing to a walk, I move up the driveway, patting the hood of my Mercedes when I pass it. I maneuver around the array of hockey gear and dog toys scattered on the concrete pad in the garage before shaking my hair free of rain and opening the door that leads to the mud room, stepping inside.

The mud room is as big of a mess as the garage, with large piles of laundry stacked in front of the washing machine and a collection of shoes everywhere but the designated rack. I've been telling myself I'll get this room cleaned up eventually, but I may have put it off a bit too long.

"Coop?" I yell, slipping off my wet sneakers.

Taking a step out of the mud room, I wince when my socks make a squelching noise and water seeps to the floor. With rushed movements, I pull off my socks and add them to a pile of dirty clothes before collecting all of it in my arms and tossing everything in the washing machine. I'm throwing in a pod of detergent when I hear the familiar click-clack of nails on the floor.

"You're lucky Dad wasn't home to see that, East. You would have had to sleep outside—" Cooper's words cut off when he enters the mud room.

Chuckling, I start the washing machine and turn around. Easton, the ninety-pound German shepherd we adopted when

Cooper was five, flops onto his back immediately, his tongue lolling out of his mouth and paws folded beneath his chin.

"Yeah, that's not suspicious." I snort and look at Cooper as he rocks back and forth on his heels. "What did he do?"

Cooper is the spitting image of me. Staring at him is like going back in time and looking in the mirror.

His milk-chocolate-coloured eyes have the same green flecks around the irises as mine do, and his puffed bottom lip twists to the right just enough to rest in a half-smirk that's gotten me in trouble once or twice over the years. He's tall for his age, coming in at just under five foot four—just like his dad was.

"Uh . . ."

"Cooper," I groan. "Let's do this the easy way, please. What did he do?"

His eyes roam around the room, focusing on everything but me. "He might have eaten one of the jerseys you had lying in that pile." He points to the laundry on the ground.

"He might have? Or he did?"

Cooper gulps. "Okay, he did. But in his defence, he probably thought it was going in the trash anyway. It had been sitting there for at least a couple of weeks."

He's not completely off base there. It's been over a week since I brought WIT's spare jerseys home to wash, and they have yet to see even a dollop of detergent. I'm sure they smelled ripe for the picking.

"Did he eat the entire thing?" I ask with a weighted sigh.

Cooper shakes his head. "No. Just the sleeve. And he puked it up in the backyard already."

Flicking my gaze to the dog wrapped around Cooper's foot, I give my head a shake. The troublemaker is smiling at me.

"Fine," I say. "But make sure he doesn't do it again, Coop. This room is off limits, yeah?"

"Got it, Dad."

I nod before checking my watch for the time and muttering a curse. Cooper raises a curious brow.

"No bike today, bud. I'm gonna drive you before you're late for school. Get your stuff, and I'll meet you in the car as soon as I change."

My boy doesn't put up a fight, despite how excited he was to ride his bike to school. Instead, he raises his hand in a salute before grabbing his backpack from its hook and slinging it over his shoulder. Once he heads into the garage, I take off toward my bedroom.

Despite the chaos that is our laundry room, the rest of the house is clean and organized. I've never been a messy person, but being a single father is no easy feat. Between chauffeuring Cooper to band practice four out of seven days a week, art lessons another two, and owning and managing a booming business, I've allowed myself just one room to not give a crap about. One room where I can shove everything I don't want or don't have time to deal with away where I can't see it.

Out of sight, out of mind, right?

My bare feet thump against the cold wood planks lining the hallway before meeting the plush carpet in my bedroom. The walk-in closet is too extravagant for my taste, with the built-in maple shelves and drawers and collection of mirrors that make it impossible to avoid staring at yourself, but it came with the house, and I haven't had the time to change anything yet.

I quickly change into a pair of black track pants and a hoodie, both featuring the White Ice Training logo, before slipping on a pair of socks. Stepping in front of the mirror beside the rack housing my suit jackets, I shake my hair out again and run my fingers through the brown curls.

Every day that passes where I don't find a grey hair on my head is a day to celebrate. Knowing that my father went grey in his early thirties has been hanging over me like a piano on a thin wire since the day I turned thirty. It's been three years since, and every day, I count my blessings.

The beeping of my smartwatch has me quickly flicking off all lights and jogging through the house to the garage. Easton watches me run down the hallway from his place on the couch, and I flip him off before heading outside.

Cooper is already waiting for me in the car, and when I slide into the driver's seat, he levels me with a disapproving stare that makes him look far older than he is.

"Are you finally ready, beauty queen?"

With a quick burst of laughter, I reach over the console and ruffle his hair. "Careful, tough guy. I might drop you off on the side of the road and leave you there."

"I dare you," he sniffs, slapping my arms.

I pull back and start the engine. "Triple doggy dare me and you have a deal, bucko."

White Ice Training is a hockey arena located a few minutes from East Vancouver, housing a half rink, a full-size gym, and several rooms specialized for position-specific training.

We coach over a hundred athletes, with ages ranging from five-year-olds learning to skate, players in their late teens preparing for their chance at the big leagues, and anywhere in between.

Besides Cooper, WIT is my pride and joy. My blood, sweat, and bucketloads of tears. I've put everything I am and have ever had into building my company, and it still feels like a dream come true to stand here—a handful of feet away from the entrance—and stare up at what I've built in utter awe.

I pull open the heavy glass door and step inside, welcoming the slight chill that settles on my cheeks from the busy rink. I'm very late this morning, and after having to call Banks, my second-in-command, and deal with his chiding when I asked him to come in early and open the building, I've already determined it'll be a hellish day.

"Good morning, Adam," Brielle, one of our front desk workers, greets me with a smile.

"Hello, Brie. How was your morning?" I ask, closing the gap between us and leaning my forearms on the half wall separating me from her desk.

Brielle is a young single mother of triplets. Her ex-boyfriend left before the three girls were even born, and although she has a lot of help from her parents, I've offered to help her out whenever necessary.

Usually, a couple of days a week, I pick her girls up for school since I'm already taking Coop in that direction, but she's been adamant recently that she can handle it on her own. It's not my place to push her on it. Lord knows I didn't love taking handouts when Cooper was young, even if that's not what I'm offering.

Brielle smiles warmly. "It was pretty good. I think we've finally worked out a good morning schedule for the four of us. One that doesn't have me rushing out of the house with my hair still up in a towel and three six-year-olds wearing Halloween costumes."

I toss my head back and laugh. "That's great. But I'm sure they're the life of the classroom in those costumes."

"Oh yes. I've heard all about how much their teachers love chasing child-size hot dogs and pickles around during morning announcements."

"I remember when Cooper was in the third grade, he went to school on Halloween with one of those Scream masks that was filled with fake blood. The tubing attached to the pump ended up ripping open, and whatever they used to create the blood squirted all over his math teacher. I received quite the scolding from the principal that day."

Brielle covers her mouth with her hand and giggles.

"I know, I know. I'm a cool dad." I wink.

She shakes her head, her lips tugging at the corners. "That's exactly what I was thinking."

I push myself back and plant my hands on my hips. "I better get to work before Banks sees me slacking off. There are three interviews on the schedule today. Just page me to my office when the applicants get here, yeah?" It's been a long search for the perfect addition to our team, and at this point, I'm losing hope that we'll find anybody worth hiring.

She nods. "Sounds good, boss. Good luck with Banks today. He's already nearly thrown down with Brooklyn Danvers."

Great. One of our best clients and an Olympic gold medalist. Mornings and Banks don't mix, so as much as it might annoy me, I'm not surprised.

"Thanks, Brie. I'll see ya later." I throw her a grateful smile before spinning around and heading for my office.

As I walk through the busy halls of WIT, I can only hope to make it out of this day in one piece.

Craving The Player

Braden has never been the type to dream about settling down.
Just the smell of commitment is enough to chill him to the bone.

And after finally being free of a toxic, long-term relationship,
Sierra plans on staying single for as long as she can. With her
sights set on climbing the corporate ladder at her dream job, it
seemed like a straightforward plan.

But after one spontaneous night spent tangled up in Braden's
sheets, will it be as easy as both of them expected to continue on
with their normal lives? It is just sex, after all.

One risky agreement later and their lives are intertwined.

**Is it really possible to keep the lines between lust and love
from blurring? Or are they just postponing the inevitable?**

CHAPTER 1

Braden

Sharp nails tear their way down my back, ripping through the sensitive skin and drawing blood. The blonde beneath me moans in my ear, begging me to pick up the pace.

We've been going at this for what feels like hours now. She's come more times than I can count, quite the opposite of myself. I've been unwantedly edging my self.

"Just like that!"

My frustration is obvious as I pull out of her in one swift movement and lean back on my legs, dick starting to sag.

"What are you doing?" she whines, lips jutting out in a juicy pout.

"Sorry. I just remembered that I have to go pick up my grandpa's friend's dog from the vet." My tone is dry and careless. I move off of the silk red sheets left in a disarray on her bed and toss the unused condom into the nearby trash can.

"You could say my name, you know." Her breathless voice only frustrates me more. In all honesty, I don't remember her name.

I try to block her out and focus on finding my clothes. I can just about plant a thank you kiss on the lamp in the corner of her room when I spot my button-up hanging from it. "And you expect me to believe that you have to pick up this dog in the middle of the night?"

She doesn't spare me an unconvincing frown as she wraps the blanket around her otherwise naked body—a wise decision on her part. It was her hot body that enticed me enough to come here in the first place, and as much fun as it is to stare at her smooth, olive skin, I already have a terrible case of blue balls. The thought makes me reach down and anxiously rub at my limp cock with a deep, aggravated sigh.

"Sorry, what?" I slide my arms through my shirt. My back burns when the material rubs across the new cuts in my skin.

"What is your deal?" she snaps.

I run a hand through my messy hair and pull my phone from the pocket of my jeans. As soon as I switch it on, I'm met with several texts asking about my whereabouts and disappearance.

"You're unbelievable!" she scoffs, pulling the blanket tighter around her. In a flurry, she rushes into the ensuite bathroom, slamming the door behind her.

Well, that makes things easier.

I pull my keys out of my pocket and the cold metal bites into my palm. The nauseating smell of her fruity perfume wafts throughout the house, making me rush to the front door even faster. I slide my sneakers on and fight back the urge to kick myself in the ass for letting my dick get me in trouble again.

I'm out the door and in the driver's seat of my car before my stomach has a chance to start swirling with disappointment.

"If you keep dropping your arms like that, I'll gladly bruise up that pretty face, Clay."

Clayton takes another risky swing at my chest and I roll my eyes at his poorly placed move. "C'mon, buddy. You gotta do better than that." I grab and twist his arm behind his back. I turn the six-foot ginger around and shove his face into the boxing bag in front of us.

Poor guy didn't stand a chance in hell with that sloppy throw.

"Your mouth twitches before every swing. That needs to stop. Anyone who studies you even in the slightest will know your tells. You'll never win like that. *Ever.*" I move back a step and lift my arms into position before nodding for him to try again.

His eyes narrow as he bounces on his feet, observing me. Trying to learn *my* tells. As if I would put them on display for him. Less than a second later, his top lip lifts just the slightest bit, causing mine to lift in a grin.

In an instant I'm tucking myself under his right hook and swinging my left arm. I make contact with his abdomen, and the air is pushed from his lungs in a raspy wheeze. He clutches his stomach and curls over.

"Fuck you," he coughs.

"Damn, I guess I should have put my gloves on. My bad." I shrug.

"Remind me again why I can't have another trainer?" He asks me the question like he doesn't already know the answer while pushing himself upright again. After a few seconds, his grimace slowly evens back out into a scowl.

"Because nobody else wants your whiny ass," I snicker, walking toward my gym bag and pulling out my gloves. The gold stripes wrapping around the slick black material never fail to make my chest swell with pride. I worked day and night to afford these babies, and damn are they *ever* worth it.

"We both know that you just don't want to get rid of me."

"Yeah." I snort. "That's it."

Sliding my hands in my gloves, I clench my fingers and

tighten the Velcro strap. Patting both gloves together, I raise my brow and nod for him to try again.

The balls of my feet tap against the concrete floor as I bounce, keeping my eyes locked on my best friend. He's finally got his arms in the correct position, at least, but the tension in his shoulders worries me.

"Drop your shoulders!" I bark. "You're going to hurt yourself."

"I'm trying," he snaps but drops his shoulder slightly, most likely to humour me more than anything.

Without a second thought I send my fist toward him, but stop mid-throw when he drops his arms just enough to expose his face to me.

I warned him. Pushing my arm forward again, I hear a loud *smack*.

"What the fuck!" he shouts with eyes full of fire as he grabs his now bleeding nose. I bite back my laugh.

"It's not broken. Relax." I grin to myself and give my head a quick shake. "I told you that if you dropped your arms again, I would mess with your pretty face."

I turn away from him and reach into my gym bag, pulling out two towels. After I toss him the darker coloured one for his gushing nose, I keep the lighter one for myself. The sweat covering my bare torso is wiped away quickly before I discard the towel.

"What if you would have broken it?" he groans.

"Then you wouldn't have dropped your arms next time. Take the pain as a learning experience."

"You were coming for my stomach!"

"It looked like I was aiming for your stomach. You would have no idea if that were a trick or not. That's why you don't drop your arms," I say with unwavering confidence. I've trained to be a boxer nearly my entire life, learned almost everything there is to know about the sport. He needs to gain a bit of confidence in me. If my ego weren't the size of

Texas I would have been offended. "Anyways, pizza for dinner?"

"Sure," he replies, voice nasally from the pressure he's applying to his nose. His ability to go with the flow is one of the reasons we get along so well.

"Come on, if you get blood on the floor Dad will kill me." I lead the way to the showers.

"Maybe I'll leave a trail then."

I scowl.

Working for your dad has its benefits, but dealing with his rage when you break one of his rules is not one of them. No bloodshed is the most crucial rule in this gym. It has been since before I can remember. We Lowry men don't follow many rules, but the ones we do, we live by. As if by breaking a single one would throw the entire universe off kilter.

"If you want to go that far, I might as well get a couple more hits in. Soak the floor in your misery," I half-heartedly threaten.

He just scoffs, shaking his head. "I'd like to see you try."

"Yeah? Want to bet on how long you'd last in the ring with me?" I tilt my head and straighten my back so all six-foot-three of me tower over him.

Clay gulps but keeps his lips pressed together. "Whatever. Arrogant bastard."

I laugh. "Always full of compliments, Clay. So, stuffed or regular crust?"

"Grab me a beer, would you?" I shout as I drop back on the couch. My words are muffled as a slice of pepperoni stuffed-crust pizza is clenched between my teeth.

"Do I look like your damn mother?" Clayton calls back.

I shove my hand between the couch cushions and grab hold

of the TV remote. My greasy fingers fiddle with the remote before finding the power button and the familiar sound of my favourite, hot as hell sports announcer fills the room.

"Pretty please can you bring me a beer?" I try again, snickering to myself when I hear the fridge door slam shut.

"Here."

I catch the cold can midair when he throws it toward me like a softball. I turn to face him and crack it open nice and slow. I take a long swig and rest my head back against the couch. "Thanks."

"Don't mention it," he grumbles and sits down beside me, holding out a paper plate. He wears a look that dares me not to use it, so I take it with a huff and set it down on my lap.

My attention drops to my phone when it vibrates, shaking the glass coffee table it's lying on. Reaching for it, I notice the several names spread across the screen.

I lean back and unlock the phone, grinning. A picture of a naked body fills the screen, and my eyes narrow. The girl's athletic, toned figure lies outstretched on what looks to be a bed, with a sheer, white, silky robe sagging off of her narrow shoulders. Her knees are bent, legs are spread wide open, the soft pink skin of her bare pussy glistening between them.

"What are you smirking at?" Clay asks. When I don't answer, he leans over my shoulder to look for himself. "Holy shit. Who is that?"

Locking my phone, I roll my eyes. "Fuck off and go find your own."

"I have my own." He sounds less than mildly confident in that statement.

"Then what are you waiting for?" I raise a brow, testing him before he flips me off and pushes off the couch. "Maybe if you got laid, you wouldn't be so damn uptight. You're acting like a twenty-seven-year-old virgin."

"Not everyone wants to be a 'fuck it and chuck it' kind of guy until the day they die. We're not all that young anymore, dude."

Registering his words, I nearly blow chunks all over the living room. "I stopped ageing when I turned twenty-four, remember?"

"Right." He snorts.

The reminder of how old we are was unnecessary. It's not like I don't know how close I am to reaching my thirties. With Clay getting his shit together with most things, I'm reminded nearly every damn day of the week. The thought of becoming someone that needs to start meeting society's standards makes a knot form in my stomach the size of Texas and my blood run ice cold.

I feel proud of Clay for realizing what he wants in life goes farther than a good fuck and a cold beer afterward. But his path will never be mine. The whole idea of going to a job I hate five days a week before coming home to a wife and three identical kids waiting on the porch of a two-story suburban home makes me want to kneel and pray to be shipped off to another planet.

Nah, I'm happy with staying twenty-six forever. Society can kiss my pearly white ass for demanding a change

I've just wrapped a towel around my waist when Clayton pushes open the bathroom door, eyes droopy and dull as he shoves past me, stopping in front of the sink.

He follows the same routine as every night: wets his toothbrush with cold water, smears a thick line of spearmint toothpaste onto the rough bristles before shoving it into his mouth and brushing his teeth for precisely two minutes. I'm no shrink, but I would confidently diagnose Clay with a case of obsessive-compulsive disorder any day of the week.

We've been living together for two years now, and I'm still trying to come to grasps with his overly cleanly, organized ways.

After exactly two minutes of scrubbing every square inch of

his mouth, Clay spits into the sink and wipes a fresh towel across his lips. He doesn't tear his concentration from the small container of dental floss pinched between his fingers as he mumbles, "I forgot to tell you that there's some sort of concert tomorrow night at SP, and you need to be there."

I raise my brow. "There's a concert? At Sinners? Since when do they do that shit there?"

"Don't know. Ethan got tickets or something from one of the bouncers last week. There's one for both of us."

"Could be fun." I shrug and rub at the sting in my eyes, exhaustion stepping on me with its dirty shoe. I don't give the invitation much thought. Ethan is an eighteen-year-old boy stuck in the body of a twenty-six-year-old man. This isn't the first time that we've been *told* to go to out with him, and it won't be the last. I just nod my head and follow along. Night clubs aren't my venue of choice anymore, but a beer is a beer regardless of where you drink it.

Clayton gives me a nod but doesn't look away from the mirror.

"I'm going to bed. Don't forget that I need you ready to go to the gym at eight," I remind him before leaving the bathroom. I don't get anything more than a brief grunt in response, and I chuckle.

Our two-bedroom apartment—if you could call a full bedroom and a small den without a window two bedrooms—is so damn tiny that it only takes me a whole two seconds to walk down the hallway and reach my room.

I was lucky enough to earn my right to the actual bedroom by sucking back two more shots of tequila than Clay at a pub on Halloween the night before we moved into this place. I'm damn grateful for my stomach of steel, too, since there's no door or a lick of privacy leading to the den Clayton calls the Boom Room. But boom, it does not.

Where I might seem picky about the women I bed, Clayton damn near refuses anyone that doesn't meet his iron-set criteria to the absolute T. It's safe to say the Boom Room is filled with more tepid echo than anything else.

I don't bother turning on the light as I quickly swap out the towel for a pair of briefs that I find in a rare, clean basket of laundry and crawl into bed. When I get under the covers, I close my eyes and pray to God himself that I'll pass the fuck out soon.

Acknowledgements

I don't know what is more surprising to me. The fact that enough of you beautiful people loved my first book enough for me to launch my second without wanting to throw up, or that writing has become a career for me. All because of you.

I owe the biggest of thank you's to the readers. This was a dream that I never expected to become a reality and now it is. I love each and every one of you.

Mitch, my amazing fiancé, thank you for the countless hours spent listening to me vent and gush about Tyler and Gracie without complaint. You have no idea how much your support means to me.

To Mia for being the best PA in the world, thank you. I love you.

To my family and friends, I know that I said you weren't allowed to read this book, but I'm going to thank you anyway. Dad, thank you for always sharing my Facebook posts even though some are a bit risky in the sex department. I love you all.

Booknmoods, thank you for giving life to these stories with the phenomenal covers. They are everything.

About The Author

Hannah is a twenty-something-year-old indie author, mom, and wife from Western Canada. Obsessed with swoon-worthy romance, she decided to take a leap and try her hand at creating stories that will have you fanning your face and giggling in the most embarrassing way possible. Hopefully, that's exactly what her stories have done!

Hannah loves to hear from her readers, and can be reached on any of her social media accounts.

Website: hannahcowanauthor.com
Facebook Group: Hannah's Hotties

Made in the USA
Monee, IL
02 January 2024

51054328R00167